ADRIFT

ALSO BY WILL DEAN

The Chamber
The Last One
First Born
The Last Thing to Burn

ADRIFT

A NOVEL

WILL DEAN

EMILY BESTLER BOOKS

ATRIA

NEW YORK AMSTERDAM/ANTWERP LONDON
TORONTO SYDNEY/MELBOURNE NEW DELHI

EMILY BESTLER BOOKS

ATRIA

An Imprint of Simon & Schuster, LLC
1230 Avenue of the Americas
New York, NY 10020

For more than 100 years, Simon & Schuster has championed authors and the stories they create. By respecting the copyright of an author's intellectual property, you enable Simon & Schuster and the author to continue publishing exceptional books for years to come. We thank you for supporting the author's copyright by purchasing an authorized edition of this book.

No amount of this book may be reproduced or stored in any format, nor may it be uploaded to any website, database, language-learning model, or other repository, retrieval, or artificial intelligence system without express permission. All rights reserved. Inquiries may be directed to Simon & Schuster, 1230 Avenue of the Americas, New York, NY 10020 or permissions@simonandschuster.com.

This book is a work of fiction. Any references to historical events, real people, or real places are used fictitiously. Other names, characters, places, and events are products of the author's imagination, and any resemblance to actual events or places or persons, living or dead, is entirely coincidental.

Copyright © 2026 by Will Dean

All rights reserved, including the right to reproduce this book or portions thereof in any form whatsoever. For information, address Atria Books Subsidiary Rights Department, 1230 Avenue of the Americas, New York, NY 10020.

First Emily Bestler Books/Atria Books hardcover edition February 2026

EMILY BESTLER BOOKS / ATRIA BOOKS and colophon are registered trademarks of Simon & Schuster, LLC

Simon & Schuster strongly believes in freedom of expression and stands against censorship in all its forms. For more information, visit BooksBelong.com.

For information about special discounts for bulk purchases, please contact Simon & Schuster Special Sales at 1-866-506-1949 or business@simonandschuster.com.

The Simon & Schuster Speakers Bureau can bring authors to your live event. For more information or to book an event, contact the Simon & Schuster Speakers Bureau at 1-866-248-3049 or visit our website at www.simonspeakers.com.

Interior design by Kyoko Watanabe

Manufactured in the United States of America

1 3 5 7 9 10 8 6 4 2

Library of Congress Control Number: 2025949006

ISBN 978-1-6680-8005-4
ISBN 978-1-6680-8006-1 (ebook)

 Let's stay in touch! Scan here to get book recommendations, exclusive offers, and more delivered to your inbox.

For unheard people in unseen towns

I have love in me the likes of which you can scarcely imagine
and rage the likes of which you would not believe.

—MARY SHELLEY

How did I escape? With difficulty. How did
I plan this moment? With pleasure.

—ALEXANDRE DUMAS

Author's note: This book is set in a fictional town, by a fictional canal, in the Midwest, someplace close to Cairo, Illinois.

TWENTY-ONE YEARS BEFORE

ANDREW JENKINS, AGED 15

Illinois-Indiana-Kentucky tristate area, Fall 1973

When I was younger I would burn butterflies.

Holding Dad's magnifying glass at arm's length on a summer's day. The scent of cut grass and wild mint in the warm, unmoving air. It was important to catch the sunbeam just right.

My parents should have known.

It took me several minutes to rinse out the peanut butter jar. I wanted it real clean.

I told them I'd do it.

They should have listened.

I hid the jar under their bed early this morning. I placed their room key inside the jar. Screwed the lid tight.

Maybe they will find it in time.

These past months Dad has treated me like a fungus growing inside the walls of his house. One punishment after another. Mom hasn't put a stop to it. If anything, she's encouraged him.

Not my fault.

I can hear him snoring in their bedroom. It is a familiar sound.

Mom never complains. I open their door quietly as I can. Striped sheets from Macy's. Matching drapes covering the locked window. Dad's jeans and thick leather belt over the chair in the corner. I am all too familiar with that belt.

Mom stirs.

I watch her.

They had every chance.

I stare at their bodies in the bed. The sheets rising and falling. Their breathing seems synchronized, as if they are one.

They can still save themselves.

The key's right there. It wouldn't take much.

I don't say goodbye or anything like that. Dad would think that soft. I close the door gently and leave them to their slumber.

I use the spare key to lock them in.

Click.

The gasoline can is green. Dark green. Dad keeps it in the garage with the lawn mower, his chain saws, and hammers. Wrenches. Just like his dad before him, he looks after his tools. Won't let me touch them.

But I do touch them.

I touch them all the time.

I study them and sometimes I write about them.

More snoring from their room. I work carefully. Don't want to wake them. Splash the carpet, the drapes, the walls. The smell is pleasing. Sweet and electric. I breathe in the fumes and then I soak the upholstered chair—a sibling to the one his jeans and belt hang on in the master bedroom—and wedge the chair under their door handle because Grandpa taught me you can never be too careful.

Retreating down the passage, I remove my rubber boots and raincoat and place them on the saturated carpet.

Almost ready.

I hesitate, lifting my chin, breathing it all in, taking note.

I can't fail now. This is my one chance to change my destiny, or at least nudge it in a good direction. There are certain decisions in life that determine which route you'll take at an intersection. I guess this is one of them.

The Slazenger tennis ball is one from a tube of four I found in the garage with his tools. I push it into the wet fibers of the carpet, careful not to dampen my pajamas, and then I walk down a few stairs and turn to face their door. I can only see the top half and it is as if the chair isn't there jammed under the handle. I set fire to the tennis ball with Dad's Zippo lighter and then I throw it, gently, underarm, toward the door.

I turn around.

Heat at my back.

Light.

They expected certain things of me. It was baked into the cake I'd turn out like they did. But now I have changed that.

Relief, and a sense of overwhelming calm. Revisiting summers past. The magnifying glass and the butterflies. Peace, descending like a heavy blanket. I wait downstairs, their screams muffled, their banging short-lived. I had planned to go back to bed for a while, I'm not sure why. I had imagined it, I suppose: the scene, the poetry of that action, but there is too much smoke.

I take my jacket from the hook.

And then I walk outside to watch it burn.

PART I

1

PEGGY JENKINS

Robertson's Marina
Illinois-Indiana-Kentucky tristate area, Fall 1994

My name is Peggy Augusta Jenkins.

As of last month I live with my husband and son on a forty-year-old narrow boat. I do not possess a birth certificate. The sheets on my bed are damp from condensation and my husband is sitting with his back to our woodburning stove at the far end of the vessel, naked, save for his socks, writing his novel.

This is our last chance.

A train passes in the distance. Fortunate souls leaving this town to venture north toward Chicago, or south toward Memphis. Others, misguided, arriving.

My son sleeps on the converted dinette sofa at the center of the boat and I worry every day that he may not make it to adulthood. Mothers profess how they would kill for their offspring, but I know I would go further still.

I would not hesitate.

Moonlight splinters through swaying poplar branches. The boat shifts gently in the water, almost imperceptibly, as the grebes and swamp sparrows outside our walls ready themselves for their nests.

The creak of wood over steel hull. Is he coming this way? My shoulders are tight and I am aware of the pulse in my ears.

Another creak.

My breath clouds in front of my eyes.

The door to our room opens.

The man I married fifteen years ago steps inside. He shaved his head before his writing session and now his porcelain skin glistens with sweat.

"You made noise." His face is as expressionless as a pebble worn smooth in a river.

I frown.

"Tell me why," he says.

I sit up. Offer a smile. "Drew, I don't think I made any noise, I swear. Not a sound."

He closes the door gently, unnaturally slowly, and positions himself next to the bed, looming over me.

"It wasn't the boy. I just want to know *why*. So we can move on."

"What noise?"

He swallows.

His bald head shines.

"I'm out there trying to get words down, for the good of this family, sweating next to the fire for you and him, and you're back here wrecking my concentration. Was it on purpose?"

I shake my head.

"By accident then, was it?"

I have been here before, so many times. Lost in his maze of backward logic. There is no escape. I have tried. There is no winning.

I cringe.

A bulge beneath his lips. His tongue moving slowly over his teeth.

"Night of work wasted but at least you owned up to it, Peg."

"I didn't think I made any noise," I say. "I apologize if I did."

"You didn't *think* you made a noise, but I *know* you did. That's the difference we're looking at. Plain as day. Thinking versus knowing."

He sits down lightly, slowly, softly, on the bed.

"Who was that fella you were talking with earlier?"

"Sorry?"

"Fella with a bicycle. Beer gut."

"Oh, he has the next boat over, the blue one. I was just talking about the fridge."

"That right?"

"He was an electrician, Drew. Before he retired. It just came up."

"Just came up."

More sweat emerging from his pores.

"I thought he could fix it and save us some money."

"How come he can fix the fridge and I can't?"

"He was an electrician."

His nostrils flare. "This old boat's not perfect, far from it, but if there's things to fix it'll be me who does it. Boy can watch, learn something useful. I won't have strangers coming in here, gawping at my papers when I'm at the yard working."

"He never came inside, Drew."

"He never will."

I am so tired.

"What did he say, this electrician?"

"Nothing much."

"That right?"

"He said that he'll take a look if we need him to. That he's a little out of date but he can look at our wiring, too, our batteries."

The scent of soap and sweat. Engine oil.

"And what did you say?"

"I said . . ."

"Word-for-word."

"I said I'd talk to you."

He grits his teeth. "I'll move us away tomorrow morning. Give us some privacy. We can't afford the marina anyhow, not with the boy's school uniform. It's time we were away, you said so yourself, and you were right."

"I don't think I ever said that, Drew. I like it here. And Samson's starting to make friends."

"Boy doesn't need friends around here, he needs to learn how to work for a living. You want coffee?"

I take a moment.

"I said, do you want coffee?"

"Please."

He stands up and wipes his face with his rough palms and walks out, his footsteps deliberate and noiseless.

The moonlight reflects off the canal surface and shimmers on the ceiling. There is no railroad noise now.

We would not even have this decrepit British-made boat if it wasn't for Mom, but he does not see it that way. She died fifteen years ago, six months before our wedding, a year before Samson arrived, and it still breaks my heart she missed those two events. She would have walked me up the aisle proudly, she had it all planned out, her outfit paid for in installments. I thought she was doing well. She pined for her family in England, what was left of it—my cousins, her old friends, her childhood town—but I had thought she was content. She seemed to be as besotted with Drew as I was. She had read his short stories and said encouraging things. Then, on the night before my twentieth birthday, she swallowed pills when we were out, and she never woke up. That's how we came to live in her bungalow. When we could no longer afford the bills we sold it for this three-hundred-square-foot boat and now all our money, *her* money, what little was left, is tied up in this vessel.

Every dime.

This, here, now, is our last chance.

I am determined to make it work.

For Samson's sake.

I hear Drew fill the pan and place it on the gas burner. Life isn't too bad here in the marina. Propane bottles for cooking, public water, and fuel for the woodstove at the far end of the boat by his bureau desk. Between the woodstove and the desk sits Mom's pale gray rug we took from the bungalow. We have electric from a cable. It is all easy here in Robertson's Marina and, more importantly, there is some minimal sense of safety, of community.

The pan begins to boil. That is the thing with living on a boat six feet wide and fifty feet long. You always know what is happening. There is no privacy or distance or personal space like there is on bigger houseboats. Our model isn't unique in the United States, but it is pretty rare. The godsend is that Samson manages to sleep through almost anything. He has the worst of it in many ways: right next to the kitchen on a bed that only comes into existence at nighttime. And yet he sleeps the sleep of the dead.

Drew takes out milk from the well deck at the front of the boat. We have a box out there that serves as our makeshift fridge thanks to this reliable November chill. A minute later he brings through two stained cups half full of coffee.

We sit side by side listening to the silence between us.

The coffee is hot.

"I do it for you and the boy."

I nod.

"Not out there writing for myself. Doing it for this family. But a man needs the right conditions, Peg. I'm working on the new book, and I need it to be perfect."

I place my hand down on his.

He flinches.

"Bathroom," I say. "Won't be long."

I slide the dark wooden bathroom door and lock it and breathe out. A blessed moment of escape. The porthole window is cracked open against the condensation and I close my eyes and worry that the dream I have had all these years, of a real family, bonded together, each of us leaning on one another, protecting each other, may morph into what finally sinks us. Drew's head is mere inches from mine on the other side of the mildewed plywood. Can he read my thoughts? Or does he seed those himself and water them till they set roots, ready for me to one day stumble over?

I wash my hands and tiptoe into the main room of the boat. In the warm glow of the fire I take in our home. Three folding Walmart camp chairs by the woodstove at the far end. His writing desk locked up securely. The steel boat doors, also locked. Our kitchen with its broken fridge. And then, closest to me, the dinette sofa and table converted into a bed containing the most precious and faultless thing in the whole wide world.

I watch him breathe.

Stardust, manifested.

I stare at him.

All the abstract love in the universe distilled into one human.

Tufts of red hair like sparks on the pillow. I bend down close to his cheek. He smells different from how he smelled as a young boy but the base notes remain. His essence. The purest scent: an aroma so powerful it makes me want to shield him with my body.

I kiss his beautiful forehead and he does not stir.

Sleep well, my boy.

2

SAMSON

I wake to the smell of bacon being expertly fried mere feet from my head.

"Thought that'd wake you, boy. You don't hear us talking, but I start frying bacon and you spring to life."

It sizzles and spits.

My bed is warm.

Dad's nodding to himself. Paint-splattered overalls and a Band-Aid where he shaved last night before writing. One of his many rituals.

"Get yourself up. Catch a worm."

I can't move because it'd be obvious I was woken mid-dream, and that the subject of said dream was private in nature.

"I'll get up when Mom's finished in the bathroom."

"So you can put your makeup on?"

I sigh and check my Walkman's still in its place, and then I carefully maneuver myself off the bed.

"Turn it back into a table. Your mother might want to sit there."

I hear the bathroom door slide open and then the bedroom door shut. I scamper into the bathroom and lock the door behind me.

My belly rumbles.

I wash my face with Irish Spring hand soap and spike my hair with the gel I received for my birthday. It makes my hair look darker, I think, almost brown, and, in theory, in my head at least, that could mean I'll have less trouble today at school.

Dad always fries our bacon. The only other thing he cooks is beans because he claims she overcooks them. *Only need heating up, cook 'em too long and you ruin it.* Everything else is woman's work according to him. I know Mom wouldn't agree, but she does it anyhow because of how he can be.

He doesn't believe in cereal. Other kids have Lucky Charms and Cheerios. None of that sweet goodness here.

I put my bedding away and pull on my school uniform. Sometimes I resent the scholarship I got, the one set up long ago by some rich Indiana family who used to own the local mine. I was told the school would be fancy. It's not like that at all. It's lots of kids with lake houses and campaign signs on their perfectly manicured lawns, but it's nothing special. Same bullshit just with neckties and rules about how you can wear your hair.

"It's wet again," I say, looking out of the window.

"Won't hurt," says Dad as he places crispy strips of bacon on sliced whole wheat toast, always whole wheat. No eggs today. No ketchup either.

A train thunders by in the distance. Pigeons erupt from the gnarled oaks on the towpath and beat their wings above our boat. Mom told me once how both pigeon parents care for their young, and how they mate for life. She said that was important. They manage to stay strong together come what may.

"Diseased pests," says Dad, glancing up at the roof. "Be better where we're moving to. Less tree vermin."

"Moving?" I say.

"Breakfast," he booms, ignoring me.

She emerges with wet hair and a towel wrapped around her head, looking like a movie star from the silent era.

"Smart mother you've got making the most of these convenient amenities while we're still in the marina. If you had any sense, Samson, you'd take a leaf out of her book. Won't be much water where we're headed."

"Leave him," says Mom, cupping my cheek with her palm, and taking the plate of bacon and toast.

The other boys in my class don't have these conversations. Eyebrow, so-called because of his one panoramic eyebrow, has two bathrooms in his house and his cousin Mickey has three. Eyebrow doesn't talk to me much anymore. At elementary school we'd play baseball and touch football, but now he's wary to be seen close. The other kids would say to him: *Why you hanging around with that redhead trash, you two going steady or what? Why you chatting with Noodles?*

They call me Noodles because of my arms.

Because they're so thin.

Breakfast is delicious. Better than Mom's pancakes, even. Dad fries the bacon until the fat crisps.

"Are you serious about moving the boat?" she asks.

Dad puts down his bacon and slowly turns his head to her.

"You asking me that?"

"It's just that . . ."

"It's just that . . ." he says, mimicking her. "I told you we're moving. Maybe if you weren't running around with some electrician with a bicycle we wouldn't need to. We reap what we sow, Peggy."

We finish breakfast in silence. Mugs of coffee and the sense that moving from the bungalow, Nanna Ruth's two-bedroom bungalow, to this boat was one thing, but moving from Robertson's Marina to some distant empty stretch of canal is quite another.

I'm beginning to experience the familiar sense of dread that comes with every weekday morning.

They'll be there, see.

Waiting.

"How will I know where to walk home to from the library tonight?" asks Mom. "And Samson, from school?"

"You'll figure it out," he says. "The *Lady Brett Ashley* is a fifty-footer, woman, you can't miss it. Name's painted on the side, clear as day. Use your eyes, both of you."

Other boys my age don't have to contend with this. School is challenging enough in this town without having to go search for your own home each night, a home named after an Ernest Hemingway character.

"Just don't moor it up too far from the road," says Mom. "We need to get to the bus."

"I'll moor it where I see fit."

Mom goes to the bedroom to finish getting ready. She works at the municipal library, but they don't actually pay her. She's a volunteer. Dad doesn't want her to have a paying job because he says it'd be too much stress on her. Because of her nerves, and what happened to Nanna Ruth before I was born. And he claims the bosses would take advantage of her better nature.

"You training later, Dad?"

"What is it to you?"

"Thought we could do some together, once I've finished my assignments. Maybe back and chest."

"*Back and chest*," he mutters, shaking his head, glancing at my white shirt, gray in places, hanging off my shoulders like it'd hang off a hanger if we owned any. "You've got Mr. Turner tonight. Make sure he pays you in full."

One day we will train together. I'll be more like him by then. Strong, and living life on my own terms.

I drag on my school blazer, three sizes too big, and my shoes, also several sizes too big. Hammer Adams says I look like I'm wearing my grandpa's suit. I told him I don't have any grandpas, and he said it's a good thing because they'd be ashamed to have a scrawny carrottopped grandson with clown shoes.

ADRIFT

The walk to the bus is all right as it goes. Local hit music show on my Walkman radio, the foam headphones stopping most of the wind reaching my ears. R.E.M., Depeche Mode, and two songs by George Michael. I keep my hand loose around the plastic shell of the Walkman in my jacket pocket in case I stumble and fall. I would rather fracture my wrist than lose my Walkman.

No kids from school on this local bus. Sometimes there are older guys from other schools: seniors too poor to drive in, too old to be seen dead on a yellow bus. Dad doesn't like school transport just like he doesn't like food stamps or voting or welfare. Hates anything that might make life easier. The big kids don't bother me too much but they're aware that everyone in ninth grade hates me. They see what happens in the cafeteria and on the football field each week. They don't interfere with me directly, but I can see a mixture of pity and dismissal in their glances, and this morning I am relieved not to witness it. Window seat to myself. A call-in game on the radio followed by Nirvana. The raucous drumbeat of "Smells Like Teen Spirit" echoes in my unsettled stomach as we approach the bus station. This is not a good place. Understatement. There is no supervision to step in if things turn, no teachers to help. I disembark and walk fast with my head bent, avoiding downtown, heading around the Salvation Army store and past the Baptist church. A pair of girls from St. Benedict's approach so I cross the street.

They are probably laughing at me.

They probably know.

I turn off my Walkman, wrap it in a long sock, and stow it safely in my bag. There are boys from my school everywhere now, swarms of them. My throat tightens. I'm sweating as I pass the church and head to the candy store. The owner is a middle-aged woman from Wales, which is someplace in Europe. Her family came over because of their mining expertise, so goes the rumor.

The store is small.

A converted room in a row house.

I am sick with the anticipation of what this day might bring. I can never predict exactly what it'll be, that's the worst of it. I'm OK at handling stuff if I can think it through beforehand, like the times Dad makes Mom upset. But this first year at high school is a series of unpredictable life-and-death challenges, one after the next. I have done nothing to them; I have not hurt them or called them names. I have never broken their stuff. And yet they despise me.

I look up at the candy options. It's all loose in big glass bottles.

As I'm waiting, a boy behind me steps on my heel. I ignore it. He does it again.

"Eighth of an ounce of lemon drops, please."

The boy kicks the back of my knees. Nothing hard but it causes me to stumble forward and the lady tuts.

She measures out an eighth of an ounce and then removes one lemon drop, a misshapen one so no great loss, and slides them from the gleaming steel scales into a paper bag, and with a flick of her wrist, she twists the bag to close it.

I pay her and the boy behind me steps on my heel again.

Just ignore him.

My palms are damp and the day hasn't even begun yet.

While he's paying for gum or baseball cards I walk out quickly and then I sprint toward school. I need to put distance between us. It's not easy running in these long shoes.

I approach the gates by the gym building, the set of gates I consider to be the safest at this time of day.

They are waiting for me.

3

PEGGY

"You'd better set off for the scrapyard, Drew, or you'll be late."

He turns to me and smiles.

"You telling me when to leave now?"

"Didn't mean it like that."

"I've changed my hours. I told you I did."

"Oh."

"Told you yesterday. Mind like a sieve, you've got. Like a leaky bucket."

I wipe down the windows one more time and wring out the cloth into the sink. Canal water that condenses inside only to be returned to the canal for the endless cycle to begin again.

"What are your new hours?" I ask.

"Is there any peace?"

I do not say anything to that. There is a family of ducks outside the window, seven in total, each chick with a dash of dazzling orange on its beak, and they look like they exist in harmony. Floating lightly atop the water and watching out for each other. Their feathers shine in weak sunbeams and I enjoy how they seem to constantly check in with each other, keeping the group whole and safe.

"Working ten till three for now. You want me to write that down for you?"

"But, I mean, can we afford that?"

He walks toward me, his bulk filling the space between the slowly rotting kitchen cabinets and the dinette, and then, gradually, he comes to a halt in much the way a houseboat would: gently, inevitably, culminating at my face.

"You ever missed a meal under my roof?"

I shake my head.

He breathes slowly. Controlled exhalations.

"There you go."

I do the dishes. Scheming. Scent of Dawn dish soap. Plotting what might come next. Coping mechanisms and strategies; tapping into another stratum of resilience I never knew I had. Plans. Ways to keep Sammy happy until he's old enough to do it for himself.

"You'll have to be mindful of water from today. No more splashing it about like you're doing now in that sink. We'll be down to the boat's tank from now on. No public water. You and the boy will have to watch yourselves."

We have been watching ourselves for years.

Me watching him and him watching out for me.

I pull on my long jacket.

"Goodbye then."

He sits at his desk.

"Might walk you back home later."

So he can keep an eye on me. Monitor who talks to me. Who looks at me.

"How will I know where the boat is, Drew? Later today, I mean, in case you don't come collect me at the library."

He looks up from his desk and holds my gaze.

"You'll open your eyes, Peggy. Walk along the canal. The exercise will do you good."

"Bye then."

Walking away from him.

Leaving.

I am minded to keep on walking and never look back, but I know by now that I always look back eventually. Not because he has the bankbook or the boat in his name, it's not that. It is because of what he told me all those years ago. It is because of the man he is deep inside that Sammy and I stay tethered to him. It is Samson who would suffer if I was to disappear, and he is not built for that challenge. He is hardly built for what we have now.

Along the towpath. Up the hill. The sweet scent of wet, brown earth. Pigtail moss and decaying leaves. The landscape slowing down into the cold, still months.

Past the railroad footbridge and on to the bus stop.

I like this time of day. The schoolchildren are all safe in their tidy classrooms by now and the workers are busy in their offices and stores. It's me riding with five senior citizens and a new mother. I help her with her stroller and we exchange a tired look of solidarity and understanding. No words needed. The bus engine drones, and as the fields and transmission towers blur outside I ponder what I will write about on my lunch break.

He lets me volunteer.

Lets me.

If it wasn't for Sammy I would leave in a heartbeat. Set up someplace else and never look back. I could clean houses in Missouri and keep my head down. But there's no good that comes from thinking that way. I have to set my boy free first and then I can think about myself.

The small concrete library is crammed between a community health center and a dollar store. Four computers, thousands of books, one photocopier, three librarians, and me. This building is the opposite of our narrow boat. Not that it is square, though it is. But it is heavy and rooted; wedged securely between two other buildings like it's never going anyplace. Quiet and warm, a modern-day church.

I hang up my jacket and start work on the children's area display. Picture books and props. A broken toy ship with a pirate flag.

Fred comes in.

"Good morning, Peggy."

"Morning, Fred. Cold out there."

"Bitter."

His fingernails are black and his hair is clumped into accidental dreadlocks. He has pockets full of plastic bags and there is no gentler man in the whole county. I give him five minutes to settle in and then I sit down opposite.

"What is today, Fred?"

"*Chuzzlewit.*"

"Again?"

"Third time, that's all. I favor *Martin Chuzzlewit* in the wintertime when the nights are drawing in. It's good and familiar."

He flinches.

"Your mouth?"

He nods.

"How's DeeDee?"

"She's moved on to the next town. Said she'd had enough of this place."

"I'm so sorry."

"Me too, Peggy. Me too. I worry for her in that big town. There's meanness over there by the interstate. I never did like it."

I leave him to read like he does every day. Warming up takes time. By lunch he will be outside again with his paper cup and his flag, holding his piece of cardboard detailing his war record, thinking about the story he read, the characters and dialogue, hoping for God knows what.

Entering the new members' details onto the computer takes a little more than an hour. When I type their names and addresses I wonder who they are and what they might be dealing with. They will have their own mailboxes in their own front yards whereas all our mail is sent to the scrapyard office. I never have a chance to see it.

Mrs. Appleby approaches.

An old-fashioned perfume with notes of vanilla, notes of rose.

"It's about that time. Go on, be away with you, I know you're itching. It's nearly done, isn't that right?"

"Last two chapters."

"We launched a poet's collection here before your time. An anthology." When she smiles she has dimples. "Poet from Poplar Bluff. I told you, didn't I?"

"Yes, Mrs. Appleby."

"A dozen or so in the audience. We put out chairs, borrowed some from Chuck at the health center. Platters of home-baked oatmeal cookies. Questions and answers, it was a good night. We'll do the same for you, Peggy, if you want, when the time comes. Be nice to meet your family."

I shiver at the thought. "Thank you."

My usual computer is taken by a tall man still wearing his military surplus hat so I take another one. I manage to write for a solid hour even though people ask me for books or sections or simply drop by to chat. I don't mind the interruptions, not like Drew. He says his style of prose demands complete focus. He will not compromise. Ironically, that is one of the things I was attracted to when we met. The other guys back then were half-hearted and directionless, whereas Drew knew exactly what he wanted. He says he will not write anything less than that which he is capable of. No room for weakness. Whereas I seem to write about the same with or without interruptions.

I save my chapters to a floppy disk and go back to work in the children's area.

The afternoon passes with me still pondering the climax of my book. Worrying about it. I had not planned what would happen and now I regret that. By the end of the week I will need to have it clear in my mind. Then, when it's the right moment, I will build up the courage to tell Drew what I have been doing. I will not jump the gun and talk to him until it is complete. If I manage to sell it one day he'll be relieved to have some extra cash coming in. Him liking the story does not worry me because I am quite certain he will not. It is not his kind of writing. He says he only really has time for Hemingway these days.

As if we didn't already know.

In some ways I write to escape, to travel, to live other lives. But I also write to confront what might be around the next corner, to visualize and prepare myself for it. I have found no better way to deal with anguish and pain than to write straight through it.

I would love to drop a quarter in Fred's cup, but he does not expect it from me. I would still like to do it, to surprise him. I know if it wasn't for us inheriting Mom's bungalow we'd be in trouble, but Drew sees to all the details. When we moved onto the boat the smell of mildew was overwhelming. That night, after scrubbing the boards with stiff brushes and Clorox, we ate cold take-out pizza by the fire and all in all it was a hopeful moment. Samson made a root beer toast to his Nanna Ruth, thanking her for our boat, and at that point Drew fell quiet. A face as hard and unmoving as basaltic rock. He stopped chewing and he turned to me and asked, *What's been said?* I told him nothing had been said. He asked Samson to stand up. Then he stood up himself to face our boy, and looked down on him, and explained how this was our boat and that was that. For the family. Nothing to do with Nanna Ruth or anybody else outside. He provided the boat for us from his work at the scrapyard, the dairy, and the construction site, all cash in hand. Later that night, his shoulder turned away from me, I asked him if the leftover money from Mom's bungalow helped a little with the boat and he ignored me and stayed still as a statue in a crypt. Since then he's mentioned the old mortgage and other bungalow repair costs. He says the boat was paid for out of his labor and it's for his family. Us against them.

Nothing is straightforward living with Drew, it never has been. He is a man of artistic integrity, his own words, and that isn't easy. But his writing is genuinely extraordinary. The story he submitted when we were dating is still the most achingly beautiful work I have ever read. It haunts me to this day. There was never any doubt in my mind he would win the Hugh Higgins Memorial Prize. The $500 check and the bronze paperweight mounted on black granite. There was never any hesitation. But his brilliance comes at a steep price. His art can sometimes turn our home life into a waking nightmare, and it is my job to navigate us through those periods for the sake of Samson. It is not always plain sailing when you are fourteen. I remember those days. The hormones and self-doubt. The endless reimagining of yourself, your reality, and your dreams.

    I am just grateful he likes his new school as much as he does.

4

SAMSON

The other boys can relax.

They play and laugh and talk about MTV and make plans for the weekend. The other boys move through each school day like water running through a smooth gully. There are no obstacles for them. Their daily lives are frictionless. I observe them doing this thing and that: buying their lunch in the cafeteria, handing in their assignments at the end of biology class, placing their textbooks back in their bags. I watch them as they thrive, and they do not even realize how fortunate they are.

I am a whole different species.

Take James Kendricks Jr. Known to us as Jim. He's the kind of boy who will become a senator someday. His blond hair is always perfectly in place, and his shirts are always clean. White collars that glow. At the end of each day, Jim looks relaxed. He has laughed his laughs and he is drifting through the final minutes of his final period, calm, almost sleepy. Whereas I am on my knees and I daren't show it. Looking over my shoulder, hour after hour, class after class, watching my back, takes it out of me.

"Jenkins, what are you loitering about for?"

"Sorry, Mr. Davenport. I'm looking for my bag, sir."

He walks closer. Dennis Davenport. Head of Lower School. Decent enough.

"Why would it be here, Jenkins? You haven't had gym today, have you?"

"No, sir."

He frowns.

"I lost it, sir."

They moved it.

"You lost your own bag?"

They hid it.

"It'll be around here someplace."

"We're locking this building soon, Jenkins. Wake up, find your belongings, and get off home."

"Yes, sir."

Ten minutes later I find my bag stuffed inside a planter. The base is wet but my Walkman is still working. It is intact inside its sock cover.

They laugh as I head out the doors by the gym. They laugh as I walk away to the school gates. Passing through with dozens of other boys, a sea of black polyester blazers, they laugh in the distance. After I've walked for ten minutes past the candy store and the bakery, they're still laughing. Inside my head I can hear them clearly. Laughing at me and my damp bag. At my life.

My spirits lift on making it past the park with the empty public pool. I see a tall sophomore on a bike. He's even skinnier than I am. I've heard his classmates call him Sniper's Nemesis.

I walk on.

A safe zone.

Neighborhood of my oldest, most unlikely friend.

Mr. Turner lives at 34 Bakersfield Avenue. His bungalow is larger than the one we used to live in. One extra room, a bigger garden, and a garage.

I ring the bell.

I found the advertisement in the classifieds. *Senior gentleman requires help in the house and boat one day a week. Light duties, grocery shopping, dog walking, odd jobs.* Mom came with me to see Mr. Turner to make sure he wasn't a pervert.

I ring the bell again.

A full minute passes.

"Come in out of the cold, Samson. Come in, boy."

He ushers me inside and the bungalow smells of unwashed sheets and the heating turned up too high, TV dinners and cigarette smoke. There are Walmart bags stuffed inside a cardboard box on the kitchen table. On either side of the box is a steaming cup.

"Nice cup of hot milk after your schooling. Sit down. You want a KitKat?"

"Yes, please."

"There you go."

He places it down next to my mug. Two fingers. He gives me hot milk because that's what he had as a boy.

"You want me to go out to the store for you, Mr. Turner?"

"After. You sit down and rest a while. Get that milk inside you. Hot drink will fix most things, my old mama used to say, God bless her soul. You see the fire truck, did you?"

"No."

"About ten minutes ago, it was. Heading up toward the levee. Lights and everything. Hope nothing too serious."

The milk is sweet and my throat loosens a little. I use my fingernail to run along the foil wrapper and then I offer Mr. Turner a chocolate finger.

"Oh, no, they're for you, Samson. I'll put my supper on when you've gone. Chicken potpie night, one of my favorites. Listen, how's the boat? Newer than mine, isn't it? British design: long and thin. How are you taking to life at sea?"

"Just a canal, Mr. Turner."

"I know it is, boy, I'm yanking your chain. You like it, though? Cozy life, isn't it?"

"Dad doesn't like the marina. Says it's too noisy."

"Yeah, well, it can be that."

"Dad's moving us."

"Where to?"

"Robertson's is too expensive, he says. He wants us to be on our own out of town. Wants to be in nature for his book writing. Maybe onto the river, even."

Mr. Turner stands up and rinses his cup and places it upside down on the drainer. He's wearing new sheepskin slippers.

"Not easy being out cruising full-time. Not having a base. People think it'll be a grand life but it's not straightforward even if you're good with motors."

"I don't want to go on the river."

"Don't blame you for that. The size of the barges these days. The currents."

"Dad likes things that are not easy."

He looks at me. "And what does your mom say?"

"I don't know."

"All right, listen. Drain that cup and go to the store. I need a carton of whole milk, pack of pink sugar wafers, and a loaf of thinly sliced bread. You remember all that?"

I nod and hand him my warm cup.

"And two packs of Marlboro Reds."

"I can't, Mr. Turner."

He smiles. "I know, boy. I'll ask my cousin's son to buy them for me. Only a few more years, eh?"

He hands me the cash.

* * *

The owner looks at me suspiciously as I walk around his tiny corner grocery store and pick up the milk, wafers, and bread. He always looks at me suspiciously, this one, like I'm about to steal something.

When I return, Mr. Turner's in his recliner, the one with stuffing sprouting out of both arms.

"Quiz show on the TV. Let's see how you fare today, Einstein."

The theme tune plays as I put the food away. The tightness in my shoulders eases and I stare at my reflection in the kitchen window. Time stops for a full minute. I look into my own eyes and take this moment for myself. No harm can come to me in this stuffy, familiar place. He just lets me be.

Mr. Turner answers the first two questions incorrectly.

"They're making it harder, the jackasses, I know they are. Nothing stays the same, does it? Infernal TV."

I made a handsome thirty-two cents profit at the store.

The doorbell rings and the neighbor hands back Mr. Turner's dog. He's too old to walk her himself and for some reason he won't give her to me to walk yet even though I've offered. He says Amber needs to become accustomed to me first. She's a Jack Russell terrier: black and brown with a pink leather collar. Mr. Turner says she's a sensitive dog and she can be anxious around new folks.

Amber jumps up on Mr. Turner's lap and he strokes her narrow head and the quiz show keeps on playing. Her eyes close.

I'm glad they have each other.

"I was going to keep it a secret and surprise you, but I can't hold it in. I'm bringing my boat out tomorrow," he says. "My cousin's son's helping me with it. He's about your parents' age and he's good with all things practical, is Phoenix. Might come and see you on the canal, Samson."

"Is Phoenix his real name?"

"Is it his real name?" He chuckles to himself. "No. His name's Graham."

I pause to imagine Mr. Turner on the canal. "Will you manage?"

"Will I manage?" he says, rubbing Amber's chin. "Will we manage? Of course we'll manage, boy. Had my boat nineteen years, five of them with Betty. Will I manage?"

He doesn't talk about Betty much with me but there are photos of her everywhere. One time, when I arrived early, he was sat on the sofa holding a framed photograph from their wedding day and he looked like he was upset. He claimed it was hay fever.

"I'll let you know where we moor up," I say.

"You do that, Ahab."

When Dad found out it was relatively inexpensive to live on a boat, he began investigating this way of life. It's just a shame he bought the smallest, thinnest boat in America, but Mom says we're lucky to have what we got. Others around here have it much worse.

I say goodbye and he pays me ten bucks for the week. Three one-hour visits, up from one originally, that I'd willingly do for free. He is a decent man, Mr. Turner. He never had any kids, but I think he would have made a good dad.

Bus home, and then a walk along the towpath.

My schoolbag feels cold and heavy, the damp part chill against my back.

I spot a bird of prey on the far bank, hovering in the tree line, but I can't tell if it's a Mississippi kite or a goshawk.

The light is falling away and the water shines: dull and bright at the same time.

"Tiny Dancer" on my Walkman radio. Then Whitney Houston at maximum volume. Then the haunting, perfect voice of Sinéad O'Connor. Music can save a person, I'd say. Radio, especially. If I'm at rock bottom, nine times out of ten the right song will come along right when I need it.

I pass the area in the marina where our boat was once moored up and walk on. Another mile. Two more. I switch off my radio. The light is almost completely absent and there is frost in the air. My feet are frozen. I move my bag strap to the other shoulder. It's as if it's growing heavier with every passing mile. And I'm growing hungrier.

A freight train rattles along the tracks in the distance.

I keep on walking.

Looking for home.

5

PEGGY

I step carefully on the timber plank, and onto the boat.

He shows himself. "You found it then."

I move forward and offer him a cheek, but he pulls back. "What do you think?"

"It's nice," I say. "That bend in the canal. Good spot."

"Canal's like a railroad. You're either going forward or back. There's no surprise to it. Unlike the river, you know where you stand with a canal."

I hang up my jacket and wash my hands and step into my slippers. It is important I do not tread dirt onto Mom's rug. I try to keep it as clean as she did.

"Who'd you talk to at the library?"

"Mrs. Appleby and the others."

He stops moving. The sound of his clock ticking loudly on his desk. "Others?"

"The other staff. The other volunteers."

"Who's that then?"

"Deborah."

"And on your walk back. Who did you see?"

"Nobody."

He sticks his tongue into the side of his mouth.

I point. "What's that, Drew?"

He looks back at his old bureau desk. Seven weathered Hemingway novels, a copy of *Writer's Market*, multiple locked drawers, one Hugh Higgins Memorial Prize dated the year Sammy was born, and a large cardboard box.

"That might be your ticket."

"Ticket?"

His smile turns from small and stiff to broad and fixed in place.

"Ticket for you and the boy. I'm not spoiling him, though, if this new book takes off. Still needs to know his place even when things turn around. I'm not bending over on that, Peggy."

"Is it a computer?"

"A computer? You think I'm made of money? It's a word processor. Battery-powered on account of our rural circumstances. Girl in the yard will keep them charged up for me. Means I'll be able to write faster. Put the words down like greased lightning, I will. No more longhand for Andrew Jenkins, not from today."

When I met Drew at a creative writing evening class run by the community college in Carterville, he sat with a different posture from the rest of us. We were casual and self-conscious, whereas Drew sat at the front of the class with a straight back and an eager expression on his face. He took it so seriously I think he intimidated the teacher.

Sammy arrives back home. He slips off his shoes and drops his bag and runs to me.

I hold him tight and the back of his winter coat feels damp. I want to warm him. Rub his bony shoulders and support his head in the crook of my neck. He smells like my boy still and his cheeks are red and the light fur on his chin is standing on end.

"Stop smothering him, woman. Treat him like a baby and he'll always be one."

I squeeze him harder still and kiss the top of his beautiful head.

"I said stop."

Sammy pulls away.

"Hello, Dad."

"Good of you to acknowledge your old man."

"What's for supper? I'm starving."

I start to say, "Ravio—"

"*What's for supper, you're starving?* After I've moved the boat out here all on my own, done a half day at the yard, and paid for a new word processor. What's for supper? Get back there and bring in a sack of coal, that's what."

An hour later we are sat at the dinette eating Chef Boyardee ravioli with a plate of bread and butter in the middle of the table. Drew and Sammy are lit by a flickering candle and their skulls are the exact same shape.

During snapshot moments like this one, when all around us is quiet and still, and my boy is eating until his belly is full, I am satisfied with my lot.

Drew finishes first and pushes his plate away.

"Propane in the tanks for a day or two but that's about it. Electric from the batteries is limited; I'm not running engines all day to charge them up, not wasting diesel on it. Toilet habits will have to change."

"Marina was better," mutters Sammy.

"Marina's built for deadbeats. Out here it's real life. Surviving on your wits and being surrounded by nature. Birdsong and endless skies. You think Ernest Miller Hemingway would have moored up in Robertson's with all those conveniences, do you? Not a chance. This place will be the making of you, boy. You'll see."

"How will your new computer work out here, Dad?"

"Not a computer, it's a word processor, and it runs on a battery. I save my work and your mother will print it off in the library, won't you?"

I squirm in my seat. "I can do some, perhaps, but I have to be careful."

"Careful? They don't pay you a wage. Careful? You work for free, why do you need to be careful? Not like they'll fire you."

"Does this mean we can afford a new fridge?" I ask.

He stiffens up.

He does not speak.

"Or have the old one fixed?" I say.

"You want to keep on like that? Seven o'clock and I'll be writing dead on nine. You want me to go in with your nags fogging up my head, what do you think will happen? No words of any merit, that's what. No original use of language. Why do you think I wrote an award-winning story *before* I married you? Coincidence? I don't want to hear about any icebox. We'll finish supper and then you two get yourselves ready by nine so I can sit down and concentrate."

"How did we buy this boat, Dad?"

"How did we what?"

"I saw it cost eleven thousand dollars."

"Oh, you did, did you? We bought it because I've been toiling all these years, that's how. One day, when you're a grown man, you'll provide for your own family, learn the value of a dollar."

I try to hold in the thought but I fail.

"Something to say?"

"Nothing."

"Go on. I saw it in your eyes; you're itching to have your say on it. Tell the kid what you're thinking."

"Just that we're grateful to you for working hard to buy us the boat, that's all." I see his lip twitch at the corner. "It's a nice little boat, we're settling in. And, at the same time, I'm also grateful to Nanna Ruth, because she worked hard like you, not as hard as you, but all her life. Moved here from England—fled, really—with no money or friends, and worked hard for the bungalow despite her nerves. And that helped us buy this, didn't it. So I'm thankful to Mom, that's all I was thinking, Drew."

He looks at Sammy and smiles, but his thin, chapped lips are clamped tight.

"Her mother." He spits out the words like he's allergic to them, like they hurt his teeth.

"Nanna Ruth," says Sammy.

"Your nanna," he says. "Was nothing but trouble, Samson. Typical Brit. Thought she knew best. Picture of the queen above the mantel, all that. I wish you'd have met her, boy, you'd have seen straight through her. Could have henpecked in the Olympics, she could, the mouth on her. Would have won gold for the Brits."

"Drew."

"You don't remember her clearly, Peggy. Not your fault. The things she used to tell me about you. Awful things. All the moaning about your studies and your idleness, honestly, I wish you'd heard. You wouldn't have these rosy memories."

"I don't want to hear it," I say.

"Well, you will hear it, and so will Samson, because it's the truth. Someone around here needs to talk sense. It's the family history on your side whether we like it or not. Best thing your nanna ever did was give birth to your mother. Second-best thing was when she swallowed those pills."

6

SAMSON

I pull my pajamas on in the bathroom. It is the only private space I've got. And then I wipe the toothpaste smudges from the faucet because Dad will be in here next.

I leave the room pristine.

Mom says, "Hot cocoa?"

I walk toward her, and Dad passes me, our bodies scraping past each other by my dinette table bed, his body hard and angular, mine stubbornly soft and young for my age.

"Yes, please, Mom."

She stands at the gas burner, whisking the milk to make it frothy. When I look at the glow of the flame I wonder how much propane is left in the tanks and how we'll ever refill them out here in the middle of nowhere.

We sit together in front of the spitting fire. She has no hot drink of her own. We stare into the flames from the comfort of our camp chairs, Dad enclosed in the bathroom behind the door, and all is well. There is distance. My mother and me and one steaming mug. Her face outlined in orange. She's pretty. Her teeth are all over the place, true, but her face, her cheekbones, her nose, her brown hair. She looks like she could have been somebody.

"What did you watch at Mr. Turner's house, Sam? Anything good?"

"Some quiz show."

"Oh, I miss them. Especially *Wheel of Fortune*, now that's a good show. Hard, but not too hard, you know? I miss our television. Don't tell your father, but I really miss it now the days are short."

"Me too. But we have the radio, Mom. And books."

She laughs. "Are you the parent, Samson, or am I?"

I laugh back. "We look out for each other."

She looks away.

"Was it like this with your mom?"

She smiles and glances at me and then stares into the fire as if looking for an answer. I sip my milky drink and gaze sideways at her and I wait. I wish I knew what she was thinking.

"Your nanna was hilarious, Sam. Mixture of British humor and our kind. Funniest lady I ever met in my life. Funniest person, full stop."

She touches her necklace. A dented gold thing with a safety chain. I can't remember if Nanna Ruth bought it for Mom or passed it down to her.

"What would she say?"

She looks at me. "Oh, I don't know. But she always made me laugh. We had giggle fits, the pair of us. I always felt we were enough for each other. But when she died the truth hit me like a bolt of lightning. We weren't enough for each other after all. I wasn't enough for her. And with her gone she wasn't enough for me either. You need more than one person in your life, see. You need a backup, Sammy. Otherwise it's all too much of a burden."

"I only have you."

"Don't talk nonsense. You have your father; he'd die for you, your dad would. He'd take a bullet for you."

The fire crackles.

I look into the embers.

"I know."

"There, then."

I sip from my mug. "He should talk nicer, though," I whisper. "I feel like hitting him sometimes."

She rubs her eye. "Well, don't. Nothing good comes of that. Your dad's harsh on you because he wants you to grow into a fine man, that's all."

"I was talking about how he speaks to *you*, Mom."

She looks down and absentmindedly pinches the skin above her knuckle. "I'm all right. Mothers are tougher than we look."

A noise from the bathroom.

The door slides open.

Steam.

Dad remains inside.

"Enough of this," she says, patting my knee. "I'll tell you one thing. Your father's mood improves when he's had the chance to write properly. An artist like your dad, with his sensibilities, his talent, the way he can find hope in the bleakest of stories, is afforded certain liberties most don't deserve. The way he sets prose down on the page, Sammy, we must let him do it. Some success, an award or a contract, he'll turn back to how he was, you'll see. Mark my words."

Dad approaches with a small towel around his waist. It looks like his musculature has been carved from white igneous stone: every line and muscle picked out by firelight. A figure on a plinth in some faraway city.

"You want the bathroom, either of you, now's the time. Nine o'clock sharp I want no noise, not a peep."

"We know, Dad."

"I don't want to hear *oh, I forgot to wash my face*. This is it. You both done?"

We nod.

He looks at her and his face softens. "I'll be in later. I'll try to be quiet." He looks down at me. "Samson, kiss your father."

I peck him on the right cheek like I've done every night before bed since I could understand the instruction.

"Good night, boy. Not a noise now."

We retreat.

I drag the comforter up to my chin. The dinette table makes a reasonable bed, as it goes. Wider than my twin bed in the bungalow. I don't mind it. I have my own window and some storage and it rarely gets too cold, not like Mom and Dad's frozen bedroom at the far end. Dad's pulled on a sleeveless undershirt and he's seated at his desk. I listen for a while. The cadence of his keystrokes on the word processor. The gaps where I imagine him dreaming up the next metaphor. Time passes. I hear him remove his shirt. The sound of his fingertips hitting the keys faster and faster. The air is warm and my mouth still has the memory of cocoa. Dad is in his own world now. Mom will be reading a library book in her bed. Complete silence, just the way Dad needs it. Not another boat for miles around. Darkness outside save for sporadic flashes of moonlight.

Once I am confident he's completely engrossed in his own work, I carefully remove my Walkman from its sock and listen to a cassette recording I made from the BBC's World Service. *Moral Maze*. A conversation that took place live in London at BBC studios that I'm now able to listen to for free here on this forgotten stretch of water. The undeniable magic of that. Dad is oblivious. The foam pads of my headphones rest against my ears, and at low volume I listen to academics and journalists debate the death penalty. Discussions of *mens rea* and *actus reus*, of the boundary between sanity and insanity, of the irrefutability of new DNA evidence, of the inherent weaknesses of any jury-based system. I learn more from the BBC and PBS than I do at school.

My whole life feels like a moral maze some days. Holding my

tongue, tough love, lesser of two evils, lying in order to help someone, not speaking up when a classmate cheats.

An inescapable maze.

Dad types, my tape ends, and a play starts on the radio. I fall somewhere between wakefulness and sleep. Daydreaming about college. Some Elysian institution surrounded by mature deciduous trees and tolerant students sharing ideas. Princeton, perhaps, or Oxford. But then it morphs into Dartmouth, the American elms, the meandering Connecticut River, and the forested Upper Valley. I am almost too warm, but I can't move or I'll put Dad off his flow. He's working well, I can sense it. The typing is frenetic. He'll be pleased we moved so far away from the marina. I dream about friends I am yet to meet. People like me in a faraway city where nobody is aware of my past. New acquaintances who don't know me from Adam. I'll re-create myself. A true rebirth. As I drift deeper into sleep I see myself in a dorm room with posters on the wall. Thumbtacks twinkling. The door opens. He walks in, a guy my age. A friend, I guess. He waits. The room is silent. I don't say a word. Static in the air. He pulls his sweater over his head and climbs carefully into my bed. He rests next to me and I don't move a muscle. He places his nose into the crook of my neck. The warmth of his breath on my skin. The unmistakable sound of someone typing up their essay in the next room. The smell of him. Nobody trying to hurt or limit me. He breathes in and out, matching my own rhythm, and every second feels like a minute.

"Did I wake you, boy?"

I squint and rub my eyes. His face looms over mine. "What time is it?"

"Almost one o'clock. Did I wake you up?"

I shake my head.

"Hot toddy? A one-off midnight treat. What do you say?"

I frown.

"You want a hot toddy or not, Samson?"

"Hot toddy?"

"Come on. Don't tell your mother."

I wrap myself in my comforter and step outside and pee into the flat metallic waters of the canal. There are shadows dancing on the surface, and an owl hoots boldly from the far bank. He has never woken me up in the middle of the night like this.

He pours something into a mug. "That'll fix you, boy."

Was I snoring? Has he been staring at me, rage in his eyes? Does he know what I was dreaming about?

He hands me a mug of black coffee, his breath clouding in front of his lips. He has his work coat on and his beanie but he's still sweating from sitting so close to the fire.

"What's in it?" I ask.

"Don't you trust me?"

"Is it coffee?"

"Drop of Jim Beam in that. I opened the bottle I got from the site foreman last Christmas. Like I said, don't tell your mother. This is between us men."

He called me a man.

"Thanks, Dad."

We sit on the well deck of the boat, staring out into the empty night air. I don't like coffee, but this toddy is good. Not too strong. I am sitting with my dad.

"You can ask me how it was if you like."

I frown. "How was it?"

"Fair, boy. Not bad."

I take another sip and the steam rises to dampen my eyelids.

"Word processor's decent. Managed some fair work. Nice run. You and your mother were good, didn't hear a noise. And having no other boats around us made all the difference. Felt like my old self."

My shoulders loosen.

The water is otherworldly at this time of night. The birds and insects are nowhere to be found, replaced by bats and raptors; hoots and the sound of river birch limbs rubbing against one another.

I think back to the dream. How the boy was in bed with me and then later he was a girl. A grown woman. I felt there was space to be myself in that life. I wasn't preyed upon.

"What were you like when you were fourteen, Dad?"

"What was I like?"

"Yeah."

"Normal boy. Fourteen was a decent year. Football team, baseball, captain for a while, won trophies for swim meets up at the pool. Butterfly, mostly. Couple of chicks on my tail. Best time of life, right?"

I drain the last of the toddy, conscious I will have to face them again in a few hours.

"Yes, Dad. The best."

7

PEGGY

I wake in the dead of night. He has his back to me. It's been a week since he moved the boat and I've never felt it this cold. He stirs as I sit up, so I pause, holding my breath, the muscles in my thighs tensing, my temples throbbing. He settles. I wait a moment more and then I leave him.

I stand by the sliding bathroom door, looking out of the round window.

The night sky is awash with stars, more so than in the marina. Plush black velvet, with clouds moving across and me standing witness within this aging vessel, tethered to a mud bank, motionless in stagnant water.

Sammy is sleeping, his face hidden to me. I watch the duvet rise and fall with each innocent breath. Observing with the same concentration I had when he was a baby in Mom's bungalow. Watching his perfect inhalations: each one a miracle.

The fire is out.

I take kindling from next to the woodstove and place it inside the firebox. There is some warmth left in the cast iron but not enough for the kindling to take. I light a match, the sulfur intoxicating in this thick silence, and my thoughts turn to what he once told me.

He sleeps and Samson sleeps and I calculate that my son has survived fourteen years under his roof and needs four more to make his own way in this world. He is a formidable survivor and by God he will continue to be one.

The flame catches the draft from the vents and I close the door gently and watch the colors shimmy behind blackened glass. Fresh smoke in the air. The boat is motionless in dull, stagnant water and you might think I would be safe here by the fire, but I am not. It's not even what he might have done as a child that haunts my dreams; it is the manner in which he told me.

The expression on his face.

I do not sit in a folding camp chair; I remain cross-legged on Mom's rug, stealing this moment of peace for myself. My existence is a bare wall in a jail cell, each year checked off with a short, well-chewed pencil. When Samson was a baby I thought that would be our most vulnerable time. And then, when he was at elementary school, I imagined his little frame would slowly grow and become powerful and resilient. But now that he is fourteen I have come to understand the bitter truth of our joint sentence.

I return to our room because he will not let me leave the bed in the morning before he does. It is a point of principle for Drew. First up, attacking the day: the action of it choreographed and farcical.

I lie still, trying and failing to sense the temperature rise in this so-called bedroom. I am not sure it qualifies, considering the bed is damp, and smaller than a standard full, and it leads directly into the greasy engine room complete with lead-acid batteries and exposed wiring and tins of old marine paint.

Yesterday Mr. Turner arrived on this desolate stretch of canal in his own houseboat, the one that inspired Drew to make this drastic life change, and, in my eyes at least, Jeff Turner's arrival set a timer ticking. A long and inextinguishable fuse.

Drew stirs and his leg twitches.

The man who told me he burned down his own home at the age of fifteen lies beside me dreaming about only God knows what.

His leg twitches some more.

He recalled the details with no sense of remorse or regret. A flat expression. The door to his parents' bedroom was locked, same as the window. Their key was later discovered underneath the marital bed, encased in a blackened glass jar. The spare was never found. The suburban house did not burn to the ground; it was still structurally sound when the fire was extinguished, but his parents, Evelyn and Bill, perished from smoke inhalation. Drew told me how he set the fire and walked downstairs and waited. When the yelling subsided, and their bedroom door stopped rattling inside its frame, he put on his winter coat and left the house. Drew walked to a neighbor. When the firefighters found his parents his mother was still alive, but his father had succumbed. Evelyn Jenkins made it to the emergency room but she passed away later that morning. Drew explained this to me when I was eight months pregnant. He had just finished building a handsome pine crib for Sammy. He told me at the kitchen table in my late mother's bungalow and I swear there were no tears in his eyes. Drew couldn't remember if it was the police or a social worker who talked to him after the fire, perhaps both, but he told them clearly it was all his fault and they told him it was not, and he must not think that way. They said old wiring was to blame. The investigation had found faulty, out-of-date electrical cables, and signs that fuel had been improperly stored on the property. They told him he must not feel guilty for what happened, and then they explained how they were going to find him a new home. He told them *he wished the fire had taken his grandpa as well* and they told him he should not blame himself. This is what shocked Drew the most. I am not sure he expected or even wanted to walk away from what he did. He told me that night, *Police don't know what they're doing. Same as teachers and doctors and government:*

all education and no common sense. I realized I should follow my own path. I was a man after that night.

Of course, that's just the version he told me.

Who knows what actually happened.

He wakes me with a cup of sweet coffee at seven.

Freshly shaved head, glistening; sweatpants, one bloodshot eye.

"I'm off training. Have my eggs done when I get back in. Three-minute eggs, not a second more."

In later years he explained that it was all a story, fiction, something he was working on for a scene in his new novel. I didn't know what to believe. Then he told me that I had imagined the whole conversation. Once he said *he* had imagined it over and over, so it felt almost real but in reality he'd never gone through with it. Another time he claimed I was mixing up an old radio play with what had actually happened. Or that he was anxious before Sammy's birth and described his nightmare to me in the middle of the night, and now I was recollecting that as if it were fact.

He says out-of-date wiring killed his parents.

I take the coffee through and think about giving it to Sammy, but I pour it down the sink instead. I do not trust it since Mr. Turner moved his houseboat directly behind ours and sent Drew into this invisible, silent rage. I'm probably being paranoid, but I'd rather be safe than sorry.

"What time is it, Mom?"

"Past seven." I sit on the end of his dinette bed. "Your dad's out training."

He jumps out of bed, smiling, and pulls off his pajama shirt. So pale and slight. He puts on his school gym shirt and says, "Why didn't you wake me?"

"I didn't think you wanted waking."

He runs out through the kitchen and past the woodstove and Drew's bureau desk and jumps onto the bank to join his father.

The boat is warming up.

ADRIFT

I have not told anyone I am submitting my book to publishers. I have not even told Mrs. Appleby, though I think she would be pleased. Thank goodness for libraries, that's all I can say. I have sent the book to three publishers so far. I found their addresses in the back of a magazine. Three independent publishers: two in New York and one in Chicago. I used the library as my return address and Mrs. Appleby approved the printing. I had to dip into my hidden stash to afford stamps, but it was worth it, even though I have received one rejection already. Years of shopping for discount almost-out-of-date food and then carefully peeling off the discount stickers before bringing the food home. He asks for receipts these days so I can no longer save that way. Years of picking up every single coin I have ever seen. Slow accrual in the clear-sighted knowledge that one day I will need money of my own. Drew says I am not good with figures, so ever since Mom died he has taken responsibility for our account. I fought against it, of course, argued and protested, but I soon realized I had to pick my battles and play the long game. Keeping Samson alive and well had to come first. Now I have two submissions out there. One in New York and one in Chicago. Perhaps they are being read right now. Part of me would love to tell him all about it but the other part knows it would set him off.

The boat shakes.

Sammy walks back in.

"What's wrong, Sammy?"

"Won't let me train."

"Why not?"

He cannot look me in the eye.

"Says I don't try hard enough. Says they're not real push-ups. Says I look like a girl doing them."

"Come here."

"No."

"Come on."

He shuffles over to me.

"Your dad's old-fashioned, that's all. Give him time."

"I don't see how I'll turn into what he wants me to be if he won't let me train with him. I was trying my best."

"I know you were."

Four more years and you will fly free, my love.

"You quit, did you?" says Drew, appearing near the fire in his drenched shirt. "Gave up, kid. Threw in the towel, did you?"

"You told me to leave."

"And you just did it?" His chest is heaving with each breath. "First sign of friction and you folded over, went running back to your mother."

Samson stomps to the bathroom and locks the door.

"Go easy on him, Drew."

"Don't see my eggs ready."

I need the bathroom myself now. Tightness in my stomach.

"I didn't expect you back so soon."

"Didn't marry you to expect, Peggy. Married you to do what I tell you. Three-minute eggs, that too much to ask?"

"Why don't you have a shower and I'll boil them."

"Not enough water in the tank for a shower. Washcloth in the sink will do." He walks toward the bathroom. "Princess, you done in there?"

Samson walks out, his eyes to the floor.

Drew looks back and says, "Make sure—"

"Three minutes," I say. "I heard you. Do you want your bread toasted?"

He approaches slowly, pulling off his shirt. Sweat glistens all over his face. A drip on the very tip of his nose. "You interrupt me like that again and watch what'll happen. We've been over this. You agreed, or have you forgotten?"

"I remember."

"I doubt it. You interrupt me again if you like. Go on."

I don't move a muscle.

"Eggs," he says. "Three minutes."

"I need the bathroom before you wash. If that's OK."

He lets me squeeze past him.

A drop of his sweat on my arm.

I emerge a while later and his face is like thunder.

"What's wrong?" I say.

He points to the pan on the burner.

"What?"

He turns off the gas and I walk to him.

"You never put the eggs in, Peggy. No water either. Which means a fire hazard. And you know how I feel about fires. How did you forget it like that?"

I stare at the burner in disbelief. "I'm sorry. I don't even remember putting the pan on. I was going to do it after."

"What?"

"I must have . . ."

"You telling me you have no memory of putting the egg pan on? This is serious, girl. You really don't remember?"

My mouth is dry.

I rub my temples.

"I do remember now. I'm sorry I left it, my mind was somewhere else. I'll put your eggs on now."

"Don't want eggs."

"Andrew, please. I was forgetful, is all. I'll cook them. Toast?"

"I said I don't want any eggs."

8

SAMSON

I stand next to Dad's desk with its locked cabinets and individually locked drawers, and Mom looks more like me than herself. Bony. Her shoulders slumped.

"The pan was my fault, Dad."

He turns to me.

"You what?"

She shakes her head frantically behind him.

"I put the egg pan on when Mom was in the bathroom. I was trying to help. It wasn't her, see. It was me who did it."

He turns to look at her then back to me.

"Tell the truth, boy."

"I am."

He walks toward me, shoulders back, forearms tensed. "You're telling me you put that pan on the burner and then wandered off and left it. That what you're saying?"

I want to flee. But instead I stay in place and nod; some fortitude I never knew I had.

He frowns and chews his liver-colored lower lip.

I am trembling.

ADRIFT

"Drew," says Mom.

He raises his hand in the air. "Boy's come clean. Thought he was a pansy but he's showing spirit, first time in his life. You owning this, Samson?"

I nod.

"All right, then. Get over here."

I step closer.

"I said get here."

I walk to him and the power he possesses, the potential contained within his large, tightly bound frame, is palpable. I sense the force of him.

"I was about to walk up to Miller's yard to empty our toilet cassette in their septic, but now you're such a chivalrous young man you can do it. You've seen me carry them often enough. Tell Miller to add it to my tab. You can manage it, can you?"

"I'll borrow Mr. Turner's barrow."

"You'll carry it, boy."

"Andrew," says Mom.

"I could have carried two at his age. You'll take it on your shoulder. No need for Jeff Turner's barrow. I'm going to work with an empty belly thanks to you. I'll have to pay for a BLT at the yard. When I come home I expect that cassette empty, understood?"

"Yes, sir."

* * *

I call in to see Mr. Turner for my Saturday shift but instead of having to go visit his bungalow I walk all of ten yards. His boat, *Skylark*, inspired Dad to buy ours. I think he liked the idea of no neighbors to share Mom's attention with. He won't credit Mr. Turner with the idea, though; he says he knew about houseboats since he was a teenager. Says he had the idea years back and anyway Jeff Turner's boat is a completely different design from ours.

"Mr. Turner, can I come in?"

He's there at his dinette reading a *TV Guide* in his long johns and undershirt.

"Shut that door, Samson. I'll catch my death."

"Mom says if she makes stew later she'll send over a plate. Think it'll have Italian sausage in it. She went to the butcher."

"She's a princess, your mother."

"She's all right."

I wish she wouldn't leave pans on, though. The last thing I need is carrying a cassette full of waste all the way to Miller's septic.

"How much does a full cassette weigh, Mr. Turner?"

"A what, Samson? You want a KitKat, do you? I've got a drawerful."

I take one and put it in my back pocket.

"Take another one, why don't you. For later."

I don't hesitate.

"A cassette from the toilet," I say again. "How much does it weigh?"

"Too effin' much, pardon my French. I have another day on mine and then it'll need emptying. You offering, are you?"

"I thought Phoenix was going to help you. Your cousin's son?"

"He is. But he's not well. You met him yet?"

I shake my head.

"He's a good man. Studied physics at college. Planets and all sorts. I know he looks like a punk rocker and goes by that nickname, but he's one of the good guys, trust me. Phoenix isn't well, but he still makes the time to come say hi."

"I can do it today."

"All my waste? You sure?"

"I'll need to borrow your barrow, though, if that's OK."

"Course it is." He looks at me, frowning with thought, and then his face lights up. "But we can do one better, I reckon." He folds over the page of the *TV Guide* and stows it down in the magazine rack. "We can steam there in style if you're up to being captain's mate?"

"I'll get the cassette from my bathroom."

"Sorry?"

"I've got to do ours, Dad says."

"Is he still raw over Amber barking at that mallard?"

"It's not that. He just wants me to help out more now I'm older and stronger."

"We'll do them together," he says. "Two cassettes, one luxury cruise. Go get it, young man."

I collect it and when I step back awkwardly onto his boat he's wearing a captain's hat complete with mud stain and feather. I help him free the boat from its moorings and pull up the hooks and we set off. He looks unsteady at the tiller, but he smiles like I have never seen him smile before, like he's proud of motoring his boat on his own.

If I'd had a grandpa I wonder if he'd have been like Mr. Turner. When I'm with him I don't feel like I'm with an adult, really. He's more like a friend.

I empty out the cassettes into Miller's disgusting septic tank, flies everywhere, kids in the distance burning stuff and shooting at rats and aerosol cans, and then we maneuver the boat back to where it was before, directly behind ours. The only two on this stretch of the water.

"Eight foot deep around here," says Mr. Turner, securing the mooring. "Most of the canal's shallow, needs a dredging it does, but it's deep here. You could swim if you wanted."

"Too cold, Mr. Turner."

"It'll do you some good, Samson. Bit of pond weed never hurt nobody."

"Don't mention this to Dad, will you? He wanted me to carry it on my shoulder."

"On your shoulder?"

I nod.

"Far as I'm concerned that's what happened, buddy. Tank of old shit on your shoulder. What should we do next?"

· · ·

On Tuesday I take the long way home from school. I don't want to see him yet. I need time for myself and I can't have that on the boat. Dad's face is growing tighter and more etched with rage every passing day. Each time Amber barks or growls at the wading birds on the embankment he physically hardens.

Football practice didn't go so good. I walk along the side of the road trying to make sense of it, but I know deep down there is none. No logical reason whatsoever. Why do they choose *me* every time? It's like I have a target on my face that I cannot see or scrub away. When I finished practice and came out of the shower they didn't whip me with their rolled towels this time. They didn't hide my jacket or my cleats. This was worse. According to local radio it's only three degrees above freezing. As I walk my socks squelch, and my shirt freezes hard against my chest. They threw my clothes on the tiled floor by the drain. I don't know who did it, how many of them. They all yelled and laughed as I collected my sodden socks and jacket. They cried with laughter as I wrung them out into the communal shower, twisting and squeezing. When I tried to pull on my pants they cheered and some of them had tears in their eyes they were enjoying it so much. Mr. Rodriguez came in to see what all the noise was about. They shut up then. I pulled on my jacket and walked straight out of school.

The one saving grace is I left my Walkman at home this morning. Yesterday at lunch, as I was eating mac and cheese on my own in the cafeteria, Rozza Metcalfe stood behind me and told me it was a cheap knockoff Asian Walkman and I should have bought a Sony and if he ever sees it again he'll stomp on it to do me a favor. Asshole doesn't realize Sony is a Japanese company. He said I listen to queer foreign music and I should be ashamed of myself. Said I was a disgrace to his school.

The footbridge over the railroad is colder than ever. There's some synchronicity between rail and canal. It is not their shared industrial heritage, although I know all about that thanks to last year's history class. Rather it's the unusual wind they have in common. The way we have sliced through the soft curves of nature with alien lines. Gusts funneling and blowing through a cut, or along a straight platform. It is the kind of gale I relish because it burns hard. It blows the cobwebs out of your ears, is what Mom says. Resets you. The wind up here on the footbridge brings an exquisite pain with it.

The pretty girl from the bus stop is heading up the steps. I tense. My shoulders tighten. I pretend I'm looking at a sedge wren. Should I walk quickly to the other side and head home or stay where I am and ignore her? What will she think of me up here on the footbridge all on my own in a soaking wet uniform looking at wildlife? She won't pick on me, it's not that, but she's too pretty.

I focus on a discarded cardboard ticket on the ground between us. An orange rectangle. First Class. Car seven.

I don't want her to notice me.

Move along.

She wears one gold ring in her ear, but not in the lobe, up at the top. It catches the light.

I don't want to catch the light.

I don't want to be seen.

"What you staring at?"

I freeze.

"Is that an eagle?"

I shrug.

Her voice is smooth and melodic.

Not like mine.

The wind gusts and she holds her palms up to her cheeks.

I look at the far bank of the canal and can't help but smile when I notice it.

"That's an owl," I say.

"Is it?"

"Barn owl."

"You sure it's not a snowy? It's white. I think it's a snowy."

"It's pale, not white. That's a barn owl."

We don't say anything for a long time. I am transfixed by the hovering raptor and its ghostly humanlike face, the roundness of its features, the grace of it.

"What's it looking for?" she asks.

"Mice. Voles, maybe. It's getting dark, this is when they like to hunt."

She sits down cross-legged next to me.

I can hardly breathe.

Staring forward, her arm not quite touching mine, she says, "I'm Jennifer Adamu. I've seen you downtown."

"Sam," I say.

We do not look at each other.

We look at the owl.

"You catching a train, Sam?"

"No, I'm watching the owl."

"I've never sat and watched an owl."

I don't answer.

We stare into the waning light.

I can smell her shampoo. Smells like wild mint.

"There are barn owls in the Galápagos," I say. "In the Himalayas, even."

"Yeah?"

My teeth start to chatter.

"You cold?"

"No."

"You sure sound cold. Your teeth are rattling."

"Look at it glide. Look at the shape of its wing tips, its primaries."

"Is it a boy or a girl?"

"It's like a ballet dancer. No, that's not it. Scrap that. A Harrier jet. But silent. Look at its movements. Smooth, but dangerous and untamable."

"You sure know a lot about owls."

"Not a lot."

She stands up and straightens her gray skirt. She smells like bubble gum now, and I am lightheaded for a moment. "I'll see you at the bus station, Sam."

I watch her walk away across the footbridge and disappear out of sight as she descends the steps on the other side.

When I look back the owl is gone.

ID: 9

PEGGY

The morning is mild. A lone heron standing near the water's edge ignores us, living her life how she sees fit. I see her brilliant plumage with my own two eyes. Her pronounced beak. When I watch her I know my mind remains, in part at least, my own.

Mr. Turner's boat is still directly behind ours and I love it and loathe it at the same time. *Skylark* is a handsome two-bed houseboat painted royal blue, and he keeps his ropes neat and ordered. Having a close neighbor is a glorious thing. A friendly face if we ever need help. I have not really experienced that since we married. Mom's neighbors all loved her, and they were welcoming and kind to us, bringing over loaf cakes, condolence cards, and they tried to give Drew a casserole when I had my appendix removed, but he refused to answer the door. He told me it was *us against the world*. It is not even Jeff Turner who disturbs him so much as his little Jack Russell terrier, Amber. If there is a night where Drew fails to put his words down, like last night for instance, he looks as if the devil has taken him.

"Can I have lunch money, Dad?"

Drew stares at me and ignores his own son.

"Dad?"

"You never told him, did you?" says Drew.

"I thought you said you were going to."

"Can't rely on you for anything."

"Sammy, love," I say. "It's just that . . ."

He cuts me off. "There's no school lunches for a while, Samson. We're streamlining. Your mother will make you up a brown bag, won't hurt you."

"Ham or cheese?" I ask.

"Cheese," mutters Sammy.

I give him two rounds of cheese sandwiches all wrapped up in foil. "Don't eat it all on the bus."

He smiles. "As if I would."

Sammy leaves, his Walkman bulging in his pocket, his headphones atop his perfect red hair.

"You treat him too soft he'll turn into a girl, you watch."

"What he's turning into is a fine young man. He's shot up, have you seen? Growth spurt. He'll need new pants before we know it."

"Incorrect. Boy hasn't grown an inch since we moved to the boat."

"I think he has."

"What you *think*," he says, "is of little consequence, that head of yours. What you think, indeed. What I know, more like."

Amber starts to bark on Mr. Turner's boat.

"If that bitch don't shut its mouth . . ."

I hand him his packed lunch.

"Ham?"

"Ham."

"Two slices?"

I nod.

"Last time you gave me one with nothing inside it. You forgot the ham, Peggy. How's a man supposed to work on bread alone? I'll be back before you tonight, so I'll hang on to both sets of keys again. You ready?"

We step off the boat together and he locks the heavy steel and wood doors.

"Might walk you back from the library. Mind who you're talking to up there. I don't want you chatting with any electricians; we've had enough of that for a lifetime. Keep to yourself."

I could shoot him. Scream an inch from his face. Poison his damn sandwiches. When have I ever given him cause to doubt my loyalty?

"Have a good day."

"No chitchat."

He walks south toward the salvage yard and I head north to catch my bus.

When I arrive in the library Mrs. Appleby has a mischievous look on her face. I have never seen her like this.

"What is it?"

She holds up a white envelope.

I take it from her and glance at the name of the publisher.

"You think?" she says, her eyes wide and sparkling.

"I've had rejections like this before. No, it wouldn't be . . ."

"Open it quick and find out," she says. "I've got to tidy photography and self-help."

I put my bag down and slide a finger to open it. Then I stop halfway along.

My ring's missing.

"What's wrong, Peggy?"

My silver ring.

Gone.

"Nothing," I say, my voice cracking. "I just remembered something, that's all."

How could I lose my ring? What is wrong with me?

I unfold the letter.

"Well?"

I swallow hard and read on.

"It's a publishing deal, isn't it? An offer? I knew it, Peggy."

"Nothing like that. But they do want to read the rest of the book. I sent them the first three chapters, with the letter. They would like to see the rest."

Last year, during a coffee break, Mrs. Appleby told me how she had wanted to be a singer when she was younger. She comes from a musical family outside Nashville and she took classes and had some paid work in her twenties, backing singer stuff, but she knew it would never be a proper career. She said she was happy she gave it a chance, but the moment she decided to stop singing professionally she felt a heavy weight lift off her shoulders.

Perhaps it will be the same for me.

"Well," she says. "That's positive news, right?"

I look up at her. "It's . . . unexpected."

"Well," she says, straightening her collar. "I sure expected it."

"Andrew's a better writer than me. And he's not had a single request like this in all our years together. He's been doing this much longer, he has his award, but nothing like this."

"Maybe he's not so much better than you after all. Send them the whole manuscript and who knows, eh?"

"Not sure I can print it off here, though, Mrs. Appleby. It's another two hundred and something pages."

She sucks air through her teeth.

I look down.

She pulls a paper tissue from her sleeve and dabs at her fuchsia lipstick and says, "Don't tell the others, Peggy, not a word."

I print the pages and then, at the end of my lunch break, instead of writing, I run down to the post office and join the line, only to discover I can't afford stamps for such a heavy package. I walk out of there slowly, dejected, hot, people staring at me. I could ask Mrs. Appleby but she has already done so much. I cannot mention it to Drew; it would push him over the edge. He does not even know I am writing, never mind looking for a publisher. Does Samson have a few dollars hidden away? No, I couldn't. In the end I walk around in circles, running out of time, sweating in my coat. The air is chill but the longer I'm out the dirtier the envelope looks and I worry the corners of the papers inside are starting to curl. And then I notice the sign. Five minutes later I run out of Kerrigan's Pawnshop clutching the money. I will go back and retrieve it soon, I will find the money somehow, and if Drew asks where Mom's gold necklace is I will tell him I left it in my library locker.

No line in the post office this time. I hand over the money and they count it. I watch the package go. These professionals actually want to read the whole thing? All those pages? They will send back a polite rejection, I know they will, but nothing ventured nothing gained, that's what Mom used to say.

I arrive back home in the dark and the doors are unlocked but Drew is out. I find Sammy lying face down on his dinette bed screaming into a pillow.

"What's all this, love?"

He stops screaming, lifts his head, and looks at me.

"Mom."

"What are you angry at? Your father?"

He shakes his head. His cheeks are flushed and his eyes look sore.

"What is it?"

"Nothing," he says, desperately, trying to compose himself. "Nothing. School stuff. Algebra, I guess. I hate it."

"But you're good at math. Listen, you need your education, Sam. This new school is a blessing. You know how many kids around here would kill for this chance? I know it can be tough, I never liked math much either at your age, but it's important. It's your ticket."

"I know it is."

"You want to hear a secret?"

He sits up straight and wipes his nose on his sleeve. "Sure."

"Publisher in New York of all places, just a small one, pretty much a family operation in Manhattan, but they put out some really good anthologies and short stories and . . ."

He frowns.

"They've asked to read my book."

He rubs his eyes. "You've written a *whole* book?"

"Finished it a few weeks back."

Just saying that out loud fills me with warmth, with pride.

He steps over and hugs me so tight I squeak.

"Well done, Mom."

"I mean, it's probably trash, but it's something, isn't it? Best thing that's happened to me for a while. Don't tell your father just yet, though. No need to bother him with it. Have to wait for the right time."

"What's your book about?"

"Oh, it's difficult to say. Love story, I suppose. Set in Appalachia, in a mining town in the fifties. It's sad in places, at least I think it is. I cried writing parts of it. Mrs. Appleby had to come over and check I was all right."

"Same place might publish Dad's stories as well, you never know. He's got five ready to go."

"When your father is published," I say, lifting an eyelash from his freckle-covered cheek. "It'll be a literary event, mark my words. Whoever puts that book out will have a major award-winner on their hands. Your dad's writing is pure poetry. It is sublime. Puts mine to shame."

Drew walks in.

"Women's Liberation meeting?"

"I've got a school field trip, Dad. Beaver Island. For geography class."

Drew grimaces at him. "You been crying, boy?"

"No."

"How much is it?"

Samson tells him.

"Not likely. You want to go away on vacation you get yourself a paid job in the factory. You think we're made of money?"

"I'm fourteen, Dad. I can't work in a factory."

"I did, never hurt me. Worked in a factory on weekends. Worked on a chicken farm all summer. You think you're special?"

"I'm at school."

"Holidays to an island at your age, whatever next."

"It's a field trip."

We separate to complete our own chores. I cook SpaghettiOs. We drink milk and have tinned peaches and heavy cream after. Samson starts his assignment and Drew rereads *A Farewell to Arms* by the fire. At eight o'clock he announces he is going to smooth things over with Jeff Turner, take him a peace offering. My stomach is uneasy at the thought of it. This is not like Drew. We watch as he steps off the boat with a bottle of Jim Beam under his arm—the same bottle we have had in our kitchen pantry this past year, in the bungalow and then on the boat—the one his foreman gifted him last Christmas. Drew is not much of a drinker, not like his father. The atmosphere on the boat lightens in his absence. Samson runs over to the radio, a basic car stereo embedded into mahogany veneer, and we dance together to Van Halen. We laugh and jump and cheer each other on. Ten minutes later Sammy's stripped to his pajama pants and the volume's on high: Madonna, then Bon Jovi, the Cure, Erasure. I am sweating, crying with laughter, and the boat is starting to sway.

"You trying to embarrass me?"

Sammy pulls on his pajama shirt.

"How was Mr. Turner?" I ask, switching off the music, straightening my hair.

"Prancing around like two whores in a bar. Samson Jenkins, what do you call that?"

"We were just playing, Dad."

"Dancing like that on my boat. I'll not stand for it."

"I'm sorry."

"Did Mr. Turner like the whiskey?" I ask, catching my breath.

"He's drinking right now, seems to like it well enough. I stayed with him for a single. Reckon he'll shut his dog up after this. Peggy?"

I nod.

"You been at those eyebrows again?"

"I plucked them this morning."

"You overdid it, girl." He looks stern. Dead serious. "There's not much left. Go easy next time, eh? You look like a cancer patient."

I bite down on my tongue. Because I loathe him criticizing any minor change I make to my appearance—the length of my fingernails, the way I pin up my hair—but also because he shaves every single hair on his body, eyebrows included, and I have never uttered a word about it.

* * *

The next morning I wake with an uneasy feeling, as if someone has moved the furniture around when I was asleep. I hear Drew in the bathroom.

I swing my legs out of bed.

Something catches my eye.

No, that doesn't make any sense. We didn't do anything last night.

There is a condom, tied, used, sitting in the trash.

10

SAMSON

I wake to the sound of Amber barking. I sit bolt upright and peer through the wet dinette window. Water drips onto my sheets. If she doesn't settle down she will set Dad off. I climb out of bed and find him stoking the fire.

"Morning, boy."

I look around. "Morning."

He doesn't say a word about Amber. He doesn't even look tense.

"How was your writing last night?"

"You know I don't talk about that."

"Sorry."

"It was all right, as it goes. Finding your way into a fictional place, a universe that seems real inside your own head, isn't easy on a narrow boat with you two here. But I'm moving forward."

He leaves to check the batteries. We might need to run the engines for a while today to top them up and I know he'll be pissed about that.

Mom is in the bedroom, so I wash my face. I don't know why the original owners installed a tub on this stupid British boat. It takes up too much space and we never have enough water in the tank to fill it up. We've not had a bath since we moved here, and I know how much Mom enjoys them because she had one most nights back at the bungalow. She'd take a paperback in with her, a candle or a hot drink sometimes, and she'd emerge half an hour later with red cheeks and a towel wrapped around her head.

Snippets of dreams come back to me as I wipe down the windows. Woodsmoke and mildew in the early winter air. Dad came through in the dead of night and I think he whispered something to me. He stoked the fire, I remember that. Switched from wood to coal to get us through the night. I was dreaming about Jennifer Adamu, the girl on the railroad footbridge, but then she turned into Jim Kendricks Jr. I blink away the thought.

Mom steps through in her robe and slippers. She rubs the top of my head and then starts making oatmeal.

Amber barks again.

"She'll upset your father."

"I was wondering about your book, Mom."

"No," she says, abruptly, shaking her head, lowering her voice. "Best if you forget I told you about that, Sammy. Nothing will come of it, I'm sure. Ignore it, please, for me, OK?"

I shrug.

But if she does sell her novel for a few hundred dollars maybe I can go on the field trip to Beaver Island after all. They have interesting rocks, apparently. I've never been to an island before. I suppose I have on the river, but I've never traveled to a large island. We'd catch a ferry there from Charlevoix. An actual ship for cars and passengers. The price includes three nights in a guesthouse near the beach, and bus travel there and back. Maximum spending money is five bucks per student. I'd bring my Walkman for the bus and I think, what with all the excitement, the scenery, the journey, the voyage, they might just leave me alone. Who knows, with us traveling to a totally different region of the country, they might even grow to know me a little better, might start to like me.

When I think of fossils and rock formations my shoulders relax. History is thought-provoking, and lots of the grown-ups I've known are interested in it, but it is the intersection of ancient history and geology and archaeology that *really* fascinates me. That's what I do when I hide away in the school library: one of my few safe places, along with Smith's Bookstore and Stationers at the bus station. I sit close to a heater at the back and research archaeological and paleontological digs in faraway places. I lose myself in the first-person accounts of tomb discoveries, and stare at the sepia-tone photographs of Egypt and Central America.

I take out the ashes and place them carefully in the box. My breath clouds in the cold air and mingles with dust from the burnt wood. A palette of grays. This afternoon, or tomorrow, I will set off up the embankment and scatter them near birches and white oaks. Dad says it's good for nature but when I leave them by trees I feel like I am concluding some dark ritual, some incremental and unholy cremation.

We eat oatmeal in silence.

Dad leaves the table for a moment to visit his writing bureau. He checks the locks one by one.

Amber starts up barking again.

"I'm sorry about the noise," Mom says.

He grunts that away.

Why should *she* be sorry?

Mom drinks the last of her coffee and I notice that her necklace is missing from her neck. She's worn it every day since I was born, even when she gave me swimming lessons at the public pool. I frown and she shakes her head and adjusts her collar and looks intently at me as if to warn me from mentioning it.

"You cooked that well, Peggy," says Dad. "Smooth oatmeal, that was."

Amber starts howling and Mom clears the dishes to cover the noise.

ADRIFT

I set off with my schoolbag. My Walkman is in my pocket and Depeche Mode plays through the foam headphones.

Amber is sitting on the very front of Mr. Turner's boat. Her pink leather collar looks too big for her.

The sky is murky, and there is a blustery wind blowing in off the sleeping cornfields, a mean wind, whipping up, pushing the birch tops over onto themselves.

I glance over at Mr. Turner's boat. His lights are on.

"Personal Jesus" comes to an end through my headphones.

Amber howls again, her neck bent.

She barks.

I look down into the muddy waters of the canal.

It's Mr. Turner.

11

PEGGY

The sound of your child screaming is a horrific thing. What is worse is the sound of him hyperventilating, shrieking, desperate to speak but unable to form coherent words.

"What is it?" I yell, sprinting through from the kitchen. "Are you hurt?"

I step off our boat onto the towpath.

He is panting.

"Deep breaths, Sammy."

He leads me by the hand toward Jeff Turner's boat.

Down in the water.

The flannel material of his shirt, a collar tip floating on the surface. One sock on, one sock off.

I pivot to shield Sammy from it all, too late, far too late, and Drew walks up behind and immediately jumps into the water.

"Be careful."

He says nothing. Time slows. I turn my head to watch. Sammy wants to do the same but I hold him back. Drew lifts Jeff Turner's head and then, grimacing with exertion, drags him over to the bank.

"Peggy," says Drew, calm yet strained. "I need you to hold him."

I release Sammy and bend down to the water's edge. Drew pulls Jeff Turner's lifeless hands up to the towpath level.

"Go on, take 'em."

"I . . . do you mean?"

Sammy appears at my side and he holds on to Mr. Turner's hands so he doesn't slip back down under the water. The contrast of their fingers, their wrists. My God. Drew pulls himself out from the canal, shivering, covered in weeds, his breath steaming into the cold morning air. Eventually he manages to heave Mr. Turner out onto the towpath. No pulse. Gray, wrinkled skin. Cloudy eyes. I pull Sammy close to me again and Drew, out of breath, says, "You did well, Samson."

Amber circles Jeff Turner.

She is silent now.

I step back on board our boat, numb and distant, to collect a clean bedsheet. When I drape it over Mr. Turner the water saturates the fine material in seconds and it turns near translucent. Drew says, "Sorry you had to see that, Peggy," and then he puts his hand firmly on Sammy's shoulder and says, "I know he was your friend. I'm sorry, boy." He tells us he will change into dry clothes.

As soon as he has gone I inhale like I have been holding my breath for minutes, like I have been trapped beneath the dark, oil-slicked waters myself.

"He's not in any pain," says Sammy, to himself, trembling, tears rolling down his cheeks.

The little dog sits by her owner and moans solemnly. I have never heard a sound like it.

I look up the canal one way and then back the other. Nothing but comatose fields, and the reflection of clouds, and bare lichen-pocked trees. We are so far from the rest of the world it feels like this *is* the world. Like we will have to deal with it all on our own.

Drew asks me and Sammy to walk to the small farmstead off the country road and use their phone to call the police. It takes us half an hour to reach it. Muddy fields churned and hardened with frost. Thickets of prairie grass and elderberry: bleak in this harsh, wintry light. Sammy is mute. I rub his arm periodically and he pauses to scrape dirt from his shoes. The farmer's wife looks at us suspiciously, but she lets us make the call.

"Nine-one-one, what is your emergency?"

"We've found a body in the canal. It's Jeff Turner. We knew him. He's drowned."

"Where are you calling from?"

I tell her.

"Have you checked for a pulse? Any sign of breathing?"

"No," I tell her, still numb. "It's past all that. He's been gone for a while."

I look out through the old, rippled glass of the farmhouse window and Sammy is shivering out in the yard. He would not come inside.

We walk back to the canal.

A formation of geese flies high in the sky above us, a pointer leading us away from all this to some other town, some other future, but we deviate from their chosen path and head back to our floating home.

The sheriff's deputies are already there when we arrive.

Others join them.

Three men, two women, and one small white tent.

Tape runs from a sapling to a spindly river birch. Flickering in the breeze; twisting this way and that.

Drew is being questioned. They question me and they talk to Sammy. It takes hours. They ask me what I did last night, where I was, what time I went to sleep, whether or not I heard anything unusual. They take notes. One of the deputies says there might be an inquest and in any event we may need to answer further questions. They ask about Jeff Turner and who his friends and acquaintances were. His next of kin. Sammy knows far more than we do.

We are allowed onto our own boat to warm up and make coffee. Sammy heads for the LEGO box he used to play with so much in the bungalow. He told me once how rummaging with his hands deep inside the box made him feel good. The smell of the old plastic bricks: memories of simpler times.

Drew tells them he has to go to work. I let the deputies know I will not take Sammy in to school today, not with what he has seen. They explain how we cannot step foot on Mr. Turner's boat until they say so. We decide to let Amber stay on our boat until his family claim her. I put a bowl of water down for her and Drew gives me a five-dollar bill to take Sammy out for some food in town.

Mother and son. Blank-eyed, exhausted from shock, riding the bus. Senior citizens and young mothers embark, shivering, showing their passes, taking their seats. The washed-out landscape scrolls by our picture windows and the stale air smells faintly of diesel.

"Do you want to talk about it, Sammy?"

"Not here."

My memories are unreliable. They are wavy and vague, and sometimes they are difficult to pin down. Last night Drew took a bottle of bourbon over to Jeff Turner's boat, a peace offering of sorts, and then he came back to write. And then, I suppose, he came to bed and we . . . Only, I'm not sure I remember it that way. It did not feel like we did anything. In fact, I am absolutely sure we did nothing.

The sheriff or the coroner will likely conclude an old man like Jeff Turner slipped from his boat. I know I have almost fallen in a dozen times, especially when it's icy.

Sammy places his hand on mine. We both look straight ahead. He squeezes tight and the bus's engine drones beneath us.

An old man mumbles to himself from the seat in front of ours. He comments on the weather. He complains about potholes, the VA, and the vice president.

It was not long after Sammy was born that Drew told me for the second time about the fire. He looked relieved to share his childhood secret. A problem shared is a problem halved, and although I was shocked, I was also glad he had confided in me. But then, like only Drew can, he turned it upside down and inside out. Did I mention this already? He said I had misremembered on account of me being so tired from night feeds. It's true that I was exhausted at that time, like any new mother. Truths and mistruths: tangled. He talked about our family being a flawless triangle. Three sides. He explained, as I was folding laundry, how if one side was to ever break away for any reason, or become damaged, or lost, then the triangle would collapse in on itself. He kept repeating how we were a nuclear family. Drew emphasized, with Sammy fast asleep behind us in his crib, that it was us against the world. He said that is the way it is and that is the way it will always be. He did not tell me explicitly he would hurt Sammy or me if we ever tried to leave, but he did not need to.

It was clear from the intonation of his voice.

The look in his eye.

12

SAMSON

The bus station is completely different at this time of day.

It's strange being here with Mom. I look around at all the safe zones I've identified—relatively sheltered positions behind walls and advertisement screens, friendly stores where I can waste ten minutes, places I can hide—and they all seem so unnecessary.

We stop in at the library and Mom explains to an older lady what happened on the canal. I watch from a distance as she mentions the sheriff. The lady pats her on her hand and nods and glances over to me. I stare down at my shoes.

"We'll stop by at the school office so I can explain your absence." I stiffen. "No."

"Sammy, it'll just take a minute. I have to tell them."

"Call them. Please, I can't . . . go in there."

She looks me up and down. And then she calls from the pay phone by the laundromat.

Nobody else is looking over their shoulder like I am. Walking through downtown like a fighter in enemy territory, a battle-scarred infantryman trying to anticipate the next ambush. We pass by

Frankie's liquor store and the Community Bank and head up the broad stone steps into the town museum.

This is her way of shielding me. She has brought me here twice before: both times when Dad was too harsh, making her sad, scaring both of us. Mom thinks this free admission museum is somewhere I feel safe. She is right, I do. But it's not the dusty artifacts or the faded printouts of dates and biographies I like; it is being with her in a quiet place. Dad not interfering. No risk of Johnno, Eyebrow, Hammer Adams, or Gunner ruining everything. It is almost like we're not in the same town anymore.

We spend time at an exhibit explaining the history of the canal, how it used to connect to the rivers. Aerial photographs. Some testimony by a farmer about how we're in the geographical middle of the country, not considered east or west, north or south. He says how we're not truly accepted as delta people, or as mountain people, or as bayou people. We're forgotten about. He says with the rivers and our central location we should be thriving. And then he finishes by saying how even though it's a rough town that has seen better days we're all still proud to come from here. Only nobody remembers why. Amen to that. I look at cross-section diagrams of some hill in England, and a narrow tunnel where boatmen of yore would detach their heavy horses from their canal barges, boats that look like ours, and propel cargo through a tunnel using nothing but their own leg power. There are black-and-white photographs of men lying with their backs on the coal pushing their boots off the curved brick roof. When I look at the pictures I imagine Mr. Turner's final moments. I hope he didn't suffer in the water. I don't like the thought of him fighting to breathe, freezing cold, trying to scramble up to the slippery bank, failing to pull himself free.

I saw pond weed around his ankles.

"You OK, Sammy?"

I look up at her and nod.

"You want to leave? Take a walk and talk about it?"

ADRIFT

I tell her I want to stay.

We spend another half hour moving slowly from one glass case to the next. A Shawnee arrowhead found on a nearby ranch. A scale model of the church near the courthouse. There are no other visitors.

"Fresh air?" she asks.

We step outside and the town is misty. I like the way the old stone steps have been worn away over the years. Softened. The wind gusts. There are women holding on to their own hair, protecting it I guess, and a man walks past us eating a hamburger.

We turn the corner and I stop in my tracks. They are thirty yards away. Johnno and Ballbag. What are they doing outside of school? Whatever they like, it seems. They don't care about the rules. Ballbag's tie is loose, the knot down by his heart.

"They your friends, Sam?"

The boys laugh and point from the other side of the street.

"Clown shoes," yells Ballbag.

"Pennywise," says Johnno. "Pennywise loser."

"Is that a joke?" asks Mom, frowning. "What does *Pennywise* mean, Sammy?"

I feel my cheeks burn. I make myself as small as possible and continue with her down the road toward the diner.

"Samson? Were those boys your friends?"

"I don't know."

The windows of the diner are all steamed up. The room smells of leather and coffee. There are numerous occupied tables. I count twelve. Everything is hushed and slow. We sit down in the corner as far away as possible from everybody else.

"Hot chocolate and a donut." She takes off her coat. "That'll make us feel better, won't it? Whipped cream?"

"Yes, Mom."

My cheeks are hot. I wish I could fold in on myself. Disappear.

The drinks arrive in tall mugs with long spoons. She has a white chocolate donut and I have a jelly one.

She leans in. "I'm so sorry, Sammy. About your friend, Mr. Turner. It's a hard thing to get your head around."

I nod.

"Do you want to talk about it yet?"

I shake my head and I'm thankful for the steam on the window glass. They won't be able to see us if they walk past. They won't be able to find me.

The short-order cook burns himself.

He curses.

"He was very fond of you, Sammy." She pats my knee. "He used to tell me how much you kept him going. Your visits, looking after little Amber, and the talks you had. He mentioned to me that you told him all about your classes, about the plates moving on the earth's crust, and about the planets."

"I don't want to talk about it, Mom. If that's OK."

"Of course."

She finishes her donut and dabs her lips on a paper napkin.

"But he did used to say you kept him going. You and your checkers games."

I smile. "It was chess, actually. He was better than me at the start, far better. But that changed a few months back. I started getting stalemates. And then one day I beat him. Trapped his king in the corner. I thought he'd be upset about it, but he gave me a dollar bill."

"He's in a better place now, Sam. He lived a good, long life. He's in a kinder place."

I watch raindrops make their way down the windowpanes and I want to tell her everything about school, cry it all out, every last detail, about the boys, about when they soaked my clothes in the shower drain and whipped me red raw with towels, and I want to tell her about them hiding my bag at recess and filling it with sand that time and when they put glue in my hair and I had to cut it off.

It could only be a kinder place than here.

A far kinder place.

I tell her nothing.

It wouldn't help.

"Drink up, Sam. Butcher's shop, and then we'll be off home to see your father."

She buys lamb chops because they are my favorite. Then she buys me a Milky Way from the newsstand. She knows I like Milky Ways. I have liked them since I was small. Smooth, but also chewy. Perfect, really. I place the bar in my pocket and we chat as we walk back the long way to the bus station, behind the crematorium. A crane stands stationary over the horizon like a giant insect. It hasn't moved for months. The whole town's like that. I want to share the dreams I have sometimes about Jim Hendricks but how could I ever do that to her?

"What happens next with your book?"

"Probably nothing. It'll fizzle out, but I enjoyed writing it. Took me away from this place for a while."

We pause and she looks around at the warehouses and tire shops, at the old community college and the Dollar General.

"If it becomes a real book one day we can maybe go away."

She looks at me and smiles warmly.

"You mean like a vacation, Sam? I'm not sure your father would be interested."

I look over at the distant hill. At what might be over the other side.

"Just the two of us, then. It's your book. You should decide, really."

She strokes my cheek. Her eyes look tired. "We'll see."

We turn a corner and traipse toward the bus station. The temperature drops. We're heading directly into the wind and it cuts between us.

"Mr. Turner was looking out for us."

"Say what, Sammy? Speak up, I can't hear you in this wind."

"I said he was watching out for us. Mr. Turner was. That's why he came back to his boat."

Her eyes are watering from the gusts.

"You think?"

"He was far too old to be on that boat," I say, my eyes stinging.

"What?"

"He was too old, Mom. He was keeping an eye on us both. That's why his boat was so close to ours, you know."

"He was a nice old fella."

"He was the only one looking out for us," I say again, quietly, as much to myself as to her. "He was the last one."

13

PEGGY

The light is falling away as we leave the country road and walk down to the brown fringes of the water. Sammy is dragging his feet. Do his shoes look that big? I am shocked those boys called him names. Although I suppose it was mild compared to what happened to me when I was little. Nuns too quick, and keen, to use corporal punishment. I am not sure Sammy could have handled that. I stare at the pale strip of skin below his hairline as he walks in front of me. The innocence of it. The way I still sometimes kiss him just there in the morning after he wakes up if he does not have time to push me away. Thank God those kids were only calling him names.

There is a sense of walking toward something. It is not just our home, not just an isolated, unseen stretch of canal; it is the scene of an accident. You walk home on a cold day as it is growing dark and you expect to have a spring in your step. The anticipation of returning someplace safe and warm. None of that here. The opposite. Will the forensics tent still be in place? Is that what it was? Will Drew be in a good mood?

Sammy points out a red fox on the far bank, scurrying, its nose flat to the ground. My boy looks hypnotized by it. Oranges morph into grays as we begin to lose sight of him. And then he is gone as if into vapor.

The tent is also gone.

The deputies are gone.

Two boats: one of them now unoccupied.

Sammy peers at me and I say, "Come on, let's get you inside."

The sweet scent of smoke as we approach. An artist's charcoal line of it rising diagonally from our chimney pipe.

We skirt around the area where Mr. Turner's body was laid out earlier this day. We do not stray there.

Drew appears from the engine room and steps onto the dew-slicked bank. The small figure of Amber follows him.

"Who did you see?" says Drew.

"Pardon me?"

"Out in town. See anybody?"

"We went to the museum. Then the diner. The butcher shop."

"Who'd you talk to?"

"Each other," says Sammy, looking up at me.

"You have much to say, boy?"

Samson lifts Amber and holds her in his arms, stroking her, fussing over her.

"Has she had some food, Dad?"

"Wrong question."

"Can we get food for her from his boat?"

Drew nods. "Deputies said that that's fine. But not to remove anything."

Sam takes her over to Mr. Turner's boat to feed her.

"Don't get any fancy ideas," says Drew. "We don't need another mouth to feed."

I yell, "When you come home, Sam, come in through the engine room. I don't want filthy boots on Nanna's rug."

"It's our rug," mutters Drew.

I step aboard.

"Lamb chops," I say. "Sammy's favorite. A treat."

"Not tonight, Peggy. I want your grilled cheese after you mentioned it last night. I've been expecting it."

Frowning, I take my coat off and hang it up.

"But he's a bit lost, Drew, to be honest. Jeff Turner was his friend. He's quite cut up about it. Can I cook him the lamb chops?"

He steps closer and there is a chill inside the boat. I am pressed up with my back against the kitchen sink, against the tiled work top, and the floor is ice-cold.

He leans.

"Grilled," he says. "Cheese. Bouillon cube crumbled on top of the cheese the way I like it. Tomato soup on the side as usual. He'll eat it or he'll go without."

His hazel eyes look almost orange in this light. Each iris a riot of fire and silent fury.

"OK."

The tension in his shoulders eases.

"Fuel man came earlier. Left a sack of coal. It's on the roof."

"We'll be needing it by the look of these skies."

"You see any police in town?"

I shake my head.

"Leave me to sleep tonight, will you? Not like last night. I'm not complaining, it's just I'm well into act one now and I have to get the words down, and then I need good sleep. All right?"

"Of course. I didn't . . . I mean, I wasn't even sure . . ."

He stares at me.

"Of course, Drew. I'm tired anyway. Did the deputies stay long?"

He walks over to his desk and starts unlocking one of the compartments. I think it is the small cupboard at the top where he keeps spare wheels for his word processor.

"They stayed awhile. I helped them with questions, taught them a thing or two about the canal, and then they took the old man away. Two of them checked over his boat, took photographs."

I light the burner.

"Turner's nephew came around before they took him. Odd looking fella, you seen him before, have you?"

"I don't think so."

"Looks like a deviant. Biker jacket, our age, strange face like he's been in an accident. Burnt, maybe. Walks around like a queer. Skinny queer in a biker jacket with dyed black hair."

"Will he come and collect Amber?"

"He'd better."

I slice cheese into strips and take six slices of bread from the bag. After I lay the cheese on the bread I crumble over two bouillon cubes and place each sandwich in the pan.

"That doesn't smell like lamb," says Sammy.

"Over here," says his dad. "Now."

Sammy walks to him.

Drew screws his face into a tight ball. "You're lucky you got supper at all. Kids in the next town going hungry tonight, they are, last night as well. Trailer park kids not eaten all day. Boys out on the farms working till they bleed. You're sulking cos you got grilled cheese and soup."

"I'm not sulking."

"Where did you leave the bitch?"

"Amber? She's on Mr. Turner's boat. She's on his bed. She's upset, Dad."

"*Upset.*"

"Can I bring her on here tonight? She can sleep with me on the dinette bed. Dad, please."

"You lost your mind."

"She'll be no trouble."

"I'm writing act one. You know what act one means, Samson? The first third. The opening of the entire story. And you want to bring Turner's bitch in the same room as I'll be working in."

"She might prefer to stay home, Sammy," I say, moving the pan, making sure the bouillon cubes melt into the cheese. "Familiar smells, her own bed. She might prefer to be there tonight."

"I wanted her close to me," he says, his voice cracking.

"Well, the universe doesn't much care for what you or I want." Sammy swallows hard and then says, "We miss him."

Drew turns to me and lowers his voice. "If I hear any more of this I'll . . . I swear I will, the day I've had. Man doesn't need to be hearing nonsense before supper. I'm going to shave and when I'm back there'll be no more talk of dogs."

I wipe down the sink.

Sammy listens to his Walkman and stares out the window as I finish making the meal. Mine will be cold by the time Sammy's has melted. If the dinette was converted into his bed I am sure he would dive under the comforter and hide, but he has no bed. There are no hiding places on a boat like this. I know he misses having his own room, his own posters on the wall.

The wind blows and the fire roars in the little woodstove.

Raindrops tap against the windows, and where the frames do not fit properly the wind drives moisture into the boat and it streams down the walls and collects on the counter.

Three plates of grilled cheese, three bowls of tomato soup, three glasses of milk.

Goldilocks, corrupted.

Drew comes out from the bathroom, his head and face shaved so close he is shining. Smooth as a peeled egg. He says the act of scraping his razor over his skin, cleansing it, removing the hairs at their roots, the dead skin cells, sets off something creative inside him.

"More bouillon cube next time," says Drew. "More bouillon. Get it meaty."

I nod.

"This mean we can have lamb chops tomorrow, Mom?"

I glance over at Drew and, without looking up from his food, he gives a subtle nod of his head.

"Yes, love."

We eat on. The glow from the far end of the kitchen intensifies with every gust of wind and the boat is at once too hot and too cold.

The uncomfortable sound of cutlery scraping across porcelain.

"Walk the bitch after dinner," says Dad. "Walk it well, wear the damn thing out, I don't want it howling all night. I need you all silent."

"I'll walk her, Dad."

"Careful you don't fall in," I tell him. "It's slippery."

"I'm a good swimmer," he says. "It's a shame Mr. Turner couldn't swim to the bank. I wish I'd heard him last night. I wish I'd have . . ."

"Well," replies Dad. "You didn't. No point wishing this thing and that. I told you he was too frail to be on the water, especially with liquor inside him. Canals are for fit men, not old folks. He should have kept to his bungalow."

I finish my dinner.

"He was keeping an eye out for us, Dad."

"Look how that turned out for him."

He stands up to check the fire and I clear away the dishes.

Sammy goes out in his raincoat to walk Amber.

I scrub plates, staring through the steamed-up glass. Water falling into water. Darkness. Howling wind and nothing good out there to rely on. Just the three of us again. The one who holds me down and the one who keeps me up. Me in the middle trying to work out how to save us. Day after day of it.

"More bouillon cube next time."

"I heard you."

"You *think* you did. You might have expected me to say it, that's one thing. But you never heard me because this is the first time I've mentioned it. You answer me back again like that and see where it gets you. You want my book to fall on its backside?"

I look at him, exhausted.

"What?"

He's cleaning his nails with the tip of his pocketknife. Doesn't look up to meet my gaze. "You want me to write to my best ability, best I can, finest work I can put together?"

"Of course I do, Drew."

"Sometimes I doubt it. Sometimes I sense you'd rather I fall short."

"You know what I think. You're capable of the greatest things; I know it in my bones. I believe in you; I always have done and I always will."

He breathes out through his nostrils and with each exhalation he calms himself. My words have soothed him and his torso has eased.

A hollow bang inside the woodstove.

"Not keeping the bitch, Peggy. I'm making that clear now. We're not taking in a dog."

14

SAMSON

The canal is a narrow black mirror. I walk Amber, and clusters of stars float unmoving on the water's surface. She sniffs pigweed and crabgrass. Mr. Turner should be watching *Roseanne* about now. He should be crossing off shows in his *TV Guide*, and there should be a small plate of chocolate chip cookies beside him, perhaps a Twinkie or a generous slice of pound cake from the corner grocery on Bakersfield Avenue. Amber looks cold at the end of her gray leash. She stays close to my ankle.

We walk on and there is no artificial light in this direction whatsoever. No boats, no trucks, no bridges. I sense creatures in the banks peering back, but they are unmoving. Watching us trek slowly away from the two boats in the distance: one occupied, one empty. Two vessels on their own.

Nobody will have collected photocopies or printouts, or thought to let me know what the assignments are. I had chicken pox a few months ago and it was as if nobody noticed. I am invisible to the teachers, even.

We head back toward the smoke of the boat's chimney. From the air I can tell Dad's moved from wood to coal. He will be settling in now, flicking through one of his Hemingway novels, each copy littered with stickers and minuscule annotations, or else he will be reading from his own notebooks. I have been observing him ever since I was little. Other dads play arcade games with their sons or take them to Little League practice, but my father always has his head in his work.

Amber drinks from a puddle.

Mom will be in her bedroom keeping out of the way. I'm going to talk to him again about running her a bath for her birthday in May. He hates the thought of it; he even disapproves of long showers. Tells us we're to only ever use Irish Spring soap, as it doesn't scum up and block the pipes too much, and never hang around mindlessly with the water running. In and out, he says. But I know she craves a long soak. He let her have baths all the time back in the bungalow. Nanna Ruth installed a tub before I was born, a full-length one, not like ours in the boat, and Mom would take one most weekends, usually only a few inches deep. I'm going to raise it with him. She hasn't said she wants a bath because she doesn't want to set him off, especially not with his new book, and now with Mr. Turner's accident, but I'm going to bring it up when the moment's right.

I know he can be better.

We reach Mr. Turner's boat and I step up and Amber follows, but I have to pull her back.

His gray Velcro sneakers are neat inside the door.

She steps in but looks back at me and then she stands right next to my leg and won't leave. She presses herself firmly against my shin.

"You'll be all right, you're safe in here. Look, you've got a nice blanket from Mr. Turner." I squat down and pat her bed. "Come on, girl. Settle down and I'll see you again in the morning. I'm only going over there."

But she stands resolute by my ankle. Leaning into me. Is she shivering?

His Salvation Army Christmas dish towel hangs from the rail on the propane stove.

His captain's hat rests on a side table.

His copy of *The Fisherman's Almanac* sits on the same table, open to the contents page.

His fingerless wool mittens are stuffed down by the armchair.

His life, everywhere.

I say good night to him, my voice catching in my throat, and stroke Amber, rubbing under her wiry chin, and then I close the door, pushing her back inside against her will.

When I walk back to our boat I step around the area we laid him down.

"Bed," says Dad.

I make my bed out of the dinette sofa and table and then I pull on my pajamas and brush my teeth. Dad is loading up the fire with coal and kindling packets when I emerge.

"Night, boy." He lifts his jaw.

I walk to him and kiss his smooth, hard cheek and then he looks away.

After twenty minutes of Amber howling from the next boat he says, "You going to lay there and ignore it?"

I sprint to her and bring her back with me tight in my arms.

"Where should I . . . ?"

"Keep it quiet. Strangle it or lay it on your pillow, boy, I don't care which. I've got one shot at this opening act. Do you know how vital act one is?"

I bring her into my bed and lay her down and she settles and rests with her nose covered by her tail.

"It sets the tone for the whole thing."

I can't see his face from this angle. There is a glow from the far end of the boat, from the woodstove, and Amber's heartbeat echoes my own.

Dad's bare legs glow orange.

ADRIFT

"Night," I say.

He pulls off his shirt and begins to type.

* * *

I am late for school the next morning and have to run all the way from the bus.

"Look at it," says Ballbag, as I pass him by the lockers. "Sweaty, guilty clown. Skinny little peasant. Look at the armpits on it, dripping they are. Filthy little ramen noodle-armed freak."

I ignore him.

Filing into social studies they kick me in the back.

In American lit they throw glue sticks at my head and the teacher sends me outside together with Gunner and Blocko. He joins us in the corridor.

"He did it, sir," they both say.

"I don't care much who did it, you were all involved. I have a mind to send you to the principal."

"He started it, sir," says Blocko.

"You think I'm an idiot, Block?"

"No, sir."

"Do I look like an idiot to you?"

"No, sir, I never..."

"I'll see you all after class. Back inside."

He never did talk to us after class. He was busy chatting with Miss King from chemistry, so we all left.

I hid in the boys' bathroom. I took sanctuary in chess club and played Go with a friendly senior who shared his Fruit Roll-Ups with me. He told me he's going to study physics at Howard. Nice guy. Reckon he's been through some stuff. You can just tell sometimes. Then I hid in the music room during lunch and didn't eat. They think I am weak for keeping out of their way but they, predictably, misinterpret the fundamental laws of nature. A smart creature will win in the long term because it thinks strategically. It is not about short-term wins, it is not even about battle victories, it is about the entire war. Mom taught me that. Watch a beaver building a dam or a spider weave its web or a pack of wolves quietly stalk an elk. It is not the easy wins, it is the *end* win. They consider me a coward, but I have my eye on a prize their feeble minds cannot comprehend. When I am eighteen, they will be at the train station spraying graffiti on the walls or in the men's room stalls looking for a vein.

Whereas I will be on a train.

Leaving.

15

PEGGY

When I return home from the library Drew is outside training on the towpath. He is doing pull-ups on a low tree branch, the vein in his forehead protruding, pulsing.

"Planning to tell me?"

"Tell you?"

He drops down and steps closer, his sneakers splattered with muddy droplets of water that he will painstakingly clean away with a rag later this evening.

"Boat was different when I got back from the scrapyard. Something off about it."

"What was different, love?"

"Been someone on my boat, tell me there hasn't."

I roll my eyes. "Oh, that. It was just the detective came around. He was checking on Jeff Turner's boat. We got to talking and I offered him a cup of coffee, that's all."

"You offered him," he says, sweat dripping off his chin, "a cup of coffee."

"He's from the sheriff's office, Drew."

"He's a man on my boat."

I step back a little. There is no one else around for miles.

"Ten minutes, that's all it was. Coffee, one sugar. Took it black. Don't think he trusted our milk. Talked about Sammy awhile, about how he worked for Jeff Turner, helped him out."

The sinews of his forearms flex and bulge.

"What did he say, this man?"

"I think he was mainly checking on his boat. Making sure it was secure and locked up. Mentioned they were looking into whether he was alone on his boat. Establishing a timeline."

Drew sets his jaw. "Did he look at you?"

I frown.

"I said did he look at you."

"We talked. Must have been less than ten minutes."

He crosses his arms and looks me up and down.

"Were you wearing that at the time? Or something else?"

I look down at my jacket and jeans and boots.

"Sorry?"

"He touch your hand, anything like that? Console you for the sudden and tragic loss?"

"Don't be silly."

His breath steams out of his nostrils and hangs in the air between us. A jet plane high overhead. Silence.

"Did he try anything on with you, this fella?"

"He's a detective, Drew."

"I know who it was. Electrician on a bicycle and now another one. Did you sleep together, you and him?"

His grinds his teeth.

"We talked," I say, not making eye contact. "He said they were running some tests on the body. I don't know what happened to you today, but you have nothing to worry about. We just talked. Five minutes."

"Ten minutes, you said before."

"Something like that."

"Something like that."

He wipes his face on his bare forearm.

"I'm getting cold."

"Did he touch your hands?"

"Sorry?"

He steps closer, breathing, frowning. His shoulders are tensed.

"Don't have a coronary," he says, loosening his torso, smiling, transforming. "Anyone'd think you were about to get a beating. What's wrong with you?"

"Oh, nothing," I say, stepping toward our boat. "I'm tired, I guess."

"From all that heavy work down at the library, all the index cards."

I step onto the boat.

He goes back to his training.

Inside, the boat is as wide as Drew is tall. The dinette is set ready for supper and the kitchen is not far removed from a decrepit trailer or squat. The only thing that is in perfect working order is his corner. Mahogany bureau desk rescued from a dumpster. Each shelf and drawer meticulously sanded and repainted out on the towpath. Each one locked with its own padlock, with its own combination. He dusts it with spittle and a tattered T-shirt he keeps for the task. A desk with a fifteen-year-old award sitting on top, taunting him, propelling him. Not one speck of dust. No verdigris on his prize trophy. The Hugh Higgins Memorial Prize. Andrew Jenkins. *Most promising writer.*

He was charming before we married, before Mom died, before Sammy arrived. He was a focused but considerate man. Over time, he has steadily hardened.

Samson comes home with wet pants and a wet jacket and a wet schoolbag.

"You fall in the river? It hasn't been raining, has it?"

"I tripped."

"Come here."

I pull him into myself and kiss the hair on top of his head. Soon he will be taller than me and that will be concrete proof, if I ever needed it, of the passage of time. He hangs on to me. I squeeze him tighter, and he says nothing but he holds me like mammalian young have done for a thousand generations.

"Better get those clothes off. Put something warm on and I'll dry them by the fire."

He walks to the bathroom, dripping as he goes.

I know he has not eaten his Milky Way yet. It is still in his pine storage box under the dinette cushions. I have not had my Twix either.

The boat's motor starts up, so I jog through to the bedroom.

Drew is there on the other side of the door by the tiller.

"Are we heading back to the marina?"

He does not bend forward to answer me.

I cannot see his head from down here, just his chest, legs, boots.

"Are we heading back, Drew?"

"Incorrect."

"What then?"

He steps down. There is a fine cut near his ear, a shaving nick.

"What's wrong with you?"

"Are we going back?"

"You want to?"

"Closer to the marina would be nice, don't you think? Closer to the road, the store, the bus. It's a lot of walking."

"Topping up the batteries," he says. "Closer to that marina, that electrician? I'm thinking of heading the other way. Build some distance between us and Jeff Turner's boat."

"How would we get to town?"

"We'll find a way."

"What about the dog?"

"What about it?"

"The food's on his boat. All her things, her leashes."

"Not my problem."

"I know, but . . ."

"The way your brain's wired. You're not thinking straight one day to the next."

"Sammy's attached to little Amber."

"Attached?"

I make supper but the propane is running low, I can feel it. I will not raise it with Drew tonight. As I stir the pork and beans in the saucepan I think about the rejection letter I received at the library, the look on Mrs. Appleby's face as I opened it. The misplaced hope. Like she is personally invested in the possibility of me securing a private victory. *We regret to inform you that we must pass on your manuscript at this time. We wish you luck with future submissions.* I knew in my heart it was not good enough. The opening needs work and I am not sure there is a clear theme in the whole novel.

We sit at the dinette, Drew in his denim shirt and Sammy in his gym sweatshirt, and we eat our beans.

"How's football, son?" Drew asks, his food untouched.

"All right," says Sammy.

"All right, is it?"

"Yeah." He puts down his fork. "Shelby scored three touchdowns last week. Rumors of varsity already. Talked about it in front of the class."

"Nice for Shelby's father, that. Real nice. What about you, Samson? What's there for your old man?"

"I'm playing OK."

"Are you? Because we never hear anything of it. No match reports, no stories from you, no tournament invites. It'd be nice to come along and watch you on the gridiron one time, the money your cleats cost."

"Andrew."

He ignores me and keeps staring down at Sammy.

"Are you on the team? School team?"

"You know I'm not."

"Reserves, then? If someone's injured do you get to play?"

"Not at the moment."

"Not at the moment, is it? You're training, though. You're looking for a spot? Fighting for a place, are you?"

"Yes, Dad."

"Yes, Dad."

Drew slowly, almost imperceptibly, shakes his head, and begins eating his beans.

"There was a soft boy in my school, tougher school than yours, and he got knocked around every day and never fought back. Lazy kid, he was. Pansy. Never helped himself. Big baby, he was. Bent nose. Blond hair and dimples. Until some of the guys pinned him down and shaved his head with a straight razor." I can see the beans on Drew's tongue. "Don't ever be a victim, Samson. I will not have a victim for a son."

Sammy finishes his food and thanks me and asks to leave the table and I tell him he can. He places his plate in the sink and goes to the bathroom and locks himself in.

"Go easy on him."

"If I go any easier he'll melt."

"He's settling in. The assignments are tough."

"Life's tough. You call this supper?"

I frown.

"Overcooked, Peg, is what this is. Look at it. Soggy beans. Might as well put my dinner in a blender for all the texture we've got here. Slop."

"I'll be more careful next time."

"Slop," he says again.

I watch the tendons in his hands. His grip tightens on his cutlery.

"Sludge for my supper."

"Sorry."

"After the day I've had."

I say nothing.

"What did the fella look like?"

"Pardon?"

"Detective. What did he look like? Would I know him?"

"Fair hair, short. Thirty, maybe. Looked Irish."

"Redhead, was he?"

"I don't know, Drew."

"You do know."

"He just asked me some questions."

"You tell him we slept together that night?"

"No, of course I didn't."

He chews his pork and beans. I watch his jaw move, bulge, his Adam's apple rise and fall as he swallows, the knife and fork cartoonishly small in his hands.

"Why not?" he asks. "Why didn't you mention it?"

"None of his business, is it? I never would . . ."

"Should have told him, love. Jeff Turner fell in the canal, slipped, shouldn't have been on a houseboat at his age, too old he was, and you and me were in bed. Best the detective knows that. Next time the redhead comes around for a tea party you tell him what we did."

"I can't remember . . ."

"You can't what?"

"That we . . ."

He motions to smash his fist down on the dinette table but then, at the last moment, his skin almost touching the wood, he flattens his palm and places it down gently. Controlled.

"Please, Andrew."

He imitates my voice. Whispers, *"Please, Andrew."*

"I'm sorry."

"Have I ever hit you, Peg?"

I pause. "No."

"So why are you shaking?"

"I'm confused."

"You are, yes."

"You want me to tell him about that night? I'll tell him."

"What I want," he says, lifting one side of his plate, tilting it, bean juice pouring off, then probing each pork sausage with a stiff fingertip, "is for you to get your head straight and tell the truth. Not rocket science, is it?"

"I just felt..."

"Are you trying to ruin my book, Peg?"

"What? Of course not."

His eyes change. His voice deepens. He booms, "Are you trying to ruin my new book, Peggy Jenkins?"

And then Samson walks out from the bathroom and his hand is covered in blood.

16

SAMSON

Dad stops shouting.
　　She runs to me.
"What happened, Samson? Hold it up, let me look at it. What happened, love?"

I stare at Dad. "I was cutting my nails and I slipped."

"Expect you'll be more careful next time," he says.

"Put it under the faucet," she says, pulling me toward the kitchen.

The cold water stings. I watch the stream leave the tap and hit my wound. I watch the gash flare open from the pressure and the skin turn white.

"Don't waste the whole tank on it," mutters Dad.

"I think it needs a couple of stitches," she says. "From a doctor."

"If he goes there he'll only come out with something worse."

Mom gives him a look and then turns to me and says, "Are you all right, Sam?"

I nod.

She puts two Band-Aids on my finger and gives me a Tylenol. He leaves to check oil levels.

I thought all this would stop once we moved here.

Back in the bungalow they were both under a lot of pressure. Ever since I started playing with LEGO they've talked about *the bills*, the payment plans, installments, loans. I'm not sure they ever realized I was listening. They discussed the burden of running a home. Insurance. Price of gas. Dad suggested moving to the boat would cut out the stress. Cheaper than a single-wide. He said he would be able to focus solely on his writing and we would be happier. I cut myself twice in the bungalow to make him stop shouting at her. I cut myself twice, and one time I clamped my eyes shut and smashed my forehead into a mirror.

I still wear the scars.

I promised myself I would never do it again once we moved onto the boat and became a normal family again. I have failed, I guess. The choice between sitting on the cassette toilet listening to him go on, or me slicing my hand. There was no decision to make.

Mom looks at me with lines on her face. She sips from her mug. Two hands wrapped tight around it. There is no bracelet on her wrist but that's not unusual. What is unusual is that her neck is also bare.

It is dark outside.

I have four years left. Just over. Once that is over I will pack my bag and be on my way, waiting for a train, one-way ticket in hand, leaving it all behind.

If I can't afford the train, I'll take a Greyhound. Have it all planned. But in my dreams it's always a train.

She says, "Does it sting, my love?"

I finish the last of my hot chocolate and nod.

"You're to promise me you'll be more careful next time. I'll cut them for you if you like; it's nothing to be embarrassed of. Let your mother trim your nails."

"I can do it."

She smiles. "I know."

"I'm not saying you should talk to Dad about it right now, I'm not saying that, but do you think I'll be able to go on the field trip or not? I have to tell the teacher tomorrow."

She looks down at her own hands.

"Only, I think it might be good for my grades. We'll be sharing, like a college dorm, four boys to a room, and I don't need any spending money, not a dime. All the meals are included."

"Leave it with me, Samson."

"You wouldn't leave me here, would you?" I whisper.

"Sorry?"

She might have sold her necklace to someone at the library. Might have some money stashed to escape.

"You wouldn't go?"

"No, love." She strokes my cheek. "No, of course I wouldn't."

I lift my finger to my nose and take in the familiar, pleasing scent of Elastoplast. "OK."

I've settled into a routine with Amber now. As long as Dad doesn't see her too much, and she's quiet after nine, it's as if she is invisible to him. I suppose that's how we all need to be. Not setting him off. She sleeps by my feet and I can tell she likes it down there. It wouldn't be humane to lock her inside Mr. Turner's boat all on her own.

Once I have washed and changed and walked her I climb into bed and listen to the radio on my Walkman. My cut's throbbing. There is a squirrel outside scampering on the roof and I have to keep Amber looking the other way so she doesn't start chasing after it.

At five to nine Mom says good night and heads back to her bedroom.

"Here, boy."

I settle Amber and walk to him.

He is shirtless, glowing in the camp chair next to the fire. His scars are faint, but I can see them.

"Hand better?"

"Yes, Dad."

I wish you didn't have to act this way.
I love you, Dad.
You shouldn't treat her like you do.
"Kiss your father good night and I'll start work."
I stand there.
I cannot move.
"What are you waiting for?"
I cannot speak.
"Cat got your tongue, boy?"
"I'm fourteen, Dad." My voice is trembling. "I suppose, well, maybe I'm too old..."
"Yeah?"
"I think so."
"That it?"
I nod.

He chews the inside of his lip and looks over at his word processor and then back at me. He exhales out of his nose.

"Yeah?"
I nod again.
His body is red from the glow of the fire.
"That's it then, right?"
"I'm fourteen."
"That's the end, then. Never again."
"I didn't mean."
"I said that is the end."

17

PEGGY

Drew moves the boat farther down the canal to a stretch that almost looks like a natural river. The banks are overgrown and there are no water towers, transmission lines, or signs of life for miles around. At least before we had Jeff Turner's boat moored next to ours, and even though it was unoccupied it felt as if there was backup.

His writing is going well; at least we have that. There were even two days when he acted like he did in the old days. He told me his writing felt different: more powerful and less self-conscious. He asked Sammy about his science classes, and he told me he had been thinking about a family trip to Memphis next summer.

There is hope.

Just enough to cling to.

I step off the bus and thank the driver. There is a spiral of masking tape twisting and flexing down by the curb. I walk into the library. Warm and dry, the reassuring scent of institutional bleach. This is where people come to take stock for a few hours. I see them. The busker who plays his penny whistle outside the general store in all weather and the old man bent over like a question mark who dresses in his best shirt and tie to come read about colonial history and impressionist paintings. Mr. Giles, his name is. He always sits under the ecclesiastical window at the end and never uses the computer or checks out a book. Mr. Giles was once a town planner, so Mrs. Appleby says. He was a principal of the elementary school near the duck pond too. But now he fastens his tie, bent double, watching his boots, and he walks here to be with us for a while and to read up about the siege of Yorktown or the first great battleships of the industrial age.

I have no rings on my fingers, besides my wedding ring. I have no studs in my ears. I am not sure if I am misplacing them or if I have pawned more than I dare to remember. I would have recalled giving them Mom's earrings, the ones with the tiny pearls? The thing about living with no birth certificate or bankbook is that those physical items of silver and gold become your only security. I suppose, before, I had Mom's bungalow, but now that has morphed into a boat I neither drive nor control. I do not even have keys most of the time. The jewelry was my insurance, my escape in case of emergency, and now I have forgotten where I placed it.

I update the database and empty the returns box.

At lunch I save a new story outline, complete with main character details, to a floppy disk. It doesn't have much capacity left. Mrs. Appleby and Pauline come and sit with me for five minutes on account of the library being empty.

"There's a letter here for you, Peggy."

"Thank you."

They look at each other.

"Open it," says Mrs. Appleby. "If you want to, of course. It's from New York City."

"New York," repeats Pauline.

I place my sandwich down and look at the envelope.

"It'll be a no," I say. "It's all right. The odds are . . ."

"The odds are the same for everybody, honey," says Pauline.

"Someone wins the lotto every week, my Kevin always says. Every single week."

I slide my finger along the paper.

They watch.

"I'll open it later. I'm too nervous."

We go back to work and my hair is out of place on account of me losing my last grip last night. I used to have a whole jar full of them in the bungalow and now my hair is falling loose and I look disheveled. I can't even find the glass jar.

At the end of the day I ride the bus and everything has changed. The people around me are the same. The young Hispanic couple with their beautiful newborn. The smoky lady with blue hair and yellow fingertips. The man with broad shoulders and gray, patchy stubble clutching his leather bag like people might want to take it from him. His eyes are sunken, and he looks like he's clinging on. But I have fundamentally changed. I know things will never be the same from this point forward thanks to the letter I opened in the ladies' room after lunch.

The people on the bus are oblivious.

The bus pulls over and I step off and start walking along the side of the road. No sidewalks here. The world is split, I think, into those who have sidewalks and those who do not. When the grass disappears I have to cut down into the woods and make my way down to the water. It is about twenty minutes farther from town than it used to be. I do not think it even enters his head. The extra walk for me through dark woodland, or for Sammy with his heavy schoolbag full of textbooks.

Drew is cleaning the roof of the boat with a bucket, swilling canal water over the length of it and then wiping down the windows.

"Come inside," he says.

"How was your day?" I ask.

"Inside."

I take off my jacket and step in, careful not to mess up the rug. The boat is warm and the ash box needs emptying.

"Keep finding your belongings in strange places."

I scratch my upper lip and he moves closer, staring at me, not blinking.

"You can't do it, Peg."

"OK?"

He leans in.

"It's not OK, not even close."

This is of no consequence, not now I have good news. I can make it all right again. Reduce the stress levels. Turn back the clock.

"Drew, I need to tell you something."

He ignores me. "You need to stop leaving your things in odd places."

The faint scent of Juicy Fruit gum on his breath.

He walks away.

Two hours later we've eaten mac and cheese and I bring out a Sara Lee cherry pie. I've been saving it for a special occasion like this. Part of me thinks it'd be better to keep the news to myself, to hide the money, but he'd find us, quietly hunt us down, it'd only make things ten times worse. This is my chance to fix us.

I hand them their bowls and watch them eat. The silence is beautiful. Then I say, "Drew, Sam, I've got something to tell you."

I can't help but smile.

Sam looks up, eyes bright, and says, "Beaver Island? My field trip?"

Drew says, "If you mention that one more time."

"Not that, Sammy, sorry. But maybe you can go on the next one."

He looks crestfallen.

Drew says, "You look mighty pleased with yourself."

"It's nothing important, really." It is important. *Very* important. I can't not tell them. "It's for us all. Some good news."

"Good news, is it?" says Drew.

"I opened a letter today."

His breathing quickens. He is holding his fork firm in his fist.

"Nothing life-changing, well, I don't think so, not yet, but listen, there's a small publisher in New York, in Manhattan, and they want to . . ."

Drew puts his fork down gently in his bowl.

He twists his bowl a quarter turn counterclockwise.

"You know I loved lit class in school, Drew. Stories. Well, I wrote a book, and they want to print it and pay me something for it. It'll be in bookstores and everything."

"Oh, Mom, well done," says Sammy, beaming, patting me on the wrist. "That's amazing."

Drew's eyes start moving, his focus all over the boat. Everywhere but me.

"We can maybe afford a mooring in the marina again, love. Maybe get you that computer you wanted."

He smiles with clenched teeth. Rotates his bowl back to its original position.

"It's not a lot, nothing like you'd earn, but I'm quite pleased."

"You look pleased," he says, still not looking at me.

"When will they publish it, Mom?"

"I don't know. Next year, I expect. They're sending over the contract. After that we'll get a piece of the money. It should make things easier. Maybe buy you some new clothes from the thrift store?"

"Rolling in dough now, are we?" says Drew, his voice deeper than before. "No need for discipline. For caution. You're dealing with it all, I see. Well, let's wait, eh. Before we lace up our spending boots. Let's just see." He snorts. "And you come out with all this just as I'm heading into act two. You know how to throw a man off course, I'll give you that, Peggy. Act two and you go and drop this."

"It's nothing really," I say. "I should never have announced it like that. It's just a small thing, not like your book, not like your award. I should never . . ."

"I have to work on the motor," he says, standing up abruptly. "Make sure we have a home that goes where we need it to. When I'm out there, see if you can stop yourself from moving things about, will you? Hate to think of you with your book deal and losing your manuscript. Take the shine right off it, that would."

18

SAMSON

"Eighth of an ounce of white mice, please."

She adjusts her hairnet and reaches back for the glass jar. It is not a popular choice, and I ponder the last time she likely poured from this dusty container. She tips the silver bowl into a paper bag and twists it and hands it to me. I pay and leave.

A retired colonel with a moustache speaks in assembly. He talks eloquently about duty and brotherhood and sacrifice. About Korea. There's a direct question from a boy with a buzz cut about how many people the colonel killed. My chemistry teacher looks embarrassed.

The rest of the morning is uneventful. Boys kick my heels and push me through doorways but it's nothing I can't handle. It takes me longer to walk home each night since Dad moved the boat farther away. Other fathers are strict; they dominate their homes, but not to the extent of deciding where home will *be* at the end of each day. The way he has acted since her book news means it is best not to come home too early anyway. The school halls are enemy territory. The bus station is enemy territory. The streets of this unseen town are enemy territory. And then, when I am exhausted and it is dark outside and I want to rest and warm up, I have to trek back to a damp boat and my dad.

I do not have the words.

The boys in geography start to hum when our substitute teacher walks in. She tells us to settle down. We hum louder. She looks afraid. Twenty fourteen-year-old boys and one adult.

"Quiet."

The humming intensifies.

"I'm warning you."

I'm humming along with them and the abject thrill of being allowed to be part of something, a small cog in a powerful machine, a team member, one of a gang, is electrifying.

Eventually she orders us all outside for five minutes, and then, afterward, class progresses as normal. I am buzzing but Johnno keeps kicking the back of my chair. Doesn't he know I was humming like he was? I was part of this, for God's sake. How can he forget something like that? He kicks me again and the boys behind snicker.

In the cafeteria I eat turkey and cheese roll-ups Mom wrapped for me. I sit at the table alone. Smells of Lysol and bacon. My stomach aches for more food.

Gunner walks behind me and slows.

"Pritch wants to see you by the big saw. Ten minutes."

When I turn my head he's already gone.

Pritch is four inches taller than me and three inches broader. He's no friend. The circular saw in woodshop? I'll stay here, thanks. No, that won't work. They'll come. I will hide in the boys' bathroom until Spanish.

When I arrive Fenwell's standing outside.

I go in.

The scent of cheap paper and a thousand varieties of piss. On the floor and up the walls. Doors kicked in and a trail of paper leading into a stall, the toilet bowl blocked, an anatomically correct depiction of a spread-eagle woman rendered in pencil next to the paper dispenser.

I walk to the end stall, but it is occupied so I move two along and go inside and lock the door. The floor is wet. The toilet has no seat. There is excrement smeared on the wall behind the chain.

The smell is pungent, but I have grown accustomed to it.

I pull out the last white mouse from my pocket and let the dusty sweet rest on my tongue. I know I shouldn't eat in here but I need something. It takes a long time for the mouse to break down, saliva pooling around it.

The sound of footsteps.

I push the mouse up with my tongue until it presses into the roof of my mouth. Sugar and comfort. A drop of goodness in this rotten place.

Someone grunts outside.

I freeze.

My eyes widen.

Someone steps into the stall next to mine. There are noises. Banging. A large shadow on the floor.

More footsteps.

I look up and there are faces staring back down. One's chewing gum, blowing a bubble.

"No circular saw in here, is there, Johnno?"

"None, Spocky."

"No saws at all around here, is there, bud?"

"Not that I can see."

"Is this shop?"

"I don't believe so."

"What you doin' down there, Noodles?"

I shrug.

"You get lost on your way, did you? Redheads like you have trouble with directions, I heard. Saw it on MTV. Irish problem. Shall we help Noodles, Johnno?"

"Nah."

"Johnno says no, Noodles. You playing with yourself down there, buddy? Why aren't you sitting down, it's not as easy from a standing start. I can tell you that from bitter experience. Have a seat if you're gonna do that."

I shake my head.

"What's that, Noodles?"

"I'm all right."

"You are not fucking all right, little man. You are the fucking polar opposite of all right. You're skinny redhead trailer trash living on the canal with your mom and her rabbit teeth and your bald excuse for a dad. Pedo if I ever saw one, sweating every time he walks past the school gates, pervert, shiny head weirdo, and now you gone and killed the poor old boy you were paid to look after."

"I heard it was euthanasia," says Johnno.

"Euthanasia," repeats Pritch. "Johnno says you euthanized your employer, little man. You threw him in the canal. I heard he sank down to the weeds, just his colostomy bag floating on the surface. Why'd you do him in, bud?"

"I didn't."

"Lying clown," says Pritch. "You can't afford to be in our school, you shouldn't be here. Period."

They both climb down from their respective stalls.

"Open the door, Noodles. I just want to talk to you, buddy."

I'm frozen in place.

"Kick it in," whispers Johnno.

"Listen, yeah. Open up or Johnno might headbutt the door in. Do me a favor and just open the latch, dude. Save us the bother."

I do nothing.

"Save us the paperwork, little man."

I lift the latch.

My fingers are shaking.

ADRIFT

They both squeeze inside and I'm pushed back toward the toilet bowl.

"Sit down, bud," says Pritch. "Relax."

I shake my head.

Together they push me to sit down on the disgusting porcelain rim of the toilet.

"You look comfier now, Noodles. Next time come and see me at the saw like we agreed, right? Don't make me come in here sniffin' your old piss."

Johnno pushes my schoolbag behind the toilet toward the excrement on the wall.

"Don't do it again, yeah. Some old-timer bothers you, take a fucking breath and leave 'em alone. Take a breath, little man. Self-control. You heard the admiral this morning . . ."

"Colonel. He was a colonel, Johnno."

"Was he?"

"I think so. Army, I reckon. Fought in Korea, didn't he say?"

"I think you might be right there, brother."

I look up at them both.

"You heard the colonel. That generation went to war so we could come to this fine academic institution. So don't go chucking old fellas in the canal, yeah?"

They leave.

It's not that I want to hurt them; I merely yearn to be somewhere else. Almost anywhere else. I crave to be four years ahead. I want to be leaving town, and I want Pritch and Johnno to have failed their GED and for them to watch as I board a train, calmly, and I want them to see the relief on my face as I move away from the station.

"Noodles," says another voice, farther away.

I don't reply.

"What's your real name?"

I pause.

"Jenkins."

A face at the door.

"Name's Pricklett. Paul Pricklett."

He fills the entire doorframe—I mean, the entire thing. Thick glasses and hair that looks like it's already receding. I recognize him. Looks more like a teacher than a boy.

"Did you hear all that?"

"Yeah," he says. "I was about to step in."

"You never was."

He looks at my bag.

The bell rings outside.

"You need to wipe all that down, Jenkins. You'll stink the place out. Come over to the sinks and I'll pass you soapy paper."

I stand up and walk to the sinks with my bag.

"Here."

He hands me a long folded section of paper complete with pink soap.

I wipe down my bag and place the dirty paper in the trash.

"Cooties," he says.

"Yeah."

Then I dry off my pants and use some of the pink soap to mask the smell.

"What you got now?" he asks.

"Football."

He frowns.

"You?"

"Chemistry," he says. "Gases and liquids. All bullshit. Come with me."

"No."

"I said come with me."

I follow him. He walks behind the library and around the back of the science labs and slips behind the industrial waste bin near the principal's office.

ADRIFT

"Not there," I whisper. "Not that way."

He gestures for me to follow him and within seconds we're outside the school gates and passing through the churchyard.

"What if . . ." I say.

"It's all right," he says. "Trust me."

The sun emerges from behind a slate-gray cloud and the air noticeably warms. Pricklett and I walk past a nail bar and a dry cleaner. Army recruitment posters. A fire hydrant with one baby shoe balanced on top. We duck down an alley by the Pentecostal church and then we're outside a bakery Mr. Turner used to talk about.

"Yeah?" he says.

I smile at him. "I've got no money."

"You get it next time," he says, opening the door.

A bell rings and the people inside turn to look at us. Can we do this? This bakery and coffeehouse is larger than the diner Mom took me to. Paul buys two bottles of cola and two cream puff pastries. He carries the tray to the rear corner, by a door that says Private.

"Thanks for this," I say.

He bites into his cream puff.

"You done this before?"

He nods. "I'm not your buddy, Jenkins."

"I know."

"Mom says I have complex needs when it comes to social connections. I don't make friends."

I bite into my cream puff.

"We're not buddies," he says again, eclipsing the bakery with his bulk. "I don't need one. Only I don't have anyone to talk with, really. You like *X-Files*?"

"Yeah."

"I got the video last Christmas. I like Agent Scully. I got the book too. Mom got a check because she was hit by a carpet van."

"By a carpet van?"

He nods. "In her Impala."

"Is she OK?"

"You got any pets, Jenkins?"

His impressive chin is covered with powdered sugar.

"I kind of have a dog."

"What species?"

Species? It's a dog. "Jack Russell."

"Four out of ten."

"Four? Come on, she's a good dog."

"Still a four, though, objectively. Tiger is ten and we work down from there. Wild stallion is a seven. Rottweiler gets six. You been up to Chicago yet on the Amtrak?"

I shake my head and open my cola.

"On the Greyhound, then?"

I shake my head again.

"I'm goin' next year with my mom and stepdad. You ever seen a pornographic magazine? Like, a proper one?"

"Yeah. Just for a second."

"What one?"

I have never seen one.

"Can't remember."

He nods and finishes his pastry.

"How much allowance do you get?"

"I don't."

"Monthly or weekly?"

"I don't."

He nods.

Dad talked about it once. About teaching me sound financial discipline—saving, keeping a bankbook—but it never materialized. And now my independent source of income has died, literally, and we've moved so far from town I hardly have time to do my school assignments, never mind extra jobs. If I do find work I'll have to sleep less.

Last week I found Dad's secret receipts. They were in the kindling packages he makes: intricately folded newspaper enveloping thin sticks. Receipts for heavy paper with a watermark. Receipts from the printing and photocopy shop near the courthouse. Receipts for padded envelopes and special delivery at the post office. He sends out his manuscripts and, judging by those receipts, the process uses up most of our money. That and ribbons for his word processor. I don't think Mom has any idea how much it all costs him.

We leave and walk past the pawnshop.

Cash Advance.

We Buy Gold.

"You goin' back in school?" he says.

"Yeah."

"I'm not your buddy, you know."

"You said."

"I know."

"Thanks for the food," I say.

"You done the right thing today."

"Going back to school?"

He shakes his head. "Not going mental when they put shit on your bag. If you let it all out at once they'll start doing worse things. I know about that. You keep on ignoring it and one day they'll move on to somebody else."

"Thanks."

"See ya, buddy."

19

PEGGY

Quiet days and cold, quiet nights where I have lain awake listening to him tapping the keys of his word processor at the far end of the boat.

Sammy has been rummaging more in his LEGO box. I measure his sense of self and his sense of safety by how deep he pushes his hands into the plastic bricks. He has already endured too much this year.

I walk toward home, if you can call it that.

Other boats have hand-painted flowerpots and elaborate hanging baskets.

Not ours.

I pause for a moment before I board. Earlier, in my lunch break, I kissed the back of an envelope and then dropped it in the mailbox outside the library. My signature. Black ink. Acceptance of the offer to publish *my* book. I have not told Mrs. Appleby yet. I do not want to jinx it until everything is countersigned. And I will not mention it tonight either. I will wait until a good time, probably after he has finished his draft. But quietly, contained mostly within my own skin, within my own frame, there is a surge of hopefulness. Kissing that envelope and pushing it through the narrow slot. Knowing it will mark the beginning of something and the end of something else.

The canal bank is muddy.

I skirt a puddle shining with oil-slick rainbows, and step on the timber boards.

Drew's right there in his jeans and his work shirt, rag in hand, polishing his trophy.

"Good day?"

"All right," I say. "You?"

"Fair," he says, turning the trophy over carefully in his hands, his fingers wrapped around the defined, carved edges of its granite base, his fingertips unconsciously tracing the engraved words: Most Promising Writer.

I remove my jacket and hang it up. There is a torn piece of yellow paper on his desk.

"What's that?"

"See for yourself."

I reach to pick it up and it falls to the rug. I bend down. It is Drew's handwriting. *Kim*, and then a local phone number.

"New girlfriend?"

"Don't start."

"What is it, Drew?"

"You'll think it's dumb."

"What is it?"

He places his trophy down carefully and then sits on one of the camping chairs. The wind rattles the window in its frame.

"One of the guys at the yard, Big Stan. He talked about it, I don't know why, and it got me thinking."

"I don't know what you're talking about, Drew."

He sighs. "Big Stan and his old lady, they weren't seeing eye to eye like they used to. He says they went up to the health center. Talked to this Mrs. Assell, some kind of counselor, for marriages.

Kim, her name is. And they all had a chat together. It's dumb, I told you it was."

"A counselor?"

"I should never have let him give me her number."

"No, it's all right."

"Big Stan says she was the wife of a miner, he's passed now, and she understands real life. She knows our county, our town, the levees, and the barges, she knows about the old days, the good times, and the sour. And she listens, gives you time to talk things through."

"I think that sounds good."

"You would."

"Have you . . ."

"Have I what?"

He lifts his chin. Angles it.

"Have you called her yet, Drew?"

"Not my thing. But Stan's still in touch with her and he told me today there's been a cancellation. Last minute. He thinks we could go tonight if we wanted."

"I'd like that."

"I'm sure you would."

"You don't want to go?"

"I wouldn't be interested but Stan says she's decent. Can listen and smooth things, you know. He vouches for her."

"Wouldn't do any harm. Mrs. Assell, you say?"

"That's it."

"Is there an appointment slot? What time?"

"Not sure I'm going. Just letting you know it's a possibility. Thought it might be interesting for my fiction. Call it research."

I do not say anything.

A boat passes by and our home moves gently in the water.

"The slot's at seven thirty at the health center."

"Next to the library, Drew. I know it."

He shakes his head. "Incorrect. It's not that health center. It's up by the dozer rental place, near the old crane yard."

"I'll go if you want."

He nods to himself. "Big Stan says she's sensible."

I wash towels in the sink and he cleans out the bilge pump. Sammy comes home and takes three conkers from his coat pocket.

"Don't put them on the table," I say. "Good gracious, they're beautiful! Look at the shine on them."

"Biggest horse chestnuts in the state," he says, grinning. "I'd put money on it."

"How was school, Sam?"

"All right."

"Your father and me, we're probably going out tonight. You'll have the boat to yourself until about nine. Don't break anything."

"You're going out?"

"Just for a short while."

"Where?"

"Doctor."

What little color he had drains from his face. "Doctor? Mom? What's wrong?"

"Nothing like that. Nothing to worry about, my love."

There is a large crow in the alder tree by the water's edge and it is cawing. Like it is trying to warn us all.

"How was school?" asks Drew as he comes back in.

"All right. Mom says you're going into town?"

"You'll be the man of the boat. You can handle that?"

"Course I can."

"Making peanut butter and jelly sandwiches for supper," I say. "We got white and whole wheat. Which do you want?"

"Whole wheat."

He wants white. I know he does. But he also wants to impress his father. If there is anything in the world my Samson desires, it is the approval and respect of his dad.

"Peg," says Drew.

I look at him.

"I went up to the marina today after work. Filled up the tanks and emptied the cassette. Had the motor running most of the afternoon. Plenty of hot water in the tank for once. As we're going out you can run a hot bath."

Samson and I both stare at him.

"Don't get used to it."

"I'll just have a few inches."

"Won't hear of it. Go fill it up for her, boy. Up to the faucet, good and hot, and put some froth in it."

"You sure?"

"Course I am."

He makes the sandwiches and brews coffee. We eat by the fire while the bath is filling. Samson is smiling for the first time in a long time. I begin to clear away the plates, but Drew says, "Boy'll do that. You get in the tub. I'll shave by the fire like my father used to."

My stomach is uneasy. It is like someone came and turned my whole universe around. It looks the same but it is upside down now. Inside out.

The water is deep and there are bubbles and it smells like fresh-cut flowers. I slide the door shut and exhale. The tightness in my shoulders starts to ease. Roses. Warm air. The room is heady with steam and I can hardly see straight.

I undress.

Cold linoleum floor. Wet window.

Plunging my hand into the water I sense my forehead start to loosen.

This has been a good day.

We can turn things around.

I step in and the relief as I sink down and let the heat take me in its grip is immense.

Blessed numbness through every part of my body.

ADRIFT

Sammy will be outside doing his history assignment at the dinette table and Drew will be shaving with a bowl and mirror by the fire. My eyelids grow heavy. The memory of sweet jelly on my lips. I lie still on the bottom of the tub and watch the tiny bubbles flex and burst.

The warmth has penetrated deep and my brain is easing.

I close my eyes.

20

SAMSON

The boat is warmer than usual and there's more humidity in the air. It's either from the bath or Dad's shaving bowl by the fire. I've never seen him shave in here before.

Biology assignment. Photosynthesis. The process where plants convert solar energy into food. An everyday miracle, so says Mrs. Patel. Starlight to sugar. I study but I can't not watch Dad. He works slowly and deliberately, scraping the razor down his carved cheeks, up from the base of his neck to his prominent chin. The steel blade catches the light from the woodstove and illuminates him like a performer. I can hear every whisker being severed. The jawline, tracked. He works at it like a concert pianist or a needleworker. Muscle memory. Mom in the bathroom and Dad by the fire. Me in between with Amber's pink leather collar loose around my wrist.

It is quiet.

There's a bird outside that swoops down from high branches and then returns. A raven or a jackdaw. Black as night.

Dad taps his razor and scrapes it along the edge of the bowl.

He sniffs.

I read about chlorophyll and what occurs inside a leaf cell. Part of me yearns to plunge my hands deep inside my LEGO box but I am trying to resist. I need to grow out of it, Dad says.

Condensation on the windowpanes.

I stroke the pink leather with the tip of my thumb.

When we found her on the towpath she was already stiff and cold; ice crystals sparkling on her gray whiskers. Dad said she'd been poisoned, most likely rat poison from one of the nearby ranches. I did my best to dig a hole on the embankment. I cried as I dug, as I hit each root and stone, and her grave wasn't nearly as perfect as I wanted it to be. She deserved better. Mom tried to tell me she's with Mr. Turner now. All I know is I miss taking her for walks and stroking the tight skin underneath her chin. Her collar fits on my arm but I have to be extremely careful in school so nobody notices it. If Gunner or Hammer Adams spots it they'll make my life ten times harder.

Dad shaves the top of his head, guiding the razor with his free hand, dragging steel blades slowly across the bumpy contours of his scalp. He works at it and I am mesmerized. He's a living shadow.

"What are you learning?"

I look back at my books.

"Biology."

He doesn't reply.

The night sky is blank through our wet glass. Blank, with vague, moving clouds, and the wind is pushing against the long, flat side of the boat.

I think about Paul Pricklett and what his family might look like. How they live in their house. The tactics he employs to endure each school term.

Dad uses scratching movements with the razor at the crease where the back of his head turns into neck. Short, precise scrapes.

He checks the clock on the wall and he looks nervous.

Restless.

"Your mother want a cup of coffee in there, boy?"

I yell, "Mom, you want a coffee?"

There is no response.

He checks the clock again.

"Get off your butt and ask her properly."

I pull Amber's collar up my wrist and scoot out from the dinette. The air outside the sliding bathroom door is humid.

I knock three times. "You want some coffee?"

Nothing.

Dad wipes his face with a towel and looks at me, droplets hanging from his long eyelashes.

I look back.

He shrugs.

I shrug back.

"Mom?"

Dad looks into my eyes.

"Mom?"

He stares at me.

I look at the base of the door, at the sliver of light, and then I head back to the dinette. A few minutes later I return to the door. "Mom, do you know about cell membranes?"

Dad stares over at me again, then pulls his shirt on slowly over his head.

"Mom, are you OK in there?"

Dad wipes sweat carefully from his brow.

I knock again, three times, harder. "I'm coming in. I'm not looking."

Dad frowns.

I collect a blunt knife from the kitchen and use it to slide the lock off and then I nudge the door open a few inches.

Steam in the air.

An intoxicating scent. Some kind of blossom.

"Mom?"

She says nothing.

"I'm coming in. I'm looking at the ground, I swear."
I peer down at the linoleum.
The bird caws outside.
"You want anything, Mom?"
I glance up.
The water is red and her eyes are open.
I whisper, "Mom," and then I fall to my knees with my face next to hers and push her hair from her eyes.
"What's this?" he says, behind me, a pill bottle in his hand.
Dad pulls me out of the way and drags her effortlessly out of the tub, water pouring all over the floor, over his bare feet. He takes her out and he places her down gently on the dinette table.
I cover her up with a cushion.
He says, "What have you done, Peggy?"
He checks her mouth and listens for breathing.
"Mom, please."
He puts his ear to her chest. She's so pale. Thin. Veins and streaks of blood down her sides.
"Mom."
He looks at me. "Get your sneakers on, Samson. Run to the highway. To the gas station. Call an ambulance right now. Run as fast as you can, son."
I stare at her.
"Go!"
I trip over myself leaving the boat.
The night is empty.
Blank.
I sprint up the hill, through trees, tears still streaming down my cheeks, into my mouth. Salt. The air squeezed from my lungs. Heart pounding. Her, back there, naked, with him. Headlights in the distance. What has she done to us? To *me*? I can't. I run, tripping, slowing, racing.
I run.

PART II

21

PEGGY

Bumpy, shaking. Rough.
   My bones.
Where am I?
Cold.
Shivering all over.
So dark I cannot see in front of me.
"Stay with me, Peggy," she says. "Keep talking to me. Stay awake, Peggy."
Darkness.
Silence; on and off.
Inside an ambulance. The ceiling. Sirens.
"What did she swallow?"
Voices. Drew. Where is Sammy? Where is my boy?
Something cold in my arm, rushing through it.
Sleep. Dark, heavy sleep.
Bleeping.
I must try to stay awake. Is this the same day? Where am I?
Fade to darkness.
Cold, so very cold.

"What?" I scream. "What? Please! Help!"

The tube is pushed down into my mouth, down my throat. Deeper. I fight. They push it in. I squirm. They are trying to kill me. I buck. Can't see properly. Can't talk. I convulse and punch out at them. They hold me down and they force me.

Scratch.

"Just a little more, honey. Easy. Just a little more."

Is it him?

Black circles.

Quiet.

Coughing. A long corridor. Bleeping. Lights on and off. Time not working anymore, not making any sense.

"You're very sick, Peggy," she says. "We are here for you."

I try to focus, to sit up, to move away.

I can't.

I can't speak.

So cold. Weak. Can't feel my own feet. My scalp is on fire. I cannot breathe. Pain in my throat.

"Sammy?"

Cold arms.

There is nobody here for me.

Bleeping.

I try to sit up.

"There you go, Peggy. How are you feeling now? Can you hear me, dear?"

Hazy.

Asleep. I feel asleep. Maybe I am asleep.

I reach out and hold her wrist. Warmth. Soft skin. Something alive.

"That's it, dear. I'm right here."

The throbbing intensifies. Rings of pain behind my eyes. Layers of those rings.

"Take it slowly, Peggy. I'm here to help you. You're in the hospital and we're taking real good care of you."

I squint at her.

"Samson. My boy."

"He's here. He's safe with your husband. You'll see him very soon."

I nod and shrink tighter within myself. I cannot feel my fingers. What happened?

"Sammy. Please."

"I'll go see if I can fetch him. I won't be long."

Hospital. Curtains moving back and forth. Plastic jug of water but I can't focus on it. Hazy. I sit up straighter. No strength. Another nurse in the distance sits watching me. Hospital gown. Socks.

I was on the boat.

Sammy.

We were going out someplace.

On the other side of the curtain a man says, "Triage."

I see a triangle in my mind. Our family.

What went wrong?

The nurse comes back. Neat uniform. Black hair.

"They're coming through in a minute," she says. "Peggy, I said they're coming through. Your son is coming."

"I'm so scared," I whisper.

"I know you are, dear. I'm here to help you. I'm not leaving."

I am so scared.

The curtains sway in the wind as someone is wheeled past. Noise. Orderlies. Commotion. Worried voices. Raised voices.

I touch the needle taped to my hand.

"Just leave that be," she says.

The curtain twitches.

A hand I have known since the moment it was created.

Muddy shoes.

Red hair in tufts.

22

SAMSON

What did I do? How did everything suddenly change?

I look down at the dirt and leaves still coating my shoes. All I could think running through the trees was that I couldn't trip or fall. How if I fell she wouldn't live. I'd be the one responsible for her dying. I had to keep running and not stumble. I had to reach that pay phone.

A man is pushed past in a wheelchair. He has an oxygen mask on his face. An IV. His knees are bruised.

The smell of plastic. Rubber. Smoke.

Why do we live so far from everyone? That was my next furious thought. How can it be that the EMTs had so much trouble reaching Mom? What made us move so far from help?

I want to see her, but I am afraid.

The nurse tells us she's awake. She can talk to us now.

The worst thing I have ever seen in my life is her in the bath. The looseness of her facial features. The color of the water.

The second worst thing was the look on Dad's face.

I had never once seen my father scared.

He doesn't scare.

Three doctors and nurses run through and almost knock me over.

There is someone behind a curtain being worked on. Lots of stern voices. Code words. Bleeping. Nurses running out again to collect things in plastic wrappers.

My own mother.

I did not trip. I found the phone. I helped them locate our boat. When they reached her Dad had covered her with two towels, and when they lifted her onto their gurney the towels fell away and I cried out and ran to put them back in place.

Her lips were blue.

A nurse walks past me and smiles. She's carrying take-out coffee cups.

I talked to the doctor with Dad. We sat in a narrow room with two chairs and a table and an artificial plant. There was a small window high on the wall and the doctor kneeled on the floor in front of us. I did not expect him to do that. He was older than Dad, much older, looked like Sidney Poitier. He kneeled down and told me she was very sick. Dad had already handed them the empty bottles. He told me I had been brave.

I asked Dad, "Why did she do this to us?"

He just looked away and shook his head.

For a man so gifted with language, he had no words to share.

I had never imagined in my worst nightmares that this might be possible. I had conjured up awful possibilities, terrible things, tragedies, but never Mom, never her. Not Mom. It was always me and her helping someone, or helping each other, calling the police after, running away.

It was always me and her at the end.

The nurse with the accent appears and smiles. She wears an ID badge clipped to her uniform. Her dark hair is held in a bun. She ushers me through.

My stomach is heavy. Pulling down.

I push through another flimsy curtain.

"Sammy," she says, her voice a croak.

I walk to her, gently, calmly. I want to run to her but she looks so small.

"Mom."

She nods and starts to sob.

"It's OK, Mom. We're here now."

She wipes her face and beckons me closer.

"What is happening, Sammy?"

I recoil slightly. My mouth falls ajar. I look at the nurse, then at Dad.

"It's OK, Mom. We're going to make it all better."

She sighs.

She closes her eyes.

23

PEGGY

They moved me.

I fell asleep, and then they moved me here.

I am in a long room now with lots of identical beds.

I tried to leave after they wheeled me out to the second ambulance. They explained calmly how I was not going home yet and how I needed to stay to receive some help. I told them I was leaving to go take care of my son. More people arrived. There must have been ten of them. They tried to persuade me to swallow medicine. I did not know what it was, and I did not know who to trust. I still don't. I told them I would not take it just now, maybe later. I reminded them I was an adult, and a mother, and I needed to see my son. They said I was sick. I told them I knew that, I would take their medicine in time, I would see the doctors, do whatever they wanted, but I was well enough to go home to look after Sammy. He needed me. They said I was not well enough. I told them they could not hold me against my will, I had done nothing wrong. They said they could. I said I wasn't a prisoner, I wasn't a criminal. I had done nothing. What had I done? Nothing. Not one damn thing. They asked me not to shout. To settle down. I couldn't get through to them. My son needed me more than they could ever know. I had to go. I needed to watch his back and cook his supper. Breakfast? What time is it? I need to check on him. They asked me to sit down. I could not get through to them. They told me they would have to give me medicine to calm me if I did not sit. I pleaded with them to see him. For them to let me out for one day. I needed to check on him. I said Drew and I would get some help. I said I wanted Kim Assell. They stared at each other. Their expressions changed. I mentioned her name again, I screamed it, and they looked at each other again. I ran for the door. They held me down. I screamed louder. Thrashed out. Sammy! Get off me. Leave me alone. They held me down tight.

A needle.

The weight of them over me.

Sharp scratch.

I have been vague ever since.

They are not pinning me down anymore, they do not need to.

I am locked inside a thick, opaque bubble filled with heavy water. I cannot move quickly. I can't think properly. The volume of my life has been turned down.

The other patients are like me.

They are quiet and their faces are sad.

I rub my hand up and down my throat. The necklace that is no more. I have nothing in here. No hair clips or shoes with laces. I have less than before. Not even my purse. The frail, soft-spoken woman in the next bed showed me how the showers are sloping so we can't hang ourselves. There are no mirrors to smash into sharp fragments. The windows only open an inch. She explained to me how there are no metal knives or forks. The door handles are sloped like the showers. Did I mention that already? The bathroom doors are half missing so they can check on us at all times.

I will go home soon.

Tomorrow, maybe.

No, apparently they say I will need to stay longer so I can recover.

Give the medicine a chance to build up in my system. They say I need to talk to the doctors. Talk in a group. I said I would because what choice do I have? But what I really need is to see him, to kiss him good night, to make his school packed lunch, to shield him. How is he coping? What is he thinking?

Dessert is Jell-O.

Raspberry.

Soft.

The frail woman with the gray hair looks very thin. She does not eat her Jell-O. They watch her closely. She will not eat it and then they will take her away to another room again and I will cover my ears with my hands like last time.

They want me to talk about the evening of the bath, but I tell them I do not know what happened. They would like me to explain how I felt. *Draw it on paper if that's easier.* How did I feel? I felt nothing. I *feel* nothing. I am in the bubble filled with heavy water, unable to hear clearly or speak like normal.

The days are long.

Muffled.

It is all about routine.

People crying and watching the dayroom TV with the sound off. Rinse, repeat.

When an exciting program comes on the nurse changes channels immediately.

We watched Bob Ross painting yesterday, and then we watched a long documentary about the Atacama Desert.

I want to hold my child. That is what I want, and I know he needs it from me. After Jeff Turner died and I took Sammy downtown I saw how the other boys treated him. After that I waited one afternoon close to the bus stop. I stood by the Mexican restaurant, the one that closed down, watching. Sammy spent most of the time in Smith's Bookstore and Stationers, clever boy, checking out nonfiction and staying out of trouble. I saw an older kid with a faint moustache tug at his bag. I saw two other boys push him when he went to board the bus. It took all my strength to stop myself from running over there and teaching them some manners, but I did not. I knew it would make things far worse for him the next day, and the next. And now he is going home to a distant, cold boat. He has his father to deal with all on his own, and no matter how hard it is for him, I cannot do a thing to help.

I do not know what I did in the bathroom that night.

I can't remember swallowing any pills. I would not do that to Sammy. But my mind *was* playing tricks, had been for months, years, I know that. I was making mistakes. Causing trouble and losing things. The time my child needs me the most and I am failing him. I have thought about breaking out but there are so many locked doors to navigate and so many nurses and how can I break out of anything when the medicine they give me makes me this vague? Cameras everywhere. Heavy doors that lead to other heavy doors. I cannot remember the start of a sentence by the time I reach the end. My thoughts are damaged. Fragmented and broken.

The ward is quiet tonight.

Maybe I have done something wrong. More than one thing. Why would they lock me in here if I had done nothing wrong? An incident. A crazed spree. The cold air on my thighs that night as they carried me through the trees to the ambulance. The long, stiff tube forced down my throat. The fight when they held me down so hard I thought my bones would surely break.

Maybe it's all my fault.

Maybe it's me.

24

SAMSON

Wind buffets the boat and hail comes down in artillery barrages, rattling off the roof, pausing, waiting, then tapping against the windows.

I sit with my cheek against the glass. To feel the ice, and the vibrations.

Dad says she's in a different hospital now. One farther outside the town. When we lived in the bungalow our neighbor's niece spent some time inside there. He says Mom is sick but they can help her. He says she'll likely be there for a while.

Tap. Tap. Tap.

I had people in my life before. I never thought about it at the time, but I always knew they were there. Grandma and Grandpa died before I was born, so did Nanna Ruth, but I always had *people*. Mr. Turner and little Amber. I had them. Mr. Turner's drawer stuffed full of KitKats. He always let me keep the change because he knew I needed it and asked me about history lessons and whether I'd reached the World Wars yet. The thing is: We'll study them next year. Mr. Turner died before we got that far. And in the bungalow we had people all around us. Not people I loved or even knew that well, but other kids, other dads, other moms who'd ask me what I was doing out so late, checking up on me, asking after us. We had Mr. Jameson in the convenience store near the intersection. He was impatient and suspicious, but we had him close by. I had a bedroom back then. A bed that stayed a bed all day and all night.

And I had Mom.

Dad is setting the fire. I've emptied the ashes and washed the dishes and swept the dirt off the deck. I've done what he asked me to do.

When I was sweeping I heard a train in the far distance. Going north, maybe. Delivering commuters and mail and lovers meeting up after weeks apart. I heard it thunder along the rain-slick tracks.

Dad says the new hospital won't allow visits. He says they want her doing all the talking therapies and group therapies with no interruptions or distractions. When I lowered my head he said, "You want her better, boy? You want your mother better?"

He is streamlining things. His word. *Streamlining*. As if we need any more damn streamlining. He expects me to use less water. Less coal. Eat less food. He wants us to live more simply until she gets out. He says, *Just us boys now. No females. No nonsense. We'll be fine, eh?*

How scared is she right this instant? How are the other people on her ward? Does she have her own room? Can she stay warm enough? She was so cold that night.

Dad points to the folding Walmart camp chair so I walk over and sit down heavily in it.

"Pork and beans tonight, young man."

I nod.

"One of your favorites."

I nod again.

"You could show some enthusiasm. I don't have to cook, you know."

"I'm thinking about Mom."

He runs his lower teeth against his lip, dragging it sideways.

"Best place if you're sick."

He toasts bread on forks in front of the fire until the edges are singed black, and then he places the can of pork and beans on top to warm through.

"Not wasting pans when it's just us, no point. I have to make the most of this writing time before your mother gets back and I have distractions again. Anyway, beans don't need cooking, just need warming through, anyone'll tell you that. Open the can and heat them up."

"Mom cooks them."

"Your mother isn't here."

The hail stops tapping.

"When does she get out, Dad?"

"Don't know."

"Can I visit her, just a quick visit?"

He half burns the next piece of toast. He grunts at it and takes it from the heat.

"They said no."

He upends the hot can of beans and we eat, plates on our knees, by the heat of the fire. Dad says we don't need drinks because the bean liquid is the same thing. It's all liquid. He chooses to eat the burnt piece of toast.

"After school tomorrow the boat will be farther down the canal, I expect. Might even take her on the river for a change."

Not this again. "How much farther?"

"You got legs, haven't you? Walk and you'll find it."

"But how will Mom find us?"

He chews.

Swallows.

"She'll not be out for a long while, mark my words. She won't need to find us."

My heart starts to cool. I stiffen. What if she breaks out or they let her go? We have no address, no phone. How will she ever find her way back to me?

"Do you ever miss the bungalow, Dad?"

"Your nanna chose it, was never us. Didn't feel like my own home. All those bills, one after the other. No, I don't miss your nanna's bungalow. I'd rather be out here in nature, the wild, free, living on my own terms. We're luckier than most."

He finishes his toast and starts cleaning his nails with the short blade of his pocketknife.

"School again tomorrow?"

I look up at him. Brown slivers are falling from his fingernail.

"That'll be good for you. Not stuck here with me all day. Out with your buddies getting up to no good. Classes and football practice. You'll be glad to be back in that school."

The fire in the woodburner flares with the wind.

I can't catch my breath.

25

PEGGY

What is Sammy busy doing right now? What is he wearing? Is he warm enough? Is he hungry?

My days are punctuated by mealtimes. They prefer us in a set routine. Breakfast. Rec room. Lunchtime. Group therapy. Dinner. TV room. Supper. Bathroom. Bed.

Myrtle, the friendly nurse with the yellow nails, tells me it is best to stay calm. To breathe deeply when I become upset. To do coloring or go off for a short walk around the rec room. And I know she is right but if she was locked in day and night she would be angry too. I understand that the way to be released is to stay quiet and normal and timid but sometimes the steam builds and builds and I cannot stop thinking about Sam and how he is coping, and what Drew did or did not do all those years ago, and if he has moved the boat, and how I have not had a single visitor when most of the others have, and then I scream and run again for the door. I can't help it. I must see my boy, to touch his skin, to check on him.

Each day the same as the one before.

Institutional food.

The smell of decay. Slow, steady decay: the warm building and its contents.

The echo of our nightmares lingering well into the mornings.

I was fine before they locked me in here. I signed a book deal for goodness' sake. In my own name. I have told them about it over and over and they look at me like I am insane. I take care of my son; I have never neglected him, never. Not once. We are a family. A *triangle*. We are holding together for Sammy's sake. He is a fragile boy but that will change, we just need to provide a stable environment for him. Love and support. I scratch my fingernails down my face. Where is his love and support now?

Sometimes I stand alone by the big window looking out at the grass and the trees. One tree in particular. A mature Scotch pine complete with russet bark and long, slender cones. It is the most reliable, consistent thing in my life at the moment.

Three of the women sit with me during the day. We watch television together. Rachel says she does not know exactly who she is. She says, "Where is this? Where? Who?" in a low voice over and over. "Who am I, really, truly?" Rachel does not really talk to us, but she likes to sit with us while she questions her own existence. Grace is charming, a teacher by profession. Her father was a Black Panther in New York and her sister is a trial lawyer. Grace looks like any respectable woman in the line at the bank or walking down the sidewalk. Except she will not eat. They weigh Grace every day. They monitor her closely and she is barely hanging on but somehow she finds the energy to make us laugh. I would like to know her again when we leave this place. She lives up to her name. Finally, the last of our group, Fatima, receives no visitors either. We talk about it. How some of the others have so many visits and we have none. Fatima has light scars on her arms and her neck. She works at the mayor's office. She says she has seen me in the library before. Fatima has accrued more time in hospitals than the others. She has spent years locked inside.

Is Sammy at school today? Is Drew making him a packed lunch? Of course he is. Drew will make sure Sammy is fed. I cannot countenance any alternative.

He must be.

I will meet the doctor in a few days. I can only speak with her once a week and I plan to stay very well-behaved until that moment. I will make my case for leaving. It is ridiculous that I have been here so long. How long has it been? I will not demand it or scream like before; I will explain, gently, reasonably, that I would like to be home for Christmas with my family. My lip starts twitching at the thought of her politely declining my request. Her looking at me with pity and saying, *It's too soon.*

Lunch.

Medication at the hatch.

They check my mouth to see that I swallow.

I sit at a table with Fatima, coloring. I have tried to write, to start a new story. Myrtle, the nurse with the nails, brought me in some lined paper and a blunt felt-tip pen but I cannot write a word. The others make it through each day coloring and now I do as well. I have become one of them. It helps me not to think about the evening of the bath and the cut on my leg. I was told there was enough medication in my system to kill me, and there were two loose razor blades in the tub. He did it. I know full well he did it. One of his blades cut me. I was told mine was a *failed attempt.* They want me to open up about it, describe my feelings in detail, but I tell them that *it wasn't me.*

I would never leave my boy.

Never.

They don't believe a word I say.

I color in a tropical bird in a tree, some approximation of a toucan, and aside from these soft clothes my skin is unadorned. I am not allowed jewelry in here and I miss my necklace. It is hollow and only 9 karats or 14 karats gold, it is not monetarily valuable, but it holds the teething marks of my only child. And it connects him directly to his Nanna Ruth. I do not know if I will be able to buy it back from Kerrigan's Pawnshop in time. Will I still be paid by my publisher? Are they sending letters to the library, and will Mrs. Appleby forward them to me here? Is that even possible? I am overwhelmed and I have no answers.

Most people in here look normal.

That is the most shocking thing.

They are the people you walk past in Walgreens or in line at the DMV. Maybe that is what happened to me. I looked normal and then they locked me up inside here with no way to convince the guards or doctors to release me. I need the ability to make my own decisions again. I might flee. I will run as fast as I can to the boat, thundering along the towpath, breathing in woodsmoke from the other houseboats, and I will locate my boy and I will hold him so tight, squeeze him, smell him, bury my nose into his hair, and I will never again let go.

26

SAMSON

I wake up shivering.

Dad's over by the fire removing ashes.

"Snore like a steam locomotive, you do."

I stretch. Yawn. Climb out of bed.

"Like a freight train going through a tunnel."

I smile.

"Nothing to grin about, boy. Am I grinning?"

"I've got a cold coming."

"You'll have something coming."

He tips ashes into the box.

"Have you eaten breakfast, Dad?"

"Nothing in."

"Nothing?"

He stands up straight, pushes his chest out.

"Do I look like your mother? You want something, you get it. And anyway, you got a Milky Way, I've seen it."

"I'm saving it."

He steps outside with the ashes, cursing under his breath.

I wash my face and brush my teeth. The bathroom is so cold I almost expect an icicle to be dangling from the showerhead.

"What you looking for?" he says.

"My boxers. Clean ones."

He scratches his chin.

"Do we need to wash some clothes, Dad?"

He shrugs. "You need to stop snoring is what you need to do. How am I supposed to write anything decent with you sniffing all night?"

"I'll use some Vicks."

"If this book doesn't turn out how I see it in my head it'll do us no good, you understand? Your mother will be back and the book will have fallen to pieces, the noise you make."

I pull on yesterday's boxers.

"We'll clean clothes tonight. Tomorrow, maybe. You'll live. Bit of grime never hurt anybody."

The milk is off so I have a glass of water.

An ache in my stomach.

I can feel my ribs in a way I never have before. Like, I can almost push my fingers around them.

"Go easy on that water, Samson. I don't want to be filling the tank up every five minutes. Think about it, boy. Costs me fuel every time. Drink like a camel, you do, just like your mother."

I open our pantry cupboard. "There's nothing to take for lunch, Dad."

She would have made sure we had something.

"You think this is a hotel?"

"I just wanted a sandwich or something."

"*Just wanted a sandwich or something.* Me working overtime, writing at night while you're in your pit dreaming. Just want a sandwich or something."

I pull on my uniform. The shirt collar is yellow.

"Do you think Mom's all right?"

"What?"

"I said do you think she's getting better?"

"How do I know?"

I pull on my jacket and shoes. The laces are fraying.

"She's getting better," he says, softening, scratching his head. "Medicine's kicking in. She'll be back soon, you'll see."

"Before Christmas Eve?"

He sniffs. "We'll see."

"Can you ask again if we can visit her?"

He nods and then he puts his hand down deep inside his jeans pocket. There are gray flecks of wood ash hovering on his arm hairs, held in place by static.

"Three bucks for your lunch. Breakfast, whatever you want. Now, go."

I walk past the lichen-covered oak that marks the mooring spot where Mr. Turner died. Every time I pass it I look up into the speckled canopy, at whatever sky is visible through the limbs, and I think about its roots drawing water and its bark protecting the sapwood, and about how the tree grows a new ring with every passing year. The cycles of life and growth, and demise. The manner in which trees like this one watch on silently. They see us emerge, and grow old, and wither, and then they observe it happen all over again. Standing witness.

Math. English lit. British poets of the Great War. The awful, delicate carnage of their words. Dad talked about them one time. Wilfred Owen and Siegfried Sassoon. "Dulce et Decorum Est." Poetry forged like new elements in those filthy, freezing trenches. Warfare so bogged down and hellish the men scribed verses to make sense of existence. Make sense of the end of everything they thought they knew.

At lunch I go to chess club. I'm halfway through a game, winning, protecting my queen having taken my opponent's, when the teacher is called away. Minutes later three boys run in and drag me out by my jacket. I kick and fight back but they lift me and cajole me and dump me out by trash cans behind the computer room.

I am acutely aware of time. Safety margins. There's still fifteen minutes until the bell rings.

They can do a lot in fifteen minutes.

"Tell us," one says.

I look from side to side in the hope that Paul Pricklett might walk past.

"Your mom's in the nuthouse. She's British, yeah? Scottish or some shit? Tell us. Is she mental, Noodles? Has she completely lost it?"

I shake my head.

"Liar," says the tall one, grinning. "She's locked in the psych ward, my aunt's neighbor said. Your mom was hearing voices, boy. Fucking possessed or something. Demons. Your mom, Noodles, is batshit crazy."

"No, she isn't."

"Oh," says the blond one. "She isn't, eh? Then why is she locked up with the other mentals? I went in there to sing carols once at elementary school. 'Good King Wenceslas.' One old guy pissed himself. Pulled his pants down and stood there with his dick out. Your mom's in with them now, locked in with old men like him, you realize what that means?"

"I've got to go."

I start to walk away.

They block me.

"Your mom's mad, Noodles, you got to accept it. She'll be in there for years, little man. Next time you see her she won't know who the fuck you are. She'll look at you all vacant, spaced out, and she won't even remember your name."

They all laugh.

"She'll be getting lots of attention, though, there's that at least. All the filthy pillheads, the psychos, probably a group of 'em. Meth heads. You might get a crazy little brother out of it."

"Shut up."

They laugh again.

"Right now, Noodles. There'll be half a dozen of them with her. All dribbling and screeching. Locked up real tight together. You can picture it, can't you? I'm glad my mom isn't crazy."

It comes from deep down inside. Incandescent rage the likes of which I never knew I had. I charge at him. I hold my hands tight around his neck and I push him to the ground and the other two start punching and kicking me, dragging me off, but I keep attacking. Squeezing. Punching. Other boys chant *fight* but then everything blurs. Elbows to my ribs. My jacket rips. Blood spurts from his busted lip. Two teachers arrive and break us up. It is over in seconds. The tall one has his shirt ripped open. We are sent, panting, to the principal's office.

We each receive double detention, and we have to write essays about the history of the Federal Reserve. The principal didn't listen to me. It was three against one and he never even listened.

On the bus everyone stares. Ripped jacket, the school badge on my breast pocket hanging down, my shirt collar scuffed, a hole on my knee. My blood is still boiling. And now I have to return home to him.

I step off the bus and a fine drizzle moves across the sky in waves.

A truck driver hits his horn warning me to walk on the shoulder and not on the road.

I ignore him.

The back of my neck is soaking wet, rain running down my face, hiding my tears, the wind gusting, trees rustling overhead.

Headlights bleed into the horizon.

I stagger toward the middle of the highway.

I stay there for a long time.

In the middle.

White lines.

Car horns, and one man shouts something unintelligible, his words stolen by the wind.

I wander farther across.

Into traffic.

27

PEGGY

Things were going reasonably well.

I was taking my medication. The nurses were beginning to trust me, I think, and even though this place still scares me I was starting to believe I would be released to see Sammy.

They have put up tinsel.

There is an artificial Christmas tree with safe, unbreakable baubles. A menorah with fake candles painted yellow.

I try so hard to stay calm even though every day I go over and over the many reasons why I should not be locked up in here. I am a volunteer librarian, a mother, a wife, a writer. And yet I have fewer rights than a violent felon. I cannot comprehend it. People who rob and deal crack have access to a lawyer and a phone call, and I did nothing wrong and yet I am locked away.

At high school, when I was in tenth grade, I read a classic short story about a woman trapped in the walls, in yellow wallpaper, and now I cannot help seeing myself lost in *these* walls. Staring out, my mouth agape, screaming silently at the nurses to see me, to notice me, to hear my voice.

It was all going pretty well.

The medication makes me blurry but I can still form coherent thoughts, and I know deep in my bones that I did not take any pills that day. I would not. Last week I told Fatima that I am not mad, and she said, "None of us are, sugar. This whole thing is an elaborate experiment. Has been for years." I told her, "No, listen, I mean it, I am not actually crazy." She blinked hard for a few moments and then opened her eyes wide and said, impatiently, "Oh, sure, that's what they all say."

There is nothing to do here.

The air is always too warm and too stale.

Everything was bearable, though, until the meeting.

I meet with the doctor once a week. Initially it was a woman doctor. Nice lady from Virginia, reminded me a little of Maya Angelou. She was kind. I thought she paid attention to my stories and she made time for me. I was getting used to her. The mellow way she spoke. It took me all week to formulate a plan to sound reasonable and trustworthy and to ask her to be released before Christmas. I want to spend time with my son, please, if that can be arranged. Please. Thank you. I was going to ask her to be let go. Monitored at home, sure, but not kept in here. And then I had prepared to stay calm if she said no. I would not have reacted with anger. I planned to say I understood, and instead of being released perhaps I could have day leave or an overnight stay and then return here. That was my plan. It was a sound, reasonable plan.

Other patients come and go but I do not know how they manage it.

The tinsel moves gently in this artificial indoor breeze and someone over in the TV area sneezes.

The doctor was a man this time.

Pale face. Going bald but hiding it well with what little hair he had left.

I was a little taken aback by the change, but I remained composed. Smiley. I even asked him how *he* was doing. We talked through my mood, my medication, how I was eating and sleeping. I stayed calm. Sweating, my palms clammy, I asked him if I could be released by Christmas. I told him the therapy was working well, and I felt like this place was helping me to manage, and I would keep on taking the medication because even though I was initially against the idea I could now see how it helped me. He did not respond. I waited. He looked at my notes and said he thought it might be a little too early to talk about going home. He said I was still very sick. I became agitated but I did not stand up or show it. At least I don't think I did? That room has unusual wallpaper. Room 8C. Pale yellow wallpaper with hot-air balloons. The balloons are faint with baskets and stripes and netting and small multicolored triangular flags. I said I understood his concerns and maybe, with all the progress I was making, I could go home just for the day, for Christmas Day, to spend it with my son, you see, to eat Christmas turkey with my boy. He looked down at his notes again and uncrossed his legs and crossed them again. He had a considerate face. Button-down shirt. I willed him to say yes with every cell of my being. *Say yes, goddammit.* Grant me this minuscule thing. He cleared his throat and agreed I was making steady progress. I nodded and remained calm. Deep breaths. I acted reasonable. He said perhaps early in the new year I could go home for the day. My lungs seized up and I couldn't catch my breath. I could not inhale. Sammy's Christmas. I shook my head and tried, again, to remain calm. Do not look at the wallpaper. Do not stray too close to it. I said the new year would be great but just a few hours at Christmas, please, to be with my son. One meal. He needed me at home for one meal. Just a few hours of normality. And he said, *New year, new start.*

I did *not* remain calm.

I tried.

I failed.

Other people were granted leave. Some were being released forever. Back to their comfortable lives and their Chevrolets and their jobs. Was I more ill than them? No. Absolutely not. How can this doctor not see what is so patently obvious?

I told him, again, how I was improving and he nodded and said he was concerned that I was perhaps telling him things I thought he wanted to hear.

Excuse me?

I looked at the wallpaper. Stared at it. I couldn't draw my eyes away. The balloons and the clouds, almost three-dimensional. The colors. Me in a balloon. In the basket. Untethered. Drifting higher toward the ceiling. No mooring ropes or ballast.

"What?" I said, loudly, shaking my head, standing up. I told him I was telling the truth and he said I should sit back down and we would look at it again in the new year.

We?

The new year?

And then the very next day, yesterday, I think it was, I calmly walked out when the door was open and then I ran like a fugitive, like a maniac, through the corridors, through the waiting room, outdoors, into the parking lot.

Fresh air. Lungsful of it. Cold, clean, delicious air, and a real breeze.

I sprinted.

Three nurses caught me.

I was taken back.

Restrained.

I kept seeing the wallpaper with the balloons and hearing Sammy's sweet voice. The voice he had when he was four or five. His singing voice. They restrained me so tight I have bruises today.

The nurses looked disappointed.

He does not have a gift. I have never missed a Christmas with Sammy, never missed an hour of a Christmas. How can he celebrate with Drew? Just the two of them? What would that look like? He might buy him a present. Something unsuitable, unsafe: a clawhammer or an air rifle. If he buys him anything it will be too grown-up for a fourteen-year-old. And then Sammy will cherish it. They will eat together at the dinette. Two plates. Will Drew buy Christmas food? Will they have a tree and hang lights? I need to be there to make sure it is enough. How can I be stuck here, less than a half hour by ambulance, and they will be there? How is it possible?

An alarm goes off and nurses run through.

It is Babs, a woman with glacial blue eyes and blond hair. She has blood dribbling down her neck. I watch them assist her. I watch the droplets of blood fall to the floor and settle there. She has taken a stone from the garden. I know this because she told me about it. A small fragment of flint or gravel. I did not know she planned to do this to herself. Did she plan it? The nurses don't look overly concerned. It is just a scratch. Just a blue-eyed wife with three daughters and a successful mail-order business who cut her own neck with a stone.

I watch as the blood droplets on the floor dry and develop a skin.

The television shows Christmas specials. Julia Child cooking canapés and vegetable dishes from her cozy, festive kitchen.

Someone comes to clean the floor.

When Sammy was small he would help me decorate. We would put up chains made from colorful strips of paper. He would lick one end and we would form a hoop and connect it to the next. He enjoyed that. We would watch Christmas specials: Andy Williams, Bob Hope, Perry Como. We would share a sliced-up chocolate Yule log from the gas station by the strip mall. It felt safe. Me and him, Drew working on his book in another room, all the while knowing that although Mom was gone, we were still together in her place. She worked so hard to buy that bungalow. When she died and we moved in as a married couple I thanked her in my mind each and every morning. Coffee machine on, and then I thanked her. Drew started off content with the place, having plans for the small backyard, plans to convert the loft, but then he soured. He would complain about the construction standards, the upkeep costs, the room layout, the drywall and brickwork. Said the windows were rotting and the walls were not insulated properly. He said Mom was too cheap to buy a proper place and it was a shame that we now lived in subpar accommodation. He actually used that phrase. But Sammy and I were happy there. He had his LEGO box in the living room so the noise would not put Drew off his work. Sammy and I would have cozy evenings in the winters: each of us wearing thick wool socks and sweaters, laughing. He would sing for me, terribly, and I would chase him around the sofa. It was as though the whole universe was contained within that one small room—curtains closed, door locked—and that the universe was fundamentally good.

I will be home for Christmas.

No.

I will not.

I will be in here.

I swallow my meds and the blue-eyed lady is back with a Band-Aid on her neck. They are searching her room and she is grinning. Babs, her name is. Did I mention that? She sits smiling at me. A small win.

What is Sammy doing now? Setting the fire? Is he warm enough?

Rachel is coloring. Two days ago she had a course of electroconvulsive therapy. That is a real thing, believe it or not. When Fatima mentioned it to me I did not believe her. I said that was something in the movies, *One Flew Over the Cuckoo's Nest*, the old ways, barbaric, and she said they still use it to this day. The strange thing is that Rachel seems a little better after. Less confused.

I did nothing wrong and yet I cannot leave.

The wallpaper, in here.

Sammy, out there.

28

SAMSON

I saw the notice in the local newspaper.

> Today, at noon, Mr. Jeffrey Donald Turner will be laid to rest in St. Christopher's Church, Shannon Avenue. No flowers. Donations to Veterans for Peace.

Dad's already left for work. Our boxers and socks are lined up on the camping chairs to dry by the dying embers of the fire. His are worse than mine. Old and gray with holes.

I lock up the boat and I'm dressed like any other kid from my school: striped tie, dark slacks, black shoes, black jacket, white shirt. But I am not going to school. As I walk along the frosty towpath that thought buoys me. I have an absurd spring in my step because I will not need to face them today.

There is a dead badger on the road. An 18-wheeler drives by and flattens it some more. Black and white. Larger than average. Broken. It reminds me of Amber before I buried her. I should move the badger to the poplars and give it a good burial, with leaves and branches and moss, but that will have to wait.

Mr. Turner used to say I could be an archaeologist or bone hunter one day if I wanted it bad enough. He said I'd get there one baby step at a time.

I spend two hours visiting the town paper and several convenience stores asking for work. I'm offered some one-off yard maintenance and painting jobs between the questions about why I'm not in school, and then I'm offered a temporary paper route for a boy who broke his arm falling off his BMX. I take the job.

The school emblem on my jacket is covered with a square of black paper. It is Scotch-taped in place. People look at it as they walk past, and I drop my gaze to the asphalt. Couples stare at me and then look each other in the eye. Some people look around trying to catch someone else's eye. I stare down. I keep my eyes, and my thoughts, to myself.

The church is small.

Unshowy.

Four cars in the lot and the wind is picking up. Roadwork outside; pneumatic drills and a yellow excavator digging up the pavement; two men shoveling and smoking, a third reading a folded tabloid.

I check the clock up by the steeple. Five minutes to twelve.

The wind eddies around the graveyard.

The sign says:

*Feed Your Faith and Your Fear Will Starve to Death.
Everyone Welcome.*

Talk about mixed messages.

I walk closer.

No flowers. That struck me as a strange request. No flowers? I would have brought some, I had planned on it. But they want no flowers.

People walk into the churchyard dressed in black and gray and navy blue. Church clothes are a real thing. One woman wears a bottle-green dress with a black shawl. The door closes. I wait awhile and then I walk in.

Candles.

An intimate church with little in the way of decoration. Stained glass immediately behind the altar but the rest of the windows are plain and domestic-looking. I've never been in here before. The sound of the drill outside fades as I walk deeper into the hushed structure. I take a pew at the back.

Fourteen people including the priest.

Fourteen.

There are numbers up on the pillar. Two hymns. And next to the pillar is Mr. Turner in his casket. Dark wood with brass handles. He's inside, poor guy. No flowers. The church is cold and Mr. Turner is inside that coffin.

They all stand.

Music from the organ. The notes: a little scrambled and blurry.

The priest says a few words and then the organist starts again. Nobody sings. The priest and the organist do their best to compensate but there is very little volume. I watch the backs of heads, and I watch the casket, and I wonder what Mr. Turner would think of all this. He never spoke to me of any religion. He liked war films and crosswords and history books; I know that. His parents passed when he was a young man. He wanted to be a veterinarian but never got the grades, so he became a seed wholesaler instead and traveled to Europe several times in the eighties. The man in the casket, cold, locked in, motionless, drowned, enjoyed Guinness poured properly into a glass, and he liked the cheeseburgers they served at the diner Mom took me to. He used to go there every weekend without fail. Cheeseburgers with curly fries and onion rings. He said their chocolate malt shakes were the best he'd ever tasted.

The priest talks about Mr. Turner's life but I can't hear him well from back here.

ADRIFT

The heads are still. I can't sense anyone crying or grieving. Fourteen people and me.

Is the value of a man's life measured by the attendance numbers at his funeral? I can say, categorically, having known Mr. Turner less than a year, that it is not.

After the service we walk out into the churchyard and the hole has already been dug. I am surprised by the depth of it. There is a mound of earth covered with bright artificial grass. We wait for a long time. The traffic noise hums in the background and the excavator keeps on digging regardless. Just another dead guy, I guess. The only person I recognize here is the gaunt man, Mr. Turner's cousin's son, Phoenix. Black leather jacket, skinny suit pants, black cowboy boots, white shirt, black pencil-thin tie. He looks at me from time to time like he's surprised I turned up. They bring out the casket slowly and carefully and they place it down inside the hole. I start to choke up a little out of nowhere. What am I doing? I cough to hide it. Turn to face the other way until I regain my composure. The sight of Mr. Turner being lowered down is worse than I'd expected. The finality of it. Phoenix glances over at me like he's checking I'm OK. I look away. The other attendees throw a little dirt down onto the timber lid, one after the other. I am last in line. I push my hand down into my pocket and pull out Amber's pink collar. The leather is soft. A few of her hairs still cling to the studs. I hold it at arm's length and two women look at each other disapprovingly and one clears her throat. I glance at the priest, but I can't read him. I look at Phoenix in his black leather jacket and he smiles.

I drop her collar.

There is an audible *tap* as metal hits wood.

The others talk in groups, mainly about the weather and the parking situation, and I hang back. Phoenix, pale, with dyed black hair that matches his leather jacket, approaches with his hands in his pockets. He looks older than my parents today.

"We're going to the bar next door if you want to come along. Private event."

I look up at him.

He has gray at his temples and his face has scars. He is very thin. Deep brown eyes.

"Just sandwiches and stuff," he says. "You're welcome. It's just us. To see him off, you know."

I have no money in my pocket. "Thanks. But I've got to get back. Thanks, though."

He nods and taps his open palm on my shoulder and walks back to join the others.

I spend the afternoon on the footbridge over the railroad counting train cars and feeling numb to the wind. I sit cross-legged and let my mind wander. To Jennifer, the girl who sat with me that one time and acted like that was normal, the sight of her in her school dress as she walked away, the way she moved inside it. To Mom, in the hospital. I try to imagine what her room looks like, but I can't. I wish she would write me a letter to say. A short note. She could send it to Dad's work or to school. I would give everything I have for a letter from her. I'd open it carefully and smell the paper and I'd hold it to my cheek and to the skin above my upper lip.

I read in the newspaper how there was an inquest held and that the coroner ruled Mr. Turner's case to be *death by misadventure*. I wish he'd stayed safe inside his boat that night. I wish he hadn't had a drink of Dad's stupid whiskey and ventured outside.

A diesel locomotive rumbles below. A freight train covered in graffiti. Bright marks. Tags and curse words. We are all angry and lost and we learn to deal with it, or not, in our own ways.

I remove the patch of black paper from my jacket, revealing my school logo, and then I walk home carrying a broken branch, tapping it against the uneven ground.

When Dad returns to the boat I've already emptied the ashes. I have folded and put away our laundry and set the fire and done the dishes and cleaned the kitchen.

"Born in a barn?" he says, walking in.

I frown.

"Door's open. Letting my heat out. I'm paying good money to heat a public towpath, am I? You know how much coal is? You know how much a sack of coal is?"

He decides he will move the boat farther up the canal tomorrow. I'm not sure if he considers this some kind of punishment, but I honestly don't care anymore. He should know that the long walks don't concern me. He can move the boat as far away from civilization as he likes.

We eat canned sardines and then we share a pack of cream of wheat.

"Fish will put hairs on your chest, boy," he says. "Brain food."

Is it chest hair food or brain food, Dad? Choose one, damn it. Commit.

We play cards and then he goes off to shave before his writing session.

Their bedroom is empty.

The boat smells different without her.

I convert the dinette into my bed and lie down listening to a Johnny Cash song on the radio through my foam headphones. There is a crescent moon and it makes the canal water sparkle and shimmy. Smoke in the air. Is she watching the same moon?

He comes out, glistening, hairless, ready.

29

PEGGY

I am trying to write my thirteenth letter, but my hand will not stop shaking. I focus on the tip of the felt pen and urge it to steady. I have sent six letters to Drew and six letters to Sammy. I mailed them to the scrapyard office. Action. I will do whatever I can with the limited options I have.

I write that I will join them in the new year and that I will miss them over Christmas, but we will celebrate together in January, our own special Christmas. I will roast a turkey, all the trimmings, stuffing, green bean casserole, cranberry sauce, mashed potatoes, eggnog, and we will do it properly, together.

Looking around the room today you would think this place is a community center or a college cafeteria. People seem normal. I thought they would be terrifying, ghoulish, berserk, but most of them are merely sad. Life is harder than we sometimes realize. Most people here just need a break from their own daily grind for a while.

The Christmas music is extremely upsetting: "Deck the Halls," "Jingle Bells," "White Christmas." The daytime TV shows talk about last-minute gift ideas, and it is like they are reaching out of the screen and pushing their fingertips into our wounds and opening them wider.

Shopping days till Christmas.

"The Little Drummer Boy."

Bing Crosby.

They talk to me about living with borderline personality disorder. They tell me it is most common among women, and that it is connected to attention-seeking and a distorted sense of self. I take that to be a barbed comment about my writing career. I told them about my publishing contract and I suspect they didn't believe me. They mentioned how strong emotional reactions can be associated with the disorder. They are talking about my recent escape attempt. They also claim that a sense of abandonment or emptiness is common, and how family history is a risk factor. They mean Mom. They know she took her own life, so they assume I tried the same thing. A generational curse. A pattern. Except, I never did. They say detachment from reality can be common. They are talking about my book again. They tell me lying is also a feature. So how on earth do I win? Please, tell me how?

I write to Sammy and explain how my drawing is still utterly appalling but it is improving, and how Fatima taught me how to hold the pencil in a different way, and how to do shading and cross-hatching. I tell him I have drawn a picture of our boat, the *Lady Brett Ashley*, moored up, a weeping willow eclipsing the well deck. It looks more like a Greyhound bus than a boat. A Greyhound bus wrecked on the interstate. I do not mention how I stare at the picture before I go to sleep, imagining him inside on the dinette bed, listening to the radio on his Walkman. I do not tell him how I yearn to fall into the picture and surprise him and hug him so tight he squirms.

There are fewer patients on the ward. Fatima says the staff try to free up beds so more people can come in. The pressure on the public system is immense, she says. There are overspills into private facilities, but she's not been to them. She has been in and out of here so many times so she knows about these things.

Band-Aid.

"Mistletoe and Wine."

Fatima says the period after Christmas can be a busy time. Lots of family stress and pressure. People spending a string of days together for the first time in the year. Drinking. Arguments about old debts and new ones. The dark midwinter.

Sammy was born after that quiet, private time. January 28. We thought he might be a Christmas baby, but he went full-term unlike his mother and grandmother before him. The pregnancy was uneventful. It was a good period for us, a hopeful period. Drew was still on a high from winning his prize, although with each passing month without an agent or publisher his confidence would fade. Sammy was a joy to carry, pretty much. I never suffered too much with morning sickness. We joked about how the baby would look like Drew, bald and smooth, but in the end he was born with spectacular red-blond hair, bright eyes, my mother's eyes, and he cried as soon as the midwife smacked his behind. Drew smiled proudly beside me. But then the midwives gathered and told me Sam needed a little extra help. Concerned expressions. They took him away from me. Another midwife said I was bleeding. That I needed stitches. Where is my baby? Can you bring him? I have to see him right now. They said I needed an operation immediately to stop the blood flow. I was losing focus. "Where is my baby?" I asked them, my voice panicked. They said he was being looked after and I would see him when I woke up. My peripheral vision darkened. I did not see him when I woke up. They told me he was in the intensive care unit. A problem with his heartbeat, with his blood pressure. His tiny heart. The sight of Drew's face when I came around from the operation. The abject fear in his eyes. I knew Drew loved our son with all of his being. In that moment I knew it. Two long, awful days later Sammy was brought back to me. He needed monitoring for a while, but he was out of danger. We were together, finally, the three of us.

Our triangle.

"Last Christmas."

"It's the Most Wonderful Time of the Year."

Is it? Are you sure?

A man in the corner cries into the crook of his elbow.

I wonder if I will ever leave. If there might be an administrative error, some series of errors, so I will be locked in here for the rest of my days. An inquiry years after my death. An official apology and a PBS documentary. A congressional hearing. Lessons learned.

The Christmas special of a children's nature program is on the TV. The presenter is wearing a tie with a robin on it. Seven patients watch the screen, motionless.

They have labeled me with a disorder and now I am unsure if I will ever rid myself of it, or if I will wear it with complicated pride like a tattoo or a scar.

I write in the letter about how we can take the boat away for a vacation in the spring. How it will not be expensive, and we have canals, and thousands of miles of river, to explore. The rest of the Midwest, the Erie Canal, down to Chesapeake even. I know Sammy would like to see the East Coast one day.

"Joy to the World."

"Santa Baby."

"Jingle Bell Rock."

Will he ever find out what happened to his grandparents? Will Drew tell him? I am not even sure myself which version to believe. He twists the truth and reshapes it like a blacksmith working steel in his forge. Did he burn his house down? And if so, how can he ever explain that to his own child? To an adult, even? From the moment he told me I knew I would never be able to leave him. I felt it deep inside myself. I didn't face the notion head-on, never spoke it or wrote it, but I understood my fate that day. If Sammy is to be safe then the triangle must persist until he's old enough to leave.

Mary-Elizabeth, one of the cleaners, stops by.

"You writing your stories, Peggy Jenkins?"

Her Afro is very short. She has curious, intelligent eyes. Bright red trainers.

"No. Just a letter."

"Oh, good. We don't see enough letter-writing these days, do we? Used to have much more of it. Pen pals."

"I'm writing to my son."

"Lucky son. I'm sure he'll cherish it, Peggy."

She sits down next to me and takes off her rubber gloves.

"You know, I was thinking about what you said before, about Christmas."

I look at her.

"I might take the shift this year. Jonah's been hinting he might want to swap. Lord knows I could do with the extra money. So, what I'm saying is, I might be here that day after all."

I smile. "I hope you are."

"I done it one time before, Peggy. Years ago now when money was tighter still, when my girls were still at home. It wasn't so bad, you know. Very quiet. I think we can make it through all right."

Sesame Street starts up on the TV.

"I'd better be off before they see me chatting," she says. "They watch us like hawks. It'll be OK in the end, Peggy. Always is, you'll see. It'll be all right in the end."

30

SAMSON

I walk out of school and a police cruiser passes, its sirens screeching. It's a relief to be away, to increase the distance between me and my classmates, but I need to keep my head down, not make eye contact, remain in the shadows.

Past the auto mechanic and on up the hill. I walk through the park. Boys from the grade above smoking weed and flirting with girls from the other school. A man walking seven or eight dogs, their leashes tangling.

Exhaust fumes heavy in the dry December air.

The hill is the steepest in town. My bag weighs me down, the strap digging into my shoulder, but I am walking toward something, and that is all that matters.

I crest the peak, my heart racing. The hospital looks more like a country club or a hotel, that is, until you see the tall fence and the boarded-up door and bars on the windows and the signs in the parking lot.

ST. MARY'S PSYCHIATRIC HOSPITAL,
ESTABLISHED 1937

It's dark now, the headlights of pickups and delivery trucks coming and going as I wait outside the high perimeter fence.

I step toward the public reception.

I never expected to have butterflies in my stomach. Nerves and excitement.

The door opens automatically as I approach.

There is nobody else in the waiting room.

It's the anticipation of seeing her after all this time. But also, the sensation of taking control of a situation. Nobody gave me permission to do this. I am here because I decided to be here.

Long corridors lead off in all directions. Closed doors. Color-coded route maps.

I approach the counter. Glass screen. A lady with large blue glasses and a permanent. She pushes the screen to one side.

"Hello, son. What can I help you with?"

Son?

I am not your son.

"Can I see my mom, please? Her name is Mrs. Jenkins."

"Oh, I am sorry. You'll need to come back with your father or guardian. And you need to read about visitation hours." She points to the board on the wall.

"Can I drop something off for her? It's Mrs. Jenkins."

"OK, let me see. Mrs. Jenkins, you say?"

"Margaret Jenkins. Her friends call her Peggy."

She doesn't reply, she just checks her computer.

"Ah, yes. Here we are. Now, just a moment."

She adjusts her glasses and says, "What would you want to be leaving for her?"

I unzip my schoolbag. The smell of gym gear and damp books. I pull out my football socks. Remove my Walkman.

"It's just this. It has a special cassette for her inside. Music. Radio recordings and stuff."

She grimaces.

"What's wrong?"

She says, "Wait there a minute. I need to check on something real quick. Take a seat."

I sit down. There's a stack of magazines on the table. *Glamour*. *National Geographic*. *Cosmopolitan*.

I open the tape deck of my Walkman. It's a cassette I've had for years. I bought it as a blank, part of a pack of three, from Smith's Bookstore and Stationers. It has an hour or more on each side. Some ballads, songs Mom likes, half a radio quiz, most of a Russian play, and some classical concertos as well.

The lady comes back.

I approach the counter.

"I'm ever so sorry. It's hospital policy, see. I tried my best but there's no tape recorders or radio player machines allowed inside. Not on your mom's ward. I'm real sorry about that."

"Can I just give her the tape?"

She shakes her head. "I'm sorry, young man. If it was up to me, but it isn't. They have a radio inside and a decent TV set as well. Don't worry, she's in good hands."

"Is she OK, please? Have you seen her yourself?"

She swallows. Smiles. Purses her lips. "She's being well looked after. I'm sorry."

"Can I bring her in anything else?"

"Course you can. What a nice idea. If there's any socks or cotton undergarments, anything like that. If she needs some face cream or a toothbrush, that kind of thing is usually permitted."

"Can I write her?"

"You can write her a letter and have your father bring it in. Talk to him about it."

"Thank you."

"Take care, son."

I leave.

When I reach home Dad's already writing. He told me last night how he's deep into act two and he can't risk slowing down. He said he isn't satisfied with it, but it's moving forward, it has momentum now, and he needs to go with it, see where it takes him.

He's wearing foam earplugs from the scrapyard.

The boat is warm but it is not hot. He still has his shirt on.

As quietly as I can, I make us oatmeal. I pour on syrup but it's almost frozen from being improperly stored outside on deck. Comes out like molasses. Dad doesn't come to the table. I take his bowl to him and he doesn't acknowledge me. But then he eats as he writes, his cracked fingertips banging away at the word processor, his trophy at eye level on the bureau, visible every time he glances up. I'm pleased he is eating something hot and nourishing. He needs it.

◆ ◆ ◆

The next day I arrive at school. I receive an A- for my history assignment and a B+ for my biology project. My bag is stolen twice—once by two short kids, which really irritates me, little shits, who do they think they are? And then I was spat at from a second-story window in the music building. I was walking past, minding my own damn business. Must have been six or seven juniors all spat at once. Nothing hit me. But they laughed and jeered and it may as well have struck me right in the eye.

Two days left until the end of term.

At least there's that.

I walk to the bus station, ice in the air, and linger in Smith's, which sells more newspapers, CDs, and sodas than books these days. I look at the car magazines. One of the stories, something about a new model of Porsche, is set in Austin, Texas. Photos of them driving fast on a bridge across the Colorado River. Maybe I'll live someplace like Austin one day. Anonymity. Opportunities. The possibility of reaching the rest of the world. I look up and the woman at the cash register nods at me. She has two plaits today and I don't know if she's aware of the way she helps save my life each afternoon, never kicking me out for browsing.

I buy a two-finger KitKat and walk toward my bus stop.

Three of them.

Gunner, Johnno, and Ballbag.

I walk faster, acting like I haven't noticed.

Gunner walks straight into me and keeps on walking like a plow pushing a ridge of snow, effortlessly slamming me into a low wall.

I fall on my ass, my schoolbag pulling tight.

"How's your mom?" says Ballbag.

I try to stand up.

They push me back down.

"I said, how's your mother? Still insane?"

"Yeah."

They snicker.

"You know they do experiments up there at that place, right?" says Gunner. "Couldn't do it in a prison or a private hospital like we'd go to. But they're so out of their minds they don't have a clue. I heard there's a mortician and an incinerator up there. Burning stuff so there's no trace. People just disappear off the face of the earth sometimes."

I make a break for it and Ballbag catches me by the arm and slams me back into the wall. There are people around, staring, but nobody comes.

Blood starts gushing from my nose.

I wipe my face with my jacket sleeve.

Gunner says, "She's not coming out of there, Noodles. You know that, yeah? Your mom's never coming back to you, little man."

I grit my teeth. I'll miss the bus if they don't stop.

Gunner pulls his zipper and rests his boot on my chest.

The other two laugh and look at each other. They do the same.

I push and twist and struggle to run away but they push me back down. It's over in seconds.

A trio of girls walk past, and they pause and step back a pace.

"Animals!" yells Jennifer, the girl from the railroad footbridge. "You should be ashamed of yourselves. Cowards."

"We're just having a joke," says Gunner, helping me up. "Relax. He's our little buddy, aren't you, Noodles?"

I walk away.

Jennifer tries to follow me, but I say, "I'm fine."

She says, "Sammy. Wait."

I don't wait.

I have never felt more shame in my life. My cheeks must be bright red, and hot urine has seeped down into my socks.

Nobody sits next to me on the bus.

I stare out of the window at the lifeless fields scrolling by.

What did I ever do to them?

I walk down the towpath, my back curved, my head low, thinking what I'll write to Mom.

I'll need to wash my clothes tonight in the sink. Rub down my jacket with soap.

"Samson?"

I turn my head. It's Mr. Turner's boat. It's been moved closer to ours, only thirty yards' gap, and the fire's been lit.

His black leather jacket gleams in the warm light from the boat.

"You all right, dude?" he says.

"Yeah."

"You don't look all right."

I don't want him to move closer. He might smell me.

"Shit day, that's all." I take a step back.

He nods.

"Same here. I'm gonna move the boat up closer to yours if that's all right?"

"Do what you want."

"We all appreciated you coming to Uncle Jeff's send-off. We talked about you in the bar after. Was good of you to come, man."

I shrug.

"He liked you, you know. I think he liked you better than he did any of us."

I look at him.

"He said you were his friend."

31

PEGGY

Fatima does not believe it is Christmas Eve. She says it is, in fact, February. She claims the doctors and nurses are trying to confuse her. A friendly nurse brings over a copy of the *TV Guide* to explain, but Fatima says it is from Christmas, isn't it, two months ago.

There are eleven of us here.

The rest have gone home for the festive period. They looked excited and scared, packing up their belongings, saying their goodbyes. Some will be back in a day or two. Eleven of us remain on the ward and it is quiet and dull. They try to make us feel at home with decorations and a tree and music, and one of the male nurses wears tinsel in his hair. The thing is: we do not want to feel at home.

Why don't Drew and Sammy visit? The others receive visitors; some of them have visits every week. Did Drew spike my coffee with pills and now he is afraid to look me in the eye? Or is it that he is ashamed of what they say I did? I don't know what to think. Have he and Sammy agreed they will not visit me until I am better? Is Drew trying to shield our son from this place?

I would give anything for them to come here. Twenty minutes. I do not need gifts or letters. I just need to see them. To hold Sammy's perfect hand. The mole on his wrist that emerged when he was three and a half. I need to see that he is coping.

We watch church carols on the television. Tom is facing the other way, looking at the wall, muttering. He does not like the picture, only the sound. The singing. Fatima is working through her calendar with a highlighter pen, double-checking something.

Later we stand in the meds line. They give us our medication in a small paper cup. Two cups. The other one has water. They administer through a hatch from the drugs room. We have to open our mouths to show we have swallowed everything. Am I repeating myself? It has become routine now, like making Sammy's breakfast or sorting laundry.

The meds line.

Mary-Elizabeth cleans and I stand with her and we talk.

"People doing their shopping, so many people out today, the roads are dangerous."

"Last-minute shoppers," I say.

"What are they all buying?" she says. "Piling up trash under a dying tree just to have to spend the whole of next year paying it off. It's madness." She looks at me. "Sorry, I didn't mean . . ."

I can't help smiling.

"What are you thinking about?" she asks.

"Me?"

She cleans the floor and nods.

"I was thinking how I never expected them to take away our bras. That's what I was thinking."

"They can have mine," she says. "Damn thing. I don't want it."

"I wasn't wearing one when I came in. But I thought I'd have one here. I didn't think we'd all be left like this. They took out the drawstring from my pajamas. From my sweatpants too."

"They have to."

"I know."

"I feel bad some days that I can walk out the door at the end of my shift. Some of the people in here need to stay for a long time, to receive help, I get that, but some of you." She stares at me, her eyes sad. "I don't know, I'm not an MD, but I feel guilty I can walk home and you can't."

A nurse looks over at us. I don't think they like me talking to Mary-Elizabeth. I smile at the nurse and he looks away.

"Strange thing is," I say, "I've had nothing go missing since I was put here."

"What do you mean by that?"

"I lose things constantly back home. Jewelry, hair clips, all sorts. They just go missing one by one. My messy head."

She stops cleaning and looks directly at me again. "How long has this gone on for?"

"Months. Years, maybe."

She nods, knowingly.

"What?" I ask.

"Nothing."

"Please."

"I had something like that happen to me when I was younger."

"You were forgetful?"

"No, Peggy. I was not forgetful."

"No?"

She looks pained. "I was living with a bad man."

I frown.

"Colter, his name was. He'd move my belongings around, Peggy. He'd move them to screw with me. Sometimes it was my keys. He'd take things or hide them, especially my socks. Colter would leave me with one of each pair. He'd take one and leave one. He liked how I reacted, I guess, how I was never quite sure of anything."

"Horrible."

"Well?"

"Well what?"

"Your man, Peggy. You think he could be moving your things?"

"Drew? No, he's too busy with his work."

She starts cleaning again but she looks serious.

"Your husband strict on you, is he?"

I don't say anything.

"He like to tell you what to do? Order you around? He wants things done his way?"

"Aren't all men like that?"

"No, Peggy Jenkins. No, they're not all like that."

"I don't know."

She wipes down the floor and we move along a little way down the corridor.

"Next time you talk to the doctor tell him all about this. That doctor's forgotten more than I ever knew."

I'm not so sure about that.

"I don't think Drew would move my things."

"How long have you two been together?"

"Since I was nineteen."

"Your whole adult life. He tell you how to do things? How to dress? Treat you like a child?"

I freeze up.

My mind whirring. Looking back.

"Because there's more than one way a man can beat down on his woman, you know. Colter, my boyfriend back when I was living in Pennsylvania, years ago this was, he beat me on a daily basis without ever laying a finger. Made me feel about two inches tall."

I start to heat up, to sweat. It's difficult to take a proper breath.

"You left him?" I ask.

"He tried to persuade me that my own mama was out to hurt me. He made me cut ties with my uncles and aunties, with my friends. He wanted to see me every day but for me to never go see anybody else. I was fading away, Peggy. I stopped trusting myself. He'd beat on me every day with his words and it wore me down."

They switch on the Christmas tree lights and one woman starts to cry.

"I'm sorry he did that to you."

My mind is racing.

Jigsaw pieces slotting into place.

"Talk to the doctors and the nurses, Peggy. They can help, I'm telling you, they can help you. It was my neighbor who told me what was happening in my own life, in my own mind. She was a social worker, nice lady. She told me straight out. I was being controlled. Us women need to stick together. My boyfriend at the time was cutting me off from the world. He was making me question my own self."

32

SAMSON

Water drips from the inside of the window and I let it fall on my grazed knuckles. The boat is whisper quiet, the fire silent. Pulsating embers. Dad fast asleep on his bed.

Christmas morning.

The drops of condensation hit my fingernails and cuticles and soak slowly into my skin. They roll over veins and deviate around pores and fine hairs before running down by my thumb. Water that used to sit inside my own chest. Old breath running down glass.

He's sleeping in.

I am warm, my comforter tight around me and tucked under at the sides. I can't smell the woodsmoke. I am too used to it. Dad's desk is secure: each drawer padlocked, and the trophy glows on top like some ancient talisman.

Normally at this time Mom would be running around in her pale blue robe making breakfast, lighting a candle on the table, turning on Christmas lights, arranging gifts to look like there are more than there are. She makes English rice pudding on Christmas morning, Nanna Ruth's recipe. We eat it piping hot. Not from a can, but with skin on top, in a dish from the stove, and we eat it with grated nutmeg and ground cinnamon and crunchy brown sugar.

Another drop of water.

There's a family of ducks outside, mere inches from my head, and they squawk and preen themselves in the unmoving waters. From the boat I am afforded a rare view. They do not seem to be afraid of us. They see us for what we are: water fauna, just like them.

Phoenix has moved onto Mr. Turner's houseboat full-time. He's waiting for something called probate, but he's allowed to stay on the boat and keep it secure until then. He moved in and then he tried out the motor. He's positioned the boat twenty feet behind ours and Dad says he's taking liberties.

I stretch.

The boat interior brightens. I look at the kinked chimney of the stove. The cans of food we don't bother to put away anymore are stacked on the kitchen counter. Their lids shine. Cream of mushroom. Split pea and ham. Canned chicken. Pink salmon.

There is no tree this year.

No presents.

Paul Pricklett and I shook hands on a deal last week. He says his mom's off with a new man so we agreed we would buy each other something. We couldn't steal or borrow. We had to buy it. That was a rule. We met at the bakery: two pastries, two colas. He talked a lot about *X-Files*, like usual, and then I gave him a Mars bar and a quarter ounce of cola cubes from the candy store all wrapped in a fresh page ripped out of a *Playboy* I found by the railroad tracks. In return he gave me a pair of black wool gloves he bought in Safeway with his own money. I couldn't believe my eyes. That was a proper gift, not just a bag of candy. It was something your grandpa might buy you to keep you warm.

What I want, more than anything else in the world, is for Mom to come home today. It's been long enough, I think, no matter how sick she was. I can look after her. Not professionally, but I can make sure she's all right; keep an eye on her, help with chores and cooking and her medicines. I can't stand going to sleep and waking up with her not here.

The canal is subdued. No boats. I haven't heard a locomotive yet.

I told Dad how we should turn up there every day until they let us see her. I said we should make a fuss until they let us in. He said that would make it all worse because they wouldn't let her out if she didn't have a stable home and support waiting for her.

I left her a note instead. Dropped it off yesterday. I have no idea if she got it, but I have to believe she did. Told her about my grades and about Paul. Told her I love her.

Christmas morning and the world is at rest.

Dad comes through.

"Still in bed?"

I stretch.

"Idle."

He exercises outside on the frosty towpath. Push-ups and lunges, squats and pull-ups. He thinks this is how soldiers train. I watch him, sipping coffee from a chipped mug.

"You need to work on your physique, boy. Not just your arms, not just your chest, the whole frame. Back, stomach, legs. You need to be able to hold your own in this town."

One day I won't need to.

"I know, Dad."

"Come on then."

"What?"

"Get down here. Might as well make a start."

He shows me how to do proper push-ups. Is this his gift to me? He teaches me how to do sit-ups with my feet held down by his arm.

"Body of a boy, of a child."

"No, I haven't."

"You need to build yourself, Samson. Fight battles for yourself because nobody will do it for you. Learn that lesson quick."

I strain to do ten more sit-ups.

"You got to turn tables on them, boy. Christmas is just another day, remember that. Fight the fight. You got to transform from prey to predator."

How much does he know?

"There, I've done them."

"You haven't done them properly, though. My mother could train harder than that."

I walk away, biting my tongue.

We eat ravioli for lunch. Dad crumbles some cheddar cheese on top. We listen to *The Old Man and the Sea* on tape as we eat. Charlton Heston narrates, and his voice is like quicksilver. I watch the ribbon move around in the cassette deck and every time I try to utter something he looks at me as if to say, *Not now. Shut your mouth and listen to his words.*

I have never been away from Mom for this long. And never at Christmas. She loves Christmas. Back in the bungalow we would watch cooking shows together. I never really liked them that much, but Mom did.

After I do the dishes I listen to my Walkman.

Dad comes back in.

"What?"

"I said," he says. "You need a haircut. You look like a girl. Sit down and I'll do it for you."

"I'm not..."

"Don't answer back. Sit."

I move to the camp chair and sit down heavily. Dad stands behind.

Chill breeze at the back of my neck.

"Reckon you're old enough to have it cut close. Get that mop off."

I hold my head in my hands. "No, Dad. Just a trim."

"What?"

She might not recognize me when she comes home.

"My school won't like it, Dad. They don't want shaved heads."

He tuts and cuts my hair short with the scissors. It takes two minutes. I go out after and shake my head into the canal. Red strands float on the surface, attach to frosty leaves, form clusters. Phoenix is outside on his boat wearing his leather jacket.

"Merry Christmas, Samson."

I like that he knows my name.

I like it very much.

"And to you, man."

"Having a good one?"

I swallow hard. The words catch in my throat. "Not bad. You?"

"Quiet."

I go back inside.

"Don't get friendly with the likes of him. Looks like a queer to me with that hair, those clothes. Looks like he's been in a fire. Keep your distance."

He holds out his closed fist.

"What is it?"

"Close your eyes and hold out your hand."

I do it. Something cool and metallic drops into my palm, scraping it.

"Open," he says.

It's Dad's old pocketknife. I didn't know he still owned it. Rusty on one end. Some bone in the handle.

"I can have it?"

He nods.

"Thanks, Dad."

"Don't break it."

I open the blade and close it again.

"You'll need to clean it up and oil it. You can use my sharpening stone but be careful, I mean it, cost me a fortune. You break that stone and I'll break your legs, do you understand?"

I nod, smiling.

"Now, get off with you. Get."

I hide the knife in tufts of insulation by the dinette table. It sits next to my Walkman.

Now it is time for my mission.

There is no bus service today, so I walk the whole way into town. The sidewalks are empty and there is very little traffic. The sky is gray: no contrails or clouds. My new black gloves keep my hands warm. I sing R.E.M. and Annie Lennox songs out loud as I walk, no boys to chase me down today, no one to laugh at me. I sing timidly at first and then at the top of my voice, mouth wide open. Ultimate freedom. Liberation. I'm screaming out the lyrics, letting it all out. The walk downhill is slippery. A fine mist in the air. I sing "Losing My Religion" so fiercely birds flee from their trees. There are no other humans on this sidewalk, it is mine.

I walk through town.

Up the hill to the hospital. It's almost dark now. I see the tall fence and the signs. The parking lot and security lights. I walk inside.

It's a different woman at reception today. An older woman with bangs and green eye shadow.

The clock ticks on the wall.

There is nobody else here.

She's reading the *TV Guide* Christmas issue, a marker pen in one hand.

"Can I help you with something, young man?"

"Can I see my mom, please? It's the right time."

She bites her lip and says, "Is your dad around?"

"He's back home."

"Talk to him and arrange a visit. Your dad will sort it all out for you."

"I can't come in?"

"Not today. I'm very sorry."

"I just want to see her. Just for a minute. I want to give her a hug."

She places her palm on the glass screen and smiles. "It's Christmas. You should be home with your father, shouldn't you?"

"I came out for a walk."

She nods.

"Can I give you something for her?"

She frowns and starts to speak.

I take the Milky Way from my pocket and hand it over. I've been saving it.

She smiles. "I think we can manage that as it's Christmas. What's your mom's name, young man?"

"Peggy Jenkins."

"Peggy Jenkins. A beautiful name. I'll make sure your mom gets it, all right?"

I nod.

"Talk to your daddy about visiting. Now get off home with you and play with your new toys."

I start to leave.

"Young man?"

I turn back to face her. "Yeah?"

She smiles. "Merry Christmas."

33

PEGGY

Last day of the year.

I watch out of the window as three men use chain saws to slice up a pine tree that fell in the storm. It had become my favorite feature here. A polestar, of sorts. When it fell it came to rest at a dangerous angle. The saws scream and the teeth of the chains bite and spew out wood chips and the tree is made smaller and, piece by piece, it is taken away from this place.

Fatima was moved to the other hospital. I miss her. She developed an infection.

The men wear helmets and gloves and special boots.

The branches are shrinking.

On Christmas Day, after most people had gone to bed early, a nurse brought me a gift. We had all received presents: coloring books or packs of crayons or crossword compendiums. But this was not from the staff. It came through to me on a red paper plate. The nurse is from Mexico City, but she has lived here most of her life. She had removed the Milky Way from its packaging and cut it up. She said it was a gift from my son. A precious gift from my Sammy.

They took the stationary bicycle away today. Someone tried to hurt themselves with it.

More slicing. A tractor removing rounds. More sawdust on the lawn.

This, today, is the last day of the year we sold Mom's bungalow and moved to the boat. The year I finished my book and found a publisher. The year I was committed.

It starts to rain outside. One of the chain-saw guys walks away.

I have seen the doctor. She is back. We had a constructive conversation. I asked her about her Christmas and she looked embarrassed. She asked how I was getting on with my medication. I told her I was dizzy in the mornings. Numb. I told her I had obscene dreams that would make her blush. I told her sometimes it feels like I am being controlled from the outside.

There is a new patient here and her name is Katherine with a "K." She has dyed blond hair, almost white, and she walks with a limp. Katherine is adamant she is a qualified nurse. She tries to help the rest of us, check on us, talk to us about therapy options and the active ingredients in our meds. On her first day she tried to accompany me to the bathroom. She genuinely believes she is on the payroll here.

I have had more nightmares about the balloon wallpaper. I know I am not insane but the short story I read as a girl planted an image so vivid, so haunting, I cannot rid it from my consciousness. Me, small, hunched down inside one of the wicker baskets. Peering out over the rim at the doctor, screaming at the top of my voice for help, the balloon moving higher up the yellow wallpaper at a pace so slow it is almost impossible for them to notice. Me, trapped in the basket. Stuck inside the wall. Screaming.

The doctor says I feel strange because the medication is working. She claims it can take weeks for it to build up inside my system. She says I should feel better soon.

Better.

Soon.

Will I ever make this up to Samson? One missed Christmas. I will make it up to him somehow. I will come out of here far stronger than before, and I will repair the damage. I pledge that to him.

Mary-Elizabeth is not working here at the moment, but I think often of what she told me. I talked it over with the doctor, but she did not seem to want to discuss the subject. She said we could cover it more in our next session but that it was vitally important that I take personal responsibility for my own actions and my well-being going forward. She said I need to look after myself better.

The third man comes back and they tackle the broad trunk of the fallen tree.

I miss balling his socks. Such a small, forgettable thing. I have balled Sam's socks ever since they were tiny, the same size as the mittens I knitted him so he wouldn't scratch his face as a newborn. I miss cooking french fries. Who knew anyone could ever miss that? Slicing potatoes and sautéing them in oil on the stove. Drying them on paper and sprinkling them with salt. I miss eating them with Sammy. Our treat. I miss the look on his face as he enjoys hot food I have cooked for him.

Growing up with one parent I never felt I missed out but looking back I fear for my younger self, and for Mom. She had me and nobody else. There were no other family members stateside. Everyone else was back in England. I remember watching programs as a girl—*The Waltons*, *Happy Days*, *Bewitched*—and thinking how invulnerable those families seemed. That is why I watched them. So many layers of protection and backup. Relations, friends, colleagues, and neighbors. And I knew then, as a young girl, that I would be part of a family one day, and that I would protect it at all costs, hold it together, make it safe. But having some time away in this place I have come to doubt my childhood wisdom. I think maybe holding a family together, protecting the triangle despite my better judgment, could actually hurt those who make it up. I do not possess the energy or clarity of thought to see what comes next, but my rigid dream, keeping the family whole come what may, is not quite so rigid anymore. Perhaps, rather than trudging home along the towpath with Sammy to locate our ever-moving boat, our life, our home, perhaps we can see it moored in the distance and then walk right on past it toward some unknowable future. I do not know how I will keep Sammy safe, and myself, but I will figure it out. I will never give up.

The base of the tree falls.

I will be free from this hospital. I will walk where I like and eat what I like and breathe cool, fresh air. Nobody will accompany me to the showers or the bathroom. I will cook real food and have laces in my shoes again.

There are voluntary patients here. They are not all like me. I was shocked to hear that some people have chosen this place, but now that I see them each day I know they made sound choices. One man, Leo, hears voices. I have not talked to him much, but he says he listens to the voices in his head. He knows the name of his condition and he says he can handle it much better than when he was younger. Leo spends long periods in silence, listening to them. I asked him if he must listen to the voices or if he can choose to ignore them. He told me solemnly, calmly, that they are the only people left in his life.

The sawdust on the lawn is turning to sludge, rain intensifying, boot prints running through wet pulp. The saws scream and the old pine tree is almost completely gone.

I wrote to Sammy again this morning. I told him I miss tucking him in at night. I will tuck him in again soon.

It is possible that a place like this might have helped my mother. She was an emotional person when I was growing up. She cried easily, more easily than I have ever cried, and she laughed with her eyes. I smile to myself thinking about it. Her lovely face. The way her features would squeeze tight as she chuckled. Mom liked Drew from the first moment they met. He was nice to her. Really sweet. He took us out to the barbecue place near the town hall and he brought her flowers one time when he came to the bungalow for Sunday lunch. Drew cut her grass for her. I never suspected she was so troubled. She hid her feelings so well from me that I never suspected it. She seemed relatively content with her life, her job, her circle of friends, the man her daughter had fallen in love with. I am not sure I will ever understand why she ended her life.

34

SAMSON

Snow on the ground.

I've been visiting the hospital whenever I can. They know me there now. I watch other people coming and going, being let through locked doors, but Dad says we are still not allowed to visit; it's against her doctor's rules. All I can do is leave candy bars and paper bags of white mice for her. The lady told me they have to open everything up and check there's nothing dangerous hidden inside. I was shocked at that. Something dangerous hidden inside a Snickers? I drop them off together with handwritten notes torn from my exercise books. Even though I have so much to say I can never find the right words. So I keep the notes brief. It's the closest thing I have to talking with her.

School days. Yesterday was the best I've had in months. I wasn't interfered with, apart from breaks and lunch. I was left with a few scratches, sure, lost my essay, but nothing worse than that. I managed to spend twenty minutes in the library researching college scholarships. Premature, but I've got to get prepared. Now I'm in Smith's Bookstore and Stationers looking at atlases and encyclopedias of modern history. Mr. Turner would have enjoyed these reference books. He'd have devoured them and left dog-ears.

I leave the store and say night to Sandra. There are three of them between me and my bus so I take the long way around, by the scaffolding. I keep my head down. The ground is slippery with ice sludge and salt. As I round the corner Gunner appears in front of me. I turn back. Four boys behind me.

I am trapped.

"Where's your girlfriend to help you this time, eh?"

I don't say anything.

I walk faster.

"It's rude to ignore a question, Noodles, buddy. Nobody ever teach you manners?"

"I need to get my bus."

"You shouldn't be with her, you know that, right? She's not like you."

"Need to catch the bus."

"Needs to catch his bus, fellas."

I look around for somewhere to go, for somebody to help.

"Gay bus, isn't it, that one?"

I dash to the left to sidestep Gunner and he catches me with his arm.

"You'll slip, Jenkins, running like that, little man. We don't want that, now, do we? We don't want any broken bones, Noodles."

The others pull my bag off my shoulder.

"My bus is leaving."

"Check he's got his Walkman. Worth a couple of bucks, that is, even though it's shit."

They rummage around and then empty the contents of my bag onto the dirty gray snow. Textbooks and my pencil case and foil from lunch and my black wool gloves from Paul Pricklett.

Gunner puts his arm tight around my neck and leads me away.

"Please, bro. I have to get my bus. My dad'll be angry."

"I'm not your fucking bro, Noodles." He lowers his voice. "I'd throw myself under a truck if I was. Why did they call you Samson with those noodle arms, eh? What a fucking mismatch. Anyway, listen. I heard you've picked up a paper route. Little enterprise. I'll be fair, right. Two bucks a week. You can pay me Mondays, keep it simple for you so you don't forget. You got it?"

I nod.

He turns. "Give him his bag back, fellas. Come on. Noodles has a bus to catch, don't you, buddy?"

I take my bag and look at Gunner and then run to my stop. I bang on the door and the driver begrudgingly lets me on.

"Next time you're late I'm leaving without you."

The bus pulls away.

The motion of the chassis, the wheels, the rolling hills, the country road, makes me sleepy.

I climb off the bus at my stop, carefully, my bag in front of me, and walk down to the towpath.

Phoenix saved my life a few days ago.

Sunday, it was.

I had cleaned up my knife and hacked away some of the old filth with a wooden toothpick so not to scratch it. If I scratched it Dad would string me up. It was a bright day and there was some traffic on the canal, people out in the cold, flat sunshine giving their motorboats a ride around, first trip of the new year, first decent day for it. I finished off a bag of potato chips and had set up on the bank watching the world. It was glorious. Insects buzzing low over the water and sun on my face. Dad was out on a jog. I started sharpening my blade on his stone, grinding it one way then the next, working the edge, settling into a steady rhythm. A Mississippi kite hovered over the field on the far bank, its angled head motionless in the pale sky, waiting patiently for its quarry. I watched the bird closely. The growing rumble of a freight train approaching in the distance. The kite flapped its wings once and dove down to the ground. I stood up tall to see what it had caught and slipped and cut my index finger on the blade. No pain whatsoever. My knife was too sharp for that. But I dropped Dad's sharpening stone and it hit the frozen ground and fell into two pieces.

I'm ashamed to say I screamed.

Phoenix came out of his boat and when he saw my bleeding finger he ran to me. I did not expect that. I told him I was fine, but he helped clean and bandage my finger. He said if it was any worse I'd need stitches. We checked the stone. He said he's never used one. I told him it's my dad's. Then I sensed something behind us. It was him. Back. Sweating, his head glistening, his shirt drenched. His veins were bulging in his forearms. I started to speak. I was stuttering, tripping over my words, panicking, and then Phoenix took over and said he was taking a look at the stone as he had never seen one like it, and he accidentally dropped it. He apologized to Dad, who just stood there glaring at him. He said he would buy him a new one or write him a check. Dad said, "Samson, inside," and ushered me back into the boat.

And that is how Phoenix saved my life.

We have no power now. Dad says there's no money for diesel, so we have no hot water. He says he would move the boat to get away from the queer who smashed his whetstone, but he can't with no fuel. I'm glad. I owe Phoenix something, I'm not sure what.

Dad looks over at me and says, "What are we having for supper?"

"Mushroom soup?" I say.

"Mushroom soup?"

I nod.

"I miss your mother's cooking."

My heart lifts at this. It swells. I can't help but smile. These past months he has never once said he misses her.

"Me too. When do you think she'll be back, Dad?"

"Why are you asking that again?"

I shrug.

"She'll be back when she's ready, boy. When it's safe. Trust me, you don't want her back before they've fixed her head up at the hospital. Let them do their work."

"I've been hand-feeding a squirrel, Dad."

"Vermin."

"Two of them come to me now, take nuts right out of my hand."

"Nuts?"

"It took six days, but I worked at it and they trust me now."

"How do you pay for the nuts?"

"My paper route. What's left over."

"How much?"

"Not much."

"How much?"

"Fifty cents or something."

"Right. Put that in the house pot from now on. Feeding tree rats, I ask you, you'll be locked up on that ward with your mother the way you're going." He points at me. "Don't get any dumb ideas, now. They wouldn't put you in there with her. You'd be in a wing for deranged children. You want that?"

I shake my head.

"Get that soup on then."

I stoke up the fire and then change out of my uniform. We have two cans of Campbell's mushroom soup and the end of a stale loaf. No butter. I open my schoolbag to retrieve my textbooks. There is something sticking out of the edge of my pencil case. I hold it in my hand and open it. Bring it up to the light. There is a handwritten note in blue ballpoint. It's folded up and it has my name on it.

Inside are two brand-new razor blades.

They shine.

The note says: *Your mom screwed it up. Make sure you do it properly.*

35

PEGGY

I am going to be released.

They call it *discharged*.

The doctor said I am responding well to my medications, to therapy, and I am taking responsibility for my decisions. She said I look happier and more composed. I told her I felt myself again.

I sit watching a man my own age coloring a picture of a ranch. He is using black for the sky and dark red for the fields.

They keep asking me about how I think it will be to return home. I do not tell them that home may have moved a mile or a hundred miles. I do not tell them I am thrilled to go back, and I do not tell them I also have frequent nightmares about it. I do not tell them I have formulated a plan that I cannot share with another soul. I do not tell them how I wake up in the middle of the night sweating, my chest tight, knowing that Sammy has grown older since I saw him last. His beautiful, unselfconscious, handwritten notes have kept me going these past days, but he sounds different. He has some of the skill of his father when it comes to stitching words together, some of that same musicality, but I can see through his style. I worry I may have hurt my child so deeply that he may have changed forever.

I am still not sure how, but I will make things right.

I will shield him from what will come.

The tree has gone. There was a stump. Sawdust on the grass. But they came and dug out the stump and took it away on the back of a flatbed truck. The sawdust has been washed away by rain. It is as if the pine tree was never there.

I have hated this time but perhaps I needed it to think straight. Years of hostility and being worn down by another person can corrupt your mind.

I feel capable again.

On the yellow chair sits a woman who arrived yesterday. She told me she came in restrained. There are scars all over her legs and arms. On her neck. She is gripping the radio we never use. The staff superglue the battery compartment shut so nobody can swallow the contents. They have also removed the antenna so the radio sounds like static. She holds it tight in her bandaged hands.

I think about how to escape somewhere with Sammy, to the next county, or Cincinnati, or England, even. Sneaking away when Drew is at work in the scrapyard, leaving a long letter explaining everything, telling him how we still love him but we need to go. It is just that I cannot see that future. I cannot picture it. I search inside my head for the right words, the visuals, and there are none to be found.

They tell me there will be a home treatment team. Plenty of support. Constant review of the meds I am taking. There will be a plan for my recovery to continue: this is not the end. We have talked about packing to go home but I have so few belongings it will not take me long.

Fatima has not returned from the other hospital yet. I want to see her. I want to say goodbye.

After my shower I am told there is a meeting and I am invited.

I am led to the room with the pale yellow hot-air balloon wallpaper.

My doctor is sitting down, cross-legged, and there is a social worker I recognize, and one of my nurses, and then, in the corner, standing slowly, stiffly, is my husband.

Drew stands straight and awkwardly opens his arms.

I run to him, weeping, and he holds me. I sense the others look away, look at each other, nod approvingly.

All part of the plan.

His scent. Some essence of Sammy in there.

"You OK?"

"Yeah," I say. "I'm getting there."

He nods. "Coming home soon."

I will see my son again.

They discuss routines and appointments. Help at home. Emergency phone numbers. They talk about the importance of taking it slow, remembering some of the coping strategies I have learned in here. They talk about support. But in my head I only see Sammy. Us at the library on a weekend, him helping, then reading quietly at one of the tables, me glancing over at him, gazing at his beautiful red hair, his freckles, adoring him, hoping he lives to be a hundred.

"I said you've done really well, Peggy," repeats the doctor. "You seem much better now. But we don't want to go one step forward then two steps back, we talked about that, remember? You'll be going home soon but not quite yet."

I nod.

"Take it one step at a time, and if you ever need us you know where we are, OK?"

I nod.

Drew places his hand on my knee and pats it twice.

36

SAMSON

They do not want me to live.

I never hurt them, did I? Never trash-talked any of them. I don't go around hiding their bags or stealing their belongings. I have never sliced *their* bag straps with a blade or cut a gash in *their* shoes so the rain leaks in. I leave them well alone. If they needed my help I'd probably offer it. I'd do what I could. And yet they want me to cut myself?

Dad says she might not be out for months. Might not be until spring break. He says she's not allowed to send letters, and we still can't visit. It would set her back, the doctors reckon. It'd be too upsetting for her. But what about us?

Phoenix isn't on his boat. He left two days ago and I'm not sure if he will come back.

Some kind of fishing vessel passes by and I plunge both hands deep into my LEGO box. I move my knuckles against the sharp plastic bricks and breathe in. They smell like when everything was better, back in Nanna Ruth's bungalow, with Mom happy, me at elementary school, still mates with Eyebrow.

The razor blades are hidden inside the box. They're at the bottom, under all the bricks. I push my fingers deeper until they graze the base but then I pull them back quickly. Would they slice off my fingertips? Would they let Mom see me then? I plunge my hands in again and move them around, the bricks crunching against each other.

"They want me dead," I whisper through gritted teeth, pushing my fingers lower. "They want me dead." I swirl my hands through the sharp bricks, pushing my knuckles deeper, searching for the blades. "They want me to die." I ball my hands into fists, each one holding bricks, crushing them, and I push both fists to the bottom and scrape them around manically. "They want me . . ."

Dad clears his throat behind me.

I pull both hands out and sit frozen rigid.

"Samson?"

I look back over my shoulder at him. My heart is pounding.

He says nothing.

"How long have you been there, Dad?"

He frowns. He looks appalled and confused.

I turn my body to face him properly.

His eyes flit around the boat, to me, to the LEGOs, to the window.

"I know the boat's better with your mother here. Creature comforts. She keeps it neat."

I look at him.

He tightens his belt. It is the brown leather belt his father wore. Dad used to sharpen his knife on his stone, but he'd always finish off the edge with his belt. "I think we're due some pizza. What do you say, son?"

"Really?"

"Why not? What's holding us back?"

I stand up.

On the bus into town Dad coughs into his elbow. He coughs and coughs and people watch. Coughing isn't uncommon around here what with all the old miners. Same goes for hunchbacks. I pat Dad once on the back and he stiffens at my touch. He withdraws.

We walk up the hill past Safeway to reach the best pizza place in town. Joe's. We stand at the counter together. Gleaming stainless steel. A thickset man moves dough between his hands. A woman wearing a hairnet restocks the drinks cooler. A glass display with six kinds of hot slices. A lineup of sauces and a napkin dispenser sponsored by the town's football team.

"Two Cokes. Two large pepperoni pizzas with onion and peppers."

They take his money.

"We're going to the top of the hill."

The man nods but does not look at my father.

Dad carries his and I carry mine. The cardboard box is hot and moist and it smells like all the best things ever conceived of.

We set off up the steepest section of the hill. The wind dies down as we approach the bench. We sit side by side and open our boxes.

Hot, spicy steam.

Neither of us says a word.

The view is half the town. Steep rows of one-story houses with chain-link fence yards. The boarded-up factory with its brick chimney. Spires and white church towers in the middle distance. The tiled roof of my school. I can see the clock tower. Buses, mostly yellow, all sizes, come and go at the station. I can make out the old mine from up here, landscaped to create a wildlife preserve, but from this distance, on a clear day, you can see it was a mine.

Dad takes a bite of pizza.

"Not a bad town, is it?"

"It's all right."

He takes a second slice.

"My mother and father moved here from out East. You know that, don't you?"

"Yeah."

"Chose it on account of the factory. Dad worked there twenty-two years. Mom never worked."

I drink some Coke from the bottle.

"Would have liked you, Samson, both of them. Would have fussed over you."

"Paul Pricklett's still got four grandparents alive."

"Who?"

"Guy at school. His dad's Navajo and his mom's from Kentucky."

"Four alive?"

"Yeah."

"Your grandpa, he left school at fourteen, but he was smart. Could have been a writer if things had turned out different. He was a tough man. A lot of the time he was too tough for his own good, just like his father before him. But he'd have been proud of you."

"Me?"

"Who else?"

I eat another slice, grease running through my fingers.

We look straight ahead like we're still on the bus.

"Would have brought you up here himself, I don't doubt. Partial to a pizza and a cold beer, your grandpa was."

We look at the town and we don't say anything for a long time.

A plane leaves a mark on the sky. I watch as it fades.

Canada geese glide overhead in formation like it's been orchestrated, planned out, rehearsed. Heading up toward Mark Twain National Forest.

"Boys bothering you at school?"

"No."

He nods and finishes his slice.

"Had some trouble when I was your age. Never spoke of it before. Problem with some older kids. Real knuckleheads. Rough school, rougher than yours is."

He always says that.

"What happened?"

"This is between you and me. Do you understand?"

I nod and he turns to see me nodding. He looks back at the town.

"Boys messing with my mind. Punching me when I wasn't looking, stupid stuff like that. If I'd had a fair fight I'd have knocked their heads off but it's never fair in high school, is it?"

"No, it's not."

He swallows hard. Sighs. Chews.

"Between you and me, they roughed me up badly, some of them. Cuts and bruises. Broke my rib one time, the bastards."

"Did you get them?"

He inspects the next slice. Folds it a little.

"Not right away. I bided my time. They weren't good years for me, Samson. I know this'll be a shock for you to hear, your old man getting messed with and boys beating on me. I know you never thought you'd hear such a thing."

I take a deep breath.

I look right at him.

"I knew you were bullied."

"No." He smiles, shaking his head, chewing more vigorously. "I never told a soul, in fact. Not even my own father. Not your mother either. Nobody knows about this."

I swallow hard. "I knew."

He stiffens up, straightens his back. "No, boy." His voice is deeper. "You never did."

"I did."

He turns to me, frowning. "Cut that out. You never."

"I could tell, Dad."

He turns away and starts shaking his head, muttering.

"I could always tell, Dad."

He looks back toward the factory, and frowns so intensely I can feel it in the air. He takes in the trailer park outside the town, the traffic on the highway.

I eat a loose slice of pepperoni from my pizza box.

We don't say anything more for a long time.

"How did it end?" I ask.

"How did it end?"

"Yeah."

He chews on his lip, sniffs, closes his box. "Just did. They moved on to some other fool. Soon as I got out of that school I shaved my head so it would never happen again."

"What do you mean?"

He pulls out his worn billfold, its leather form contoured to his backside, and shows me a small, wrinkled photograph of him as a child with Grandpa Bill and Grandma Evelyn. It's the first photo I've ever seen of him as a boy. All three of them have red hair. Dad's hair looks like mine.

"You're my son. No doubt about it when you look at that picture, is there?"

I smile. "Nope."

"My boy."

I move a little closer to him and he coughs and moves farther away. Some instinct.

"Struggling with my novel, Samson. Not as good as it ought to be. Flawed. I should burn the damn thing and move on."

"You'll get there, Dad."

He squeezes the box in his hands. Holds it tight, sinews protruding. "We'll see."

I turn to him. "Why don't you, you know . . . ?"

"What?"

"Why don't you . . . like me?"

He snorts. "What did you just say?"

"I said, Why don't you like me?"

"Turn to face the town, stop gawping at me like that." He tuts. "Why don't I *like* you? What is this? *Like* you? Jesus wept, boy, I'm your father. It's nothing to do with liking or not liking."

"I know Mom likes me."

"She'd better."

"But you don't."

He coughs into his elbow. Spits on the ground. Tuts again.

"You enjoy this, don't you? All this modern talk? Feelings."

I shrug.

"Look at the town, boy," he says, sternly.

I focus on the transmission towers: electric overhead cables streaking across the horizon.

"My dad never talked to me the way you're doing," he says. "Never had a hug off him, barely even shook the man's hand. There was no talk of emotions, anything like that. Day's work then supper then TV then bed. One day, then the next. The bar near the Goodwill, when you come of age. He never grasped why I wrote what I did. Never understood my interest for Hemingway. Thought it was soft."

"Hemingway wasn't soft."

"Damn right."

I smile. After a few minutes, I say, "Thanks, Dad."

He frowns, still staring forward at the town.

"Thanks for the pizza."

"Why do you think these cowards want you hurt?"

"What?"

"Boys at school."

"I don't know. Because they have money. Because they're too scared to fight with the real tough kids, the kids from the other schools."

"They're jealous, Samson, that's why. They know you've got something they haven't."

I pause. "What?"

He turns and looks at me properly for the first time. The wind picks up and moves his collar against his neck. He says, "Talent, boy. Dreams."

PART III

37

PEGGY

They open the door.

I have had talks with the doctor, with the whole discharge team. They were kind and patient. Told me this is not the end of my recovery, of my care, that it will continue, that I have managed well. We talked more about medication and how I can get in touch if I need extra help.

I walk up to the door.

I step through it.

Fatima is still in the other hospital, the private one, the overspill. I never had a chance to say goodbye to her. To thank her for helping me through those early days.

They are here.

He runs to me.

I drop my bag on the floor and open my arms, the way I did when he was small, and he leaps into my embrace. I smell him, bring him in tighter, wrap myself around him, squeezing his frame.

"My boy. Oh, my boy."

He will not ease up. His slender arms are tight around my neck.

My heart swells.

The scent of his hair. The mole on the back of his right ear. The sharpness of his shoulders.

Drew comes over and takes my bag.

"All right, Peggy?"

I wipe my eyes. "I am now."

The outer doors open. We walk out of the building, people watching. There is a taxicab waiting with its engine idling.

Drew opens the back door of the cab.

"What's this?"

"It's for you. For all of us. I booked it."

I shake my head and smile and peer over at Sammy. He looks so proud. Drew places my bags in the trunk and we climb in and drive away. I glance back out of the rear window at the hospital. The wire fence. The missing pine tree. All the signposts.

I breathe.

A blur of a journey.

The cab slows and pulls over. We climb out and pay and then we walk down through the woods. How would this look? Stopping a cab in the middle of nowhere, no marker or crossing, no sign that this point signifies home, no address or zip code to speak of, and then walking down through trees and scrubby brambles.

The unfamiliar route is well-trodden. Samson's footprints. Broken twigs and a rotting carton of milk. Some missing child's face, faded.

The boat looks the same. Drew has maintained it, repaired the entrance cover, replaced one of the old mooring ropes.

"Welcome home, Mom."

I had to be smart to get out of that place. Smart and patient and strategic. I will do the same to get out of *this* place, when the time is right, when it is safe to do so.

The two of us.

I stroke Sammy's hair and the sensation of having him so close, so available, is indescribable.

The boat is cool. Drew takes coal from the scuttle with his bare hands and builds up the fire. He blows and tends to it.

"I missed you so much," I say to Sammy. "It is wonderful to be home."

"We missed a woman's touch around here," says Drew, wiping coal dust hands on his jeans. "Not the same just us, is it, boy?"

"Definitely not," says Sammy, grinning, his eyes sparkling.

"A few things have changed since you left. We've been low on cash what with one thing or another, so we've been stuck here a fair time. No fuel in the tank. Means we're out of propane and we can't fill up the water. No hot water, either, of course, no electric. But I've found some windfall branches farther up the embankment. It'll work well once they've dried out. Woodstove's been keeping us going, hasn't it, Sammy?"

"It's been all right," he says, quietly.

"Payday on Friday. I'll get some diesel in."

I look around. There is appallingly little food. Three large water bottles and a six-pack of ravioli on the countertop. A small cup on the table full of perfect, still-tight snowdrops.

"Those are lovely," I say.

"Boy's idea."

"I'll have my book money come through soon," I say. "Then we can fill up propane; get a new fridge in, maybe."

Rather, I can plan our escape.

Drew stiffens and looks out of the window.

"You're the breadwinner, love, I know that," I say, biting my lip. "Always will be. It's just a top-up is all. A slice of good luck."

He doesn't shift his gaze; he just nods ever so slightly.

"You must have been mixing with all sorts in that place," he says. "I saw some of them coming and going. Looked like the gates of hell, that hospital. Folks babbling and groaning. Spaced out their heads. Bedlam. Don't know how you put up with it, Peg."

"I didn't have much choice."

"Perhaps not."

I frown. I can't hold it back. "Drew, you know I didn't. I wasn't allowed out."

"Boy missed you something terrible."

My eyelid twitches. "What are you saying, exactly?"

"Been a long time is what I'm saying. We coped, though, didn't we, Samson?"

Sammy nods. He looks uncomfortable between us.

"You settle in, then," says Drew. "I'll make coffee."

I walk through the kitchen, past the dinette, and pause by the sliding door to the bathroom. My blood chills in my veins. I drag it open. The sink. The cassette toilet. The bath, now full of tools and old rope. I close the door.

When the money comes through I will be able to look after Sammy. I will have some autonomy at long last. Stage one of the exit plan.

Sammy comes in.

"It's great to have you back here. Did you get my notes? The white mice?"

I sit down on the bed and bring him close to me. "They kept me going. You write beautifully, Sammy, just like your father. Thank you, my love."

He blushes. "It's all right."

"Did you get my letters?" I ask.

"Your letters?"

I stare at him.

Tightness in my chest.

"I sent them to your father at the scrapyard office." I pause. "He never told you, did he?"

Sammy looks away and shakes his head.

I breathe deeply. Slowly. Exactly like I have been shown. "He never even mentioned them?"

"No, Mom."

"I'm going to make it all OK, Sammy."

Sammy frowns.

Drew shouts through, "Coffee's gettin' cold."

The fire is blazing hot, vents open, burning ferociously.

Ramen noodles with lots of cracked black pepper. The snowdrops are in the center of the dinette table, the exact location of my son's heart each night when he falls asleep.

"This is cozy," I say.

We eat in silence.

I do the dishes, careful not to use too much of what precious water we have.

"How's school?"

Sammy puts down his Walkman and joins me, picking up a dish towel to dry the plates.

"Not bad, really. Dad taught me a few tricks. Simple stuff. Body language, not backing down, not looking like an easy target. Sounds dumb saying it out loud, don't know why I didn't do it years ago. It's getting better."

"I wish those bullies would pick on someone their own size," I say. "They're cowards."

He dries the cutlery.

"Dad helped me. It's better now."

He converts the dinette to form his bed. We read together by the fire. Drew tells me he is approaching act three of his book, the final third, and he must not stop, must not lose momentum.

I tuck Sammy in. I do not rush it; I take my time like the old days. I perch on his bed and tell him about Christmas in the hospital and he tells me about what Drew cooked for him. He talks about Phoenix on the next boat and how he might buy himself a leather jacket on layaway when he is older. He sits up and we hug and I breathe him in.

"Night, my boy. I love you."

"Night, Mom."

Drew shaves his head and gets to work.

38

SAMSON

Dad's been paid. Sometimes I question whether it's fair for him to collect my paper route money, and, since last week, my money from Phoenix for helping him on his boat while he's sick. He only leaves me with a couple of bucks. He likes to collect it and then use it wisely, he says. He rations it so we won't find ourselves in hot water like last time.

Math followed by social studies: a unit on world religion. I feel sorry for the teacher, Mr. Norris. He tries his best. Today he's wearing a sweat suit because he'll be helping to coach football later, assistant to the assistant type thing, and the pants are too short for him. The other boys don't let him do his job. I like to hear the stories from various faiths—for me it's an extension of history class, mixed with philosophy—but the others ask him constantly about the devil and exorcisms and celibacy, and today they removed the wheels from his chair with a screwdriver when he was out collecting photocopies and projector slides from the teachers' room. I can tell from his face that it bothers him. It's not the same with the other teachers—Mrs. Cosby and Mr. Davenport—they're not affected by it; they brush it off. But Mr. Norris takes the comments and the ridicule to heart. I can sense it weighs him down. When I catch him walking to his Chevy at the end of a day, especially a Friday, I can see the toll it takes. How he drags it home with him and there's nothing I can do about it.

I talk to Dad more than I ever could before. Something's been unlocked. Or *unblocked*. We'll perform tasks together, repairing the rope fender or changing the oil in the motor, and the gap between us is different now. I'm not sure what I did to make him see me, hear me, but he does. And I like it a lot.

A couple of guys still bump into me on purpose, call me Noodles, skinny Irish queer, but it's different. No escalation or cash payments. I tell them to fuck off and, on the whole, they do. They are focused on Kavanagh now because he doesn't smell so good. His parents can't afford deodorant for him and so the predators have moved on. I know I should feel sorry for him but honestly, I don't. I am a coward, I guess. They hide his bag now instead of mine and all I feel most times is an overwhelming sense of relief.

Dad says I wasn't really bullied.

He claims what happened to me was nothing compared to what happened in his school in his day. He says I shouldn't dwell on it, should thicken up my skin. After we added pool shock to the water tank we measured oil in the motor with the metal dipstick. He said, "Your memories are skewed, Samson. It's not your fault, boy, you get that from your mother and her mother before her. That side of the family. You remember bad times, it's like your filter's busted. You forget the good parts. Your school's been good. It's been the making of you. Don't dwell on a few rough weeks, eh?"

Maybe I am misremembering it. Paul Pricklett went through worse; I know that now. Far worse. But I was attacked every day, throughout the day, and I was worried for my life at times, especially outside the school gates. I am not misremembering that.

After school I walk to the bus station with Joe Brigwell. He's not in the same class as me but his dad and brother fish from a boat on the lake so he's interested in how we live. He asks a lot of boat questions, a lot of catfish questions, a lot of sex questions, a lot of military questions, and he makes me laugh. His dad's F-150 has a bumper sticker that says Honk If You Love Jesus. I say goodbye to him.

At the bus stop Jennifer comes over, her two best friends behind her.

"All right?" she says.

"All right."

She smiles. Dimples and white teeth.

"Fools aren't bothering you anymore, are they?"

"Not really."

"What did you do to make them stop?"

I shrug.

She looks back to her friends and then turns to me and says, in a quiet voice, "Come on, what happened, really?"

"Told them to fuck off. They knew what was good for them, so they did it."

"Honest?"

In my dreams.

"Yeah," I lie.

"Yeah?"

"Ask anyone."

She glances over to her friends then back to me.

"You want to go to the park one day after school, Sam? Me and you?"

My heart races. I know this moment, I've seen it portrayed, I've imagined it, I've read about it, I've dreamed it, I've even written about it.

"Could do, I suppose."

She turns and as she does she brushes my arm softly with her hand. She walks away.

I am a brand-new person on the bus. High, floating, numb, grinning like an idiot. She wants to go to the park with *me*? Just me and her? But what then? Other guys at school have girlfriends. Relationships, I guess you'd call them. Gunner says he lost his virginity at age ten, but he talks a lot of shit so who knows. They take girls to the movie theater, take them to prom. One boy had his girlfriend stay over in his house when his parents went to their lake house for the Fourth of July weekend. Just the two of them, together, like grown-ups. He said there were fireworks that weekend, all right. I never understood how to take that leap from being a boy to a man. The logistics involved. That exact moment of change. I can't exactly take her to a restaurant or a motel, can I? The park, sure, but what then? She'll grow bored with me eventually is what. First base and then crash and burn. See that I'm a noodle-armed kid with no money who still plays with his damn LEGO bricks. She'll see right through me.

But the floating doesn't end. Every time I doubt myself I play back her words. Her skin brushing mine. Her smile. She asked *me* to the park.

If Jennifer wants to kiss I will have to act like I've done it before. I'll improvise. Make it up as I go along. Play it cool. I must ask Paul Pricklett about French-kissing, get some pointers, find out what it is exactly. He hasn't done it yet, but his big brother has.

I walk to the doors and the bus comes to a halt. It hisses. The door opens and the light is slowly returning to the skies. I skip through the embankment, weaving through papery birch trunks, my arms outstretched to touch them, heading down to the water level. I don't notice the Cheetos packets and decomposing Marlboro filters because Jennifer Adamu asked me to the park.

The park.

I glide toward the canal.

Paul Pricklett told me once how he wants to run a company one day so he can sit behind a big desk and not work too hard. He said he'd like a comfortable life with a new Buick and not too much stress or hassle. Garage full of arcade machines and a hot tub outside. You have to admire the guy's honesty.

Before I head home I call in on Phoenix.

He is on the wicker sofa in his living room area, wrapped in a wool blanket, holding a hot drink. He looks awful.

"All right, Phoenix?

"Hello, friend."

"What chores you need doing today?"

He coughs.

"Just come and sit down. Have a chat, that's all."

"What? No chores, you sure?"

His eyelids are heavy, drooping, and his Adam's apple sticks out farther than usual.

"Talking. Come talk with me, Samson."

I sit next to him. Under his blanket is his black leather jacket draped over his knees. I've never once seen him not wearing it.

Deep sigh. "Uncle Jeff asked me to keep an eye on you, you know."

"Did he?"

"He thought you were one of the good guys."

I look down at my long shoes.

"He never knew much about me as it turned out. I think he still thought of me as a young guy, never saw me as being much older than you."

"You look a *lot* older."

"Oh, thanks."

"Sorry. You look nearly as old as my dad, that's all."

He sighs again. "Jeff always knew I was gay, I think, deep down."

I tense up.

"Never talked to him about it out loud, he was that generation. I couldn't come out and say it to his face, you know?"

"Hmmm."

"Maybe I should have been more open with him."

I shrug.

He takes a sip of his drink.

"When . . . when did you, you know, find out?" I ask.

"Find out?"

"That you were, you know?"

"Teenager, I suppose. Younger than that probably. Seventh grade, maybe eighth? Some people know when they're really young. I think I was in denial or confused. I had some major crushes in school, but I'd tell myself I was just admiring those boys, looking up to them, idolizing, you know. Then I realized it was more than that."

"Girl asked me out to the park today."

"You serious?"

I break out into a broad smile. I can't help it. "Yeah. Asked me in front of everyone at the bus station."

"You gonna go?"

"Course I am. She's cute."

He coughs and says, "Good for you, Samson, man. Live your life to the full."

"Did you, sounds dumb, but did you ever, I don't know, like girls and guys at the same time, Phoenix? Or was it just guys mainly?"

He thinks for a long time. Takes a sip of broth, then another. He looks at me like he's reading my mind. "Just guys for me, really. I thought some girls were gorgeous, really beautiful, but when it came to attraction, it was guys."

I nod.

He bites his lower lip and stares at me for a long time.

"Lots like both, though. If you have a friend at school who wants to date both that's completely normal, let me tell you. I've had plenty of friends and colleagues like that."

"Yeah?"

"Lots of people like both, Samson. If you have a friend like that then just let them be, honestly. Can be tough in a place like this. Let them work it out in their own good time. Look at me, now."

I turn to him. He looks very sick. I can see too many of his veins, his blood vessels.

"There's nothing weird or wrong or different about liking boys, or liking girls, or liking both. I want you to know that."

I frown.

"Everyone's different, right. Everyone needs to find out what they like. It's not always obvious. Sometimes it's only clear once you've left home, gone to college, or work, had some space to think things through."

"I suppose."

He drains the last from his mug.

"Phoenix?"

"Yeah."

"Are you getting sick?"

"You could say that, yeah."

"What is it?"

"Virus. Complications. Don't worry, you won't catch it."

I nod.

"Don't you worry about me, Samson. I'm bulletproof. You worry about what you're going to do with this cute girl in the park. You need any pointers you come to your old friend, Phoenix."

"And what would you know about it?"

He makes a fist and waves it at me, smiling.

I take his ashes out for him and check his propane levels. He doesn't have much food in, mainly purees and soups besides all the meds bottles, so I'll get a list from him tomorrow.

"Night," I say.

"Samson, come here a second."

I walk back to him.

"Little closer."

"What is it?"

"That knife your old man gave you for Christmas. The one you were sharpening that day with the whetstone. You're not carrying that on you at school, are you?"

"No."

"You swear?"

"I'm not."

"If there's a ruckus at school and you pull that blade out your whole life can go sideways in an instant, right. You'll be taken away. Leave it at home, pal."

"I'm not stupid."

"I know you're not. Swear to me."

"I swear."

He looks relieved.

"I'm smarter than that, Phoenix. Been planning. One day I'll get the grades to go someplace else, a big city, maybe. Could be Chicago, even. I'll leave on the train. Ticket in my back pocket. I'm not going to screw it up."

Phoenix smiles and I can see one of his teeth is missing. "Mind you don't."

The smell of woodsmoke in the air as I step on the plank to the towpath and walk onto our boat. I hang my jacket up and kiss Mom.

Things are awkward between us after last night. I can sense she's still hurting. Maybe I should never have said it, but I couldn't stop. I told her, when she came through to make a warm drink, when I was already half-asleep, drowsy, *You said you'd never leave me, Mom.* She tried to answer but then she turned away and had to shut herself in the bedroom so as not to disturb Dad's writing. I know she cried in there. I don't understand why I needed to hurt her that way, to say what I said. I'll make it up to her later and do the dishes. I don't know why I said it. I don't know what's wrong with me.

I check my storage area for my gloves.

Dad comes home.

He's panting.

Wet patches on his shirt.

"How was your day, Drew?" she asks. "Coffee?"

"Samson."

I look up at him.

"No point you looking." He takes a breath. "For a Walkman in that closet."

My heart starts beating faster. "What?"

"Not there."

I raise my eyebrows.

He lifts his chin in response. "Priorities, boy. Pawned it for diesel. I'll get it back before the time runs out, so don't start complaining." I begin to reply but he cuts me off and says, his voice deep and firm, "No backchat, not a word. Oh, and Peg, you'll never guess what I saw, darling."

He never calls her *darling*.

Mom, already patting my shoulder, says, "What, love?"

He grinds his teeth and I see the sinew within his shoulder muscles flex. He says, "Have a wild guess, love."

"I don't know, Drew."

He narrows his eyes. "You do know."

She glances at me.

"Take a guess, go on," he says, his fists down by his hips.

"I don't know what to say, Drew."

"Store window," he says. "Ring any bells? Pawn store window."

She dips her head.

"Not surprised you're staring down at the floor."

She looks up at him.

"Your gold necklace for sale. One I gave you. Saved up my wages for that. Hard labor. Samson here chewed on it as a baby when his teeth were coming through. When were you gonna tell me, Peg?"

39

PEGGY

My first day back at the library.

I was worried how the staff and volunteers would look at me. If they would trust me. I need not have worried. One man, Jerry, a guy who volunteers one day a week, asked me some uncomfortably direct questions about what specific medications I was on, but apart from him everyone has been considerate. Mrs. Appleby took me to one side after lunch and told me her sister had some trouble years ago and needed rest time in the exact same place. She said her sister had been overtired, and the weeks she spent at St. Mary's helped her.

My plans are coming together in my head. Escape routes and new high schools. How I'll ration out the book money. I'm going to ask Mrs. Appleby if it can be paid into her checking account and then I'll tell Drew it's half the amount I actually received. I'll fabricate paperwork in advance using the library computer. I'd like to write a diagram of the plan, the stages, but I can't risk him finding any notes.

Unpacking new arrivals is one of my favorite tasks. Seeing which new releases we have in stock, and organizing the areas to shelve them in. I like the coding logic, the Dewey decimal system, the sense of gradually building and shaping a resource the whole community can rely on.

By four I am exhausted. I am so out of practice, not only with work, but with talking to people. I take my purse and my jacket. I say goodbye to Stephanie on the front desk and walk out clutching the envelope. Inside is an apology letter to my publisher explaining my hiatus, without going into too much detail, and expressing how excited I am about the novel making its way into the world. I didn't ask about the check, who to make it out to, whether it can be made out to cash so I can keep control of it. I'll deal with all that next. The letter is stamped. I have written the library's address on the back of the envelope in case it is not delivered.

I walk outside, cold dry air on my face, and turn the corner toward the post office.

I jump when I spot him.

Drew is waiting by a pay phone.

"All right," he says.

"You frightened me, Drew."

"Thought I'd walk you home. Keep an eye on you. Make sure you're safe."

His face is severe.

"You didn't have to do that."

We set off, and the leather hobnail soles of his work boots tap on the pavement. He walks upright, shoulders back, making the most of his size.

"I need to mail this, won't take a minute."

He looks at it and stops walking.

Him breathing. Me watching him breathe.

"About that," he says, gesturing to the white envelope.

"Yes?"

"Let's walk that way instead."

"I need to mail this first. It's important, Drew."

"I said we'll go that way."

There are people all around us, but I am trapped inside a tight, invisible cage. A shrinking cage.

He claims *he* gifted me the gold necklace. That it was a higher-quality version of the mail-order one Mom used to wear. This has been going on for so long. I am not sure which version, which truth, which perception of history, is accurate.

It is not important.

Not now.

We walk toward the bus station. We take the long way around, past the hardware store.

"You OK?" I ask.

"It happened."

"What did?"

He looks straight ahead as we walk, not at me.

"What we talked about, Peg."

"I don't understand."

He sighs impatiently. "You went into the hospital, you remember that part, yes? And then it happened. I helped you out like we'd agreed. To save face. To make sure it didn't all fall apart, you remember?"

What is he talking about? To save face?

"I don't know what you mean."

He clears his throat. "You take your meds today?"

"Yes."

He scratches his head and talks slower. "When you got sick and went up to St. Mary's I took it over to help out. Like you asked me to. Well, let's just say we weren't dealing with professionals. Bunch of cowboys."

"Cowboys?"

"Incompetents. Philistines. Wouldn't know a clean, coherent piece of work if it hit them square in the forehead."

"Drew, can you just slow down? What do you mean *piece of work*?"

He doesn't listen. We pass a drugstore. He keeps on walking at his own brisk pace. If anything, he speeds up.

"Like we talked about. You went into St. Mary's to get your head right. Well, you had a contract, didn't you, you remember that? You signed it, Peg. You had legal obligations, a time schedule, deadlines. I took it over, like you asked me to. I did my part, even though it wasn't my kind of thing, not at all. Far from it, in fact."

My heart sinks.

"Are you talking about my book, Andrew?"

He keeps walking.

Lifts his jaw.

"Deal's dead and buried," he says. "You shouldn't deal with them again. Not to be trusted."

My mouth falls open. "What . . . what have you done?"

"Did you a favor, girl."

"Tell me."

"Just did."

"The deal's dead?"

"Mutual agreement."

"I never agreed to anything. Drew, slow down a second, tell me what went wrong."

He turns to look at me and his gaze is blank. "Your head, that's what went wrong. Can't you remember that either?"

"You talked to my publisher directly? In New York?"

I jog a few paces to keep up.

"Helping you out, otherwise the whole thing would've gone down the tubes."

"What did they say?"

"Say? Didn't say a word. I found their details in *Writer's Market* and wrote them. Nipped it in the bud. Worked through your edits myself. Course, it wasn't my kind of writing, romance, genre fiction, not my wheelhouse, but I finished the rewrites, tidied it up best I could. Lots of dead wood there was, Peggy. Filler. Not your fault, your head wasn't right at the time."

I never agreed to any part of this.

I try to maintain my composure. If I scream he will have me locked away again. "Why didn't you just tell them I was sick?"

"You wanted that, you think? Tell them their new author was in the nuthouse drugged out of her skull. Not likely. My job's to protect you, love. Keep the wagon on the road."

A cyclist rings her bell and passes us.

I am faint. Unsteady.

"I don't understand this."

"That'll be the medication."

I jog again. Sweat, cold on my back.

"I'll talk to them. Explain. I can do the work again."

"No," he says, snorting. "Said they don't want any more contact. It got heated, shall we say. Letters were exchanged. Talk of lawyers. They're third-rate, Peggy, a shambles, and I told them so. Not worth thinking about. I can give you a list of worthwhile publishers if you like."

"I'll write them a new letter."

"Did you not hear me?" he says, firmly. "Strike them off the list, Peggy, and learn from your mistakes. Important lesson for any writer, that is. Know when to move on."

An ambulance drives by. Flashing lights but no siren.

I take a deep breath and say, "We never talked about this. Did they think you were me?"

"Course they did, like we talked about. You're telling me you can't remember asking? I signed letters. Your signature isn't exactly a challenge, is it? Peggy Jenkins. You pretty much write it out like a ten-year-old. We talked on this plenty before you went into St. Mary's. You don't remember, really?"

"No."

"The pills they put you people on, you don't know what day of the week it is half the time. Not your fault, Peg. Keep walking, girl. Keep up."

"I lost my deal?"

"Wasn't much of a deal to begin with. But the characters showed promise, Peggy, I'll give you that. Have another crack at a fresh piece, something with depth, voice, pathos. I'll give you a few pointers and all this mess can be avoided next time."

"We didn't discuss this. I'd have remembered."

"It's you that's mentally ill, not me."

Dry in my mouth.

I can't catch my breath.

The plan just went up in flames.

"So we won't have that check coming in?"

"We'll manage. Scrapyard wants more hours. Might take Samson with me this weekend now he's getting stronger. Have more cash coming in."

I jog another few paces.

"But. He's so young." Everything is falling apart. Moving too quickly. "Make sure he doesn't get injured."

He laughs.

"Don't laugh, Drew. I'm serious. He's fourteen."

"If it weren't for me he'd be with child welfare by now, you ever think about that? Children's home just like my cousin. Taken away forever. You hurt yourself, swallowing pills, sent up to St. Mary's all that time for a rest. All right for some. If it weren't for me he'd have been taken away, Peg. Child services doesn't take chances. So, yes, I've been looking after the boy. You might have noticed. You might have been grateful."

"I noticed." It's like I'm trapped deep inside a maze of his design, unable to see over the top. "He seems happier."

"There you go then."

We walk on for a few minutes, me trying to keep up. Past the check cashing place, past the pet store, past the boxing gym.

In how many ways can my existence be compressed? Each escape route walled in?

"I think it can be salvaged," I say. "I'll schedule a phone call, maybe, from the library, explain, come clean. They'll understand. I can still save this book."

He stops and turns to face me properly for the first time. The wind blows hard and his eyes water a little.

"Book's gone, Peggy. Let it go. Your head can't be relied on; the doctor said it to my face. You know that, right? Told me straight to keep an eye out for warning signs. Delusions of grandeur, detachment from reality, that sort of thing. So I am keeping an eye out. Trust me, that book wasn't taking you anyplace good. Would have been an embarrassment. Start again from scratch. Something stronger, something worthy of you. Genuine publisher this time. Someone with pedigree. Let's hear no more about that dead book."

40

SAMSON

I watch the heron glide and land gracefully on the water. A creature from another epoch. It is a male, I can tell by the length of his bill. I watch him wade and fish, monitoring the water, focused, composed. There are no dragonflies buzzing around him at this time of year. No bees or damselflies or tree frogs. He is completely alone. Dominant and quiet. A bird with a wingspan to rival a golden eagle. Me watching him watching the water.

Mom is subdued. She thinks it's her medication. The dosage is difficult to fine-tune, she says. She spends a lot of time alone in her bedroom.

I walk over to her by the sink.

"Can they change your tablets? Are there different kinds?"

She stops wringing out shirts and stockings and says, "They'll adjust the dose, Sammy. We'll find the right level."

Through the glass I watch the heron bend and dip its neck. The windows are crystal clear after Dad and I washed them all with newspaper and white vinegar.

"I had a plan for us, Sammy," she says in a hushed voice, almost a whisper. "Wanted to show you someplace else, another world. But that'll have to wait now."

"Outside the county?"

She smiles at me. "It'll have to wait, my boy."

"We could still do it? Dad says he'll refill the tank from a jerrican and then fill the boat's tank up at the marina, have us shipshape again."

"That'll be fine," she says, but she sounds sad.

I polish my shoes and make sure I wear my one good shirt, no fraying, little discoloration. It is almost white and I like the way it feels against my skin. I smuggle an old toothpaste tube into my schoolbag. They won't know I stole it. I am careful when I take things. Before I leave I find Dad's cologne, he's had the bottle for years and rarely uses it, and splash my cheeks.

"What's all this?" says Mom, smiling.

"Nothing."

"Come on."

"What?"

"Is it a girl?"

"No."

"You can tell me."

I run out of the boat. "Bye, Mom. See you later."

The heron flies away.

It is strange walking to the bus stop. The colors in the trees and the fallen leaves are sharper than usual. The air is cool but I am perfectly warm. I don't even care anymore that Dad pawned my Walkman. I should still be angry but today promises to be the turning point of my whole life so what is a Walkman to that?

The morning is fine. There's a brawl near the school gates, three sixth graders with bad cuts, but I'm in no way involved. Nobody tried to push me into it. Nobody blamed me for it. I was just one of the crowd. Normal. Like the rest.

At recess I avoid the spicy corn chips I'd usually buy on a Friday and chew gum instead. I can't risk bad breath. Not on a day like today.

Every time another kid is pushed, or a glue stick is thrown, I wait to be the next target. Sometimes I am, briefly, but on the whole they've moved on. It is strange how that can happen. Years of constant aggravation, in this school and the last, and then it switches. They're targeting Bower now on account of his lisp. He went under the radar all this time but now they have him in their sights. A pack moving on from one innocent creature to the next.

I don't know if I will stay untouched for much longer. Maybe I will. I feel there's been a sea change.

Chemistry. The periodic table. The teacher, Mr. Saunders, *Tony* Saunders, is shorter than most of the kids he teaches. When he's out of earshot we call him *Shetland Tony*. I shouldn't but I do. He drones on about inert gases and noble metals. But I cannot see the blackboard, the atomic numbers; I can only see her face. The shape of her fingers. I have never encountered a person like Jennifer. Her pale nail polish. Her lashes. She might just be the most beautiful girl in the world. But not only beautiful, her voice has a liquid quality. A roundness. She has a sensibility rare in this town. Jennifer is cool, much cooler than me, but also she carries herself in a certain way. Good posture and an easy, generous smile.

"Jenkins. I said, what's the chemical number of boron?"

"Sorry, sir?"

"Quit daydreaming. Chemical number of boron. Come on."

I glance at my book.

"Fourteen, sir."

He moves on to ask Gunner something about lithium.

After school I work in the library then walk to the park. The town looks better than it ever has. The cars seem to have been upgraded and cleaned. Waxed and polished. Brighter headlights. More aerodynamic, somehow. My heart is larger in my chest, higher, closer to my collarbones. I walk past the candy store, past the burned-out hair salon.

The park. Largest in the area after the old mine.

Clusters of teenagers huddle together acting nonchalant. There's no way I'd have lingered in this place even a month ago. My life has changed completely.

It's a gray day and their faces are lit sporadically by the orange tips of their cigarettes. Will Jennifer want me to smoke a cigarette? Oh, God. Why haven't I practiced? *Samson Jenkins, why have you never thought to practice? You'll cough, you know you will.*

She's not here yet. I wander down to the swings and wait in the middle of the park. It's not a huge space, it's just some bushes and swing sets and a shallow pool they drain each fall.

My stomach is all over the place. Floating, stirring, bubbling. She's meeting me here. She might bring vodka in a Gatorade bottle. Some kids do that. Others drink Sprite mixed with cough syrup. She asked me out. I have my toothpaste in my pocket just in case.

It's getting dark.

A couple walk hand in hand toward the bushes. They disappear from view.

She's not expecting . . . ? Not right away, surely. No. I mean, I'll need equipment. I must have that sorted for next time. They sell them in the drugstore. I can't go in and ask them myself, they know me. I'll find a machine. Paul will know where to find them. And then I'll practice.

I shuffle from side to side to keep warm. She will be here soon. She's ten minutes late. Playing it cool. Maybe I shouldn't have arrived on time? Where do you learn about these things? I wish I'd asked Phoenix. He'd know.

The largest group in the park leave, kicking something across the ground, an empty can, and singing a Guns N' Roses song.

Half past.

I squeeze a small drop of toothpaste onto my tongue.

Quarter to.

She's not here yet. Probably had a detention or something. I dreamed last night about holding her hand. The warmth of it. We weren't in the park in my dream; we were up the hill overlooking the town. It was an excellent dream. We talked and there was some kind of aeronautical display team flying above the train station. The Blue Angels, perhaps. We laughed and drank glasses of wine in the dream. I woke up with a strange sensation. I was worried. Maybe she'll be able to tell when we kiss? To know my secret. Is that possible?

An hour goes by, but I am patient. I'll wait for her. It'll all be worth it. I will wait all night if I have to.

A group of older teenagers come, some with skateboards, and I move away from them. They sit down with a stereo and one of the boys has a basketball. I think they might be stoners.

Maybe she isn't coming.

I'll wait.

Dad says he's never quit anything in his life.

I am cold now, so I walk around in circles.

A little more toothpaste on my tongue.

The threat of frost on the short grass.

She's not here. She's not coming, is she? I understand that now. Other groups—smoking, drinking—laugh like hyenas all around me. I can't see their faces in the dark. They could be laughing at me. This was some kind of mean prank, some kind of game. Of course she never wanted to come here with me. Why the hell would she?

I walk north from the park, drawn unthinkingly toward Mr. Turner's bungalow. Chilled to the core, I break out into a pathetic run. *Why am I so gullible?* I sprint as fast as I can to his bungalow. Streetlights. Good old Bakersfield Avenue. Cold feet. The corner grocery in the distance, lit, door always wedged open, freezing cold inside. There's a For Sale sign up outside number 34. The garden looks neat and there are no lights on in the windows. I'd have gone inside if he'd still been alive. I'd have knocked and he'd have brought me in and made me hot milk or a mug of Campbell's soup. He made me cream of tomato soup one time when my uniform was soaked through. A grilled ham and cheese to go with it. I look at the front yard, its mailbox stuffed with flyers.

"Jenkins?"

I turn.

Shit. "Mr. Davenport?"

"You know he's not there anymore, Jenkins."

"I know, sir."

He walks out of his gate. Dennis Davenport, head of Lower School, wearing slacks and a sweater. I've never seen him dressed like this.

"Everything OK with you?"

"Yes, sir."

"Good."

"I'm just out for a quick walk, sir. Heading back soon. I'm catching the bus home."

"Clear night. Frost, I expect."

"Yes, sir."

"You know we're in for some meteor showers next week? I heard it on the Weather Channel. Best display for this time of year in over a century. You interested in meteors, Jenkins?"

"I suppose so, sir."

"Your father has binoculars?"

"No, sir."

He raises his eyebrows and then he sticks out his lower lip and breathes in. "Wait there a second." He walks into his bungalow on the opposite side of the street. It looks like Mr. Turner's except there's an ornamental wishing well in the front yard and he has a two-seater porch swing painted white.

A minute passes.

I turn back to Mr. Turner's bungalow. It looks so cold now. So lifeless.

"There you are."

I turn and Mr. Davenport is holding out a pair of binoculars in a leather case.

"I couldn't, sir."

"Why on earth not? This is my old pair. I bought new ones last year, mainly for hunting whitetails. You can borrow these and drop them off at the teachers' room when you're done. It's no problem."

"You sure, sir?"

"Take them and don't damage them, OK? Now, be off home with you."

41

PEGGY

The sun has some strength today. It is rising higher in the sky and there's heat on my cheeks as I hang out laundry on the small rear deck for the first time this year. We have a rotary washing line anchored into the boards.

A few hours ago I saw a kingfisher. I could not draw my eyes away from its blue plumage: iridescent in the sharp morning light. The first one I have seen. Its beak was long and it sat atop a rock as it fished. Shades of orange in its feathers: vermilion, ochre, and coral; and it shimmered like water, like mercury.

Drew and Sammy train together on the towpath. I am still wary, but I am pleased they enjoy each other's company. For so many years he seemed intimidated by his father, scared of him, and now, seeing them so easy together is a pleasant thing. It is a surprise every time I notice. Drew is doing push-ups, showing Sammy how to execute them properly, and the breeze is traveling from them to me, from the bank to the clothes I am hanging out to dry.

"Don't know why you're surprised," says Drew, just in earshot, his nose close to the earth, his back rod straight. "Never rely on women for anything. You can't trust them, boy. Say they'll meet you down at the park and then they never show up. Probably with some other guy."

Sammy kneels down on the ground and starts doing push-ups.

"All the way down, boy, that's it, come on, put your back into it. If you don't feel pain you won't get stronger, remember that. Down. Nose to the dirt."

"I'm trying."

"Try harder."

I watch all this from the corner of my eye.

"That's it, Samson. Back straight, arms extended."

They start doing squats.

"Thing is, they're not like us. They'll say one thing and mean another. Riddles. They'll twist things around and before you know they'll be in charge. Not having that, are we, boy?"

"No, Dad."

A chill runs down my back and I know it is my responsibility to correct all this once we are away.

"Girl stood you up. Good life lesson, that is. Don't expect anything from women. Heartache and disappointment, that's about it. More bills than you could ever imagine."

"Maybe she had an accident?" says Sammy. "Or a detention?"

"Don't believe a word she says. Lesson learned."

I walk inside the boat.

Drew will not talk to me about the money side of things but somehow, miraculously, we now have a full tank of diesel and full tanks of propane and water. The toilet cassettes have been emptied. Our pantry is stocked with cans and jars and packets. We have hot water, and we can cook. The lights are back. Coincidentally, all this happened yesterday, exactly two days before my first home visit from a social worker.

I know what I need to do. Pull myself together. Sit down and write another book as quickly as possible. Send it out like before. I need to gather in a little money of my own, no matter how, and then I will move Sammy away from this.

They come inside.

I cook fish sticks and fries. Afterward I stew apples on the gas burner.

"Just because we've got gas doesn't mean you have to use it all up, Peg. Cook on the woodburner next time."

I glance over at his desk. I noticed a pack of expensive paper earlier. Heavy-grade paper with a watermark. The kind of paper you don't need to use for your manuscript but maybe it will help to get you noticed. Now I have fire in my belly again, like I did as a teenager, I'm tempted to remark on the paper.

I bite my tongue.

Not now.

"A kingfisher was out before," I say. "I saw it perch on a rock by the bank."

"Serious?" says Sammy.

I nod.

"Don't listen to her," says Drew.

"It was there for a short while, I swear. Saw it come and go. Beautiful blue it was."

He lowers his voice. "You never saw it."

"I did."

"You *think* you did."

"I saw it."

"We believe you." He nudges Sammy with his elbow. "You think you saw a belted kingfisher near the water. We believe you *think* you saw it. But, you never. It wasn't there, love. If we'd had a kingfisher out in broad daylight near the boat I would have seen it myself, wouldn't I?"

"It was there," I say, defiantly.

"You don't know your own head."

"If I'd had a camera I'd show you proof."

"You might be getting better but there's a ways to go yet, Peggy."

I look at him, gritting my teeth. "I feel fine."

"You *think* you do. We know different, don't we, Samson?"

Sammy squirms on the dinette bench. He doesn't say a word.

I hand them both their stewed apples, the bowls steaming, and Drew pushes his away. "Not eating it."

"Don't then," I say loudly. "Not my problem."

His forearms tense on the table. I see his knuckles turn white: bone pushing out against the thin skin covering his fists. "What did you just say?"

Sammy mutters, "I need the toilet."

"Not my problem," I say again, even louder, urging Sammy to stay seated. I feel an inch taller now. "Eat it or don't."

"Cook it better next time."

"You haven't even tried it."

He breathes in and out slowly through his nose. "Don't need to."

A boat passes by. The windows darken for a moment.

"We're out of money," he says. "Hope you're satisfied."

"Pardon me?"

Sammy leaves the table.

"Your nurse friend is coming by in the morning, right? Forcing us to pay out for propane so you don't get dragged back inside. Hope you're grateful, Peggy."

"I . . . am."

"You don't look it."

"Why are you like this?"

He snarls and says, "Better ask your mother. We were doing fine until she started interfering if you remember right, which you probably don't. That bungalow. Cost of repairs, pest control. Just about ruined us."

"It's her bungalow that gave us this boat and you know it."

He says nothing. He simply fixes his stare and then taps his temple with the tip of his index finger. An unspoken renewal of his threat.

I go and check on Sammy. I find him with his knife out, the knife Drew gave him for Christmas when I was in the hospital. He hides it as I enter. I shake my head desperately. He looks panicked. I whisper, "We're not arguing anymore, Sam. It's OK."

He breathes out like he's been holding his breath this whole time.

When we walk back together to the dinette Drew is sliding his stewed apples into the trash. He turns and says, "I'm writing from eight thirty so I'll need hush from then. Man can't hear himself think around here."

Sammy sits down to eat his apples and says, "OK, Dad."

Rage from my belly. I can't hold it back. "You working on your book or someone else's?"

He pivots and walks toward me slowly, his jaw clenched, his shoulders back. The energy of him, like he is prickling with static. He lifts his chin. I feel his breath touch my lips. "Say that again."

Sammy moves his arm and his bowl drops to the floor and smashes. Splinters of porcelain and raisins and apple sludge all over the floorboards.

Drew exhales through his nose. "Best place for it."

42

SAMSON

Paul Pricklett is allowed out for lunch. I am not. I have to wait until next grade for that liberty. The other boys in my class talk about how they meet up with their girlfriends at the Dairy Queen or the skate park after class. Gunner says his brother will happily drive them around in his Dodge Dakota. He says you can rent the back seat for ten minutes if you give him five bucks. He also says the brother tends to drive erratic because he's watching what's happening in the rearview mirror.

Paul wants to leave so we go out the back way past the principal's office and the janitor's shop. I'm an unlikely maverick, too wild for this small town, too independent of thought. If I want to go out at lunch, I damn well will. A modern-day cowboy in a polyester blazer who rides the bus. Paul walks heavily through the churchyard and I follow. We buy freshly made corn dogs, still warm, and hang around the back of the deli eating them, the grease turning our chins shiny.

"Let's go visit your mom," he says, pointing in the direction of the municipal library. "See if there's a section on erotic fiction."

"Are you nuts?"

"What?"

He has food on his shirt.

"She'll go mental if she catches me out of school."

"She's already mental, bud."

We walk past the post office and run into some girls from the other high school that Paul knows from his bus route. They don't want to talk to us, I can see that from their body language, but I'm impressed Paul had the guts to go approach them.

"Too skinny for me," he says, after they walk away giggling.

"Bullshit."

"Too young, as well."

"What? Paul, they were your age."

"I'm looking out for a more sophisticated lady, I guess. A worldly woman I can go to church with."

"You don't go to church."

"But I would." He coughs. "She could drive us in her car."

I laugh and place my corn dog stick in the trash.

We walk by the aquarium store. Then we backtrack and go inside. It is warm and humid and it smells weird. We peer at the azure-blue tropical fish and Paul tells me how his dad's going to build an aquarium in his new apartment once he gets around to it.

"Goldfish?" I say.

He shakes his head. "Piranhas and stuff."

I start to speak and he says, "Japanese fighting fish. Maybe a shark."

I smile. "You see him much?"

Paul doesn't answer.

We leave.

"You'd think this place would be important," he says.

"The aquarium?"

"No, dumbass. The town. With the railroad, the rivers, the mines. Right at the center of our country. You'd think we'd be important to somebody."

I don't say anything.

He heads toward the church and the pawnshop but I urge him to loop back toward the bakery. He goes on anyway. I walk with him and it is right there in the window. I spotted it last Friday when I passed by. My Walkman. I remember unwrapping the box by the Christmas tree in our bungalow. Now it's for sale at half the original sticker price. I'm surprised it's still there behind the glass. People in this town are fools. They should snap it up. Tape cassette and FM radio with headphones, excellent sound quality. It was close to Mom's necklace last Friday but now the necklace has gone, and I have to bite the inside of my mouth to stop myself from thinking about it. Dumb, I know. It was just a necklace. But it belonged to Nanna Ruth and Mom says I chewed on it as a baby when I was teething.

"What's wrong?" he says.

"Nothing. Walkman, that's all."

A girl bounces past on a pogo stick. She's younger than us. Pigtails. Her pogo stick squeaks with every jump.

"Gotta oil that thing," says Paul.

She flips him off and keeps on hopping.

• • •

After school I visit Phoenix's boat. It snowed briefly while I was on the bus, the children cheering, but it melted away as soon as it touched the dirt.

"Just a minute, Samson."

He goes to his room for five minutes because he says he needs to adjust something. I sit looking out of the window. There's little boat traffic this time of year. The canal feels more like a rural river: bare branches and nests high up in the chestnut trees. There is a silver sheen to the landscape.

He has been writing something. There are pens and envelopes on his dinette table next to his meds.

When I return home I'll have another look for my LEGO pieces.

I've been losing more and more pieces recently. Mom says she saw a LEGO man in the gas locker so I'll check in there.

"I'll just be a few more minutes," says Phoenix, from the other room. He sounds like he's in discomfort.

I flick through a copy of *National Geographic*. It is my favorite magazine; the one I always gravitate to in Smith's.

I still haven't seen Jennifer. I hung around by the strip mall place after school, but she wasn't there. Haven't seen her at the bus station either. There is a rumor she's met a boy, an older boy with a motocross bike and a tattoo on his arm. I just want to know the truth.

After washing three mugs and a small bowl and spoon, I sit close to the fire. This woodstove is larger than ours and it is backed by blue-and-white tiles that Mr. Turner once told me came from a small town in Holland, Europe. Ours is backed with aluminum foil Dad bought from Walmart. The boat smells mustier than it used to. More like ours. Dad's got some kind of plan to install moisture absorbers from Lowe's but I have no idea if they'll work. I will help him do it because I want to help, but also, to be fair, he's made my life a lot easier. I owe him. I'm not even sure how he did it, to be honest. He started looking at me different, I suppose. Talked to me in a new way. That's all it took. And then suddenly I could face the world for the first time ever. School improved. Like night and day. He says he will take me to an aeronautical show in the next town over if I maintain at least a B+ average and my teachers say good things at the parent-teacher conference.

"Sorry, Sam. I'm OK now." He's out of breath. "You hungry?"

"No, I'm fine."

"I should be honest with you. I won't need to visit the hospital anymore, fingers crossed. That part's over with now. I'll be cared for here on the boat from now on. Nice and quiet. That's how I want it. You understand?"

"That's brilliant. No more miserable hospitals. No more mush to eat. You must be pleased."

He smiles flatly and looks out of the window.

"How's your mom and dad doing, Sam?"

"All right. Why?"

He takes a deep breath. "I hear things from my boat, you know. It's not far."

I freeze with the shame of it.

How much does he know?

"It's not what you think, Phoenix."

He rubs the bridge of his nose.

"They're just . . . I don't know. Mom's been ill, you know. It'll get better."

She's livid she can't find any of the floppy disks where she saves her work. Dad says he's never seen them. Doubts she ever had disks on the boat. She tells him she wants to help out more with finances, so we don't get into trouble again. He says she's not exactly qualified for that, especially not after her medical diagnosis. She's showing her anger more than she used to. She's bold. Dad says she'll be back on a psych ward soon if she's not careful.

He says he only needs to make one call.

Says he won't hesitate.

43

PEGGY

I am going to start staying home on Wednesdays. Mrs. Appleby was very understanding when I told her I needed more time to write. I know I must do everything I can to catch up after my deal was ripped apart, to accelerate our exit. I am in a hurry. She said I should work whatever hours suited me. She said I am a valued member of the library volunteer team and not to worry if I needed to cut back for a while.

One small vase of snowdrops.

There is a sprawling glade of white specks over by the abandoned diesel tank, in the shade of the beech trees. I picked these yesterday. A smaller bunch of wood anemones sit in a cracked eggcup.

I hope the boat looks presentable.

She arrives ten minutes late and knocks on the window.

"Peggy?"

I step outside. "Are you from the hospital?"

"I'm Eleanor," she says, smiling, holding out her hand. Under her other arm is a notebook with a pen attached with string. She shows me her ID. "I'm a social worker. Just here for a chat to see how you're doing. Is it OK if I come inside for a while?"

"Of course. Come in, Eleanor."

She has tight, curly hair and thick eyeliner.

"Peggy's right, is it? Or do you prefer Margaret?"

She has a slight Texan accent.

"Peggy, please. Sorry to drag you all the way out here, Eleanor. Probably seems odd us living on a boat."

"No problem. Seems pretty wonderful to me. I parked up on the side of the road, had good directions. Scenic walk down here. You've got a nice place, Peggy. A tranquil place to spend your days."

"Cup of coffee?"

"White, no sugar. Watching my waistline. Overindulged at Christmas. Well, you have to, really, don't you?"

I didn't.

I make her a cup of coffee.

"So, how are you feeling?"

She smells like coconut oil. I like her.

"Good," I say. "Much better, thanks."

"Are you sleeping OK, Peggy?"

"Yes, sleeping fine."

She sips her coffee. "Just what I needed."

I smile and sip my own.

"Any down days? Difficult days?"

"Not really. I'm feeling quite relaxed. We've had some challenging times, but I've managed them fairly well, I think."

"Good. You look well, Peggy."

"So do you."

She smiles at that.

This conversation takes me back to St. Mary's. How many people were there desperate to numb their individual, deep-seated pain. Sad, exhausted, worn-out faces. Normal people like you and me who hit hard times. Women separated from their own children, their own flesh and blood. How does a person ever truly move on from that?

"Sometimes my belongings go missing," I say, and the words take me by surprise. I know I should not talk about things like this. I have to keep these thoughts to myself. They'll put me back in the hospital if I say too much.

"What's gone missing, honey?"

"Oh, nothing. Nothing much."

"Is it cash, or . . . ?"

"Hair things. Scrunchies and clips, hair grips. My toothbrush. ChapStick. Just things."

"Go on."

"Most of my jewelry. Over the years. This thing and that. I'm down to one pair of pearl earrings now. And I don't think they're even real pearls."

She checks around the boat with her eyes.

"Can you show me around, Peggy? I've never been on a boat like this before."

We walk around and I see her checking the pantry and the bathroom.

"Where's your fridge, honey?"

"We had to throw it away." I panic and work hard to recover. "We're getting a new one this weekend, I think."

She nods thoughtfully.

I want to tell her he stole my novel. Impersonated me. Pretended to be Peggy Jenkins and rewrote my own story. Ruined it. I want to scream at her that he says we agreed when we did no such thing. I would never have agreed to that. But then she will think I am insane and I will be committed all over again. *Detached from reality. Strong emotional reactions. A propensity to lie.* I want to tell her how he is a rare form of slow-growing cancer. He moved in and turned malignant. Spread. And he has eroded me year after year. Social Security documents going missing, him taking control of the checking account, him skewing my memories of my own mother. I do not tell her. I want to say how he has somehow managed to get

Sammy on his side. How sometimes they look like a double act and I am left on the periphery and how I worry that may make our escape more complicated.

"How's the medicine? Any new side effects? You feel OK on the tablets?"

"Fine."

I do not tell her I have cut my dose down by half, and how that has made all the difference. I feel like me again. Stronger than ever. Angry and focused. I do not tell her I will cut them out completely soon. A clear head ready to write a new book and earn enough so I can take care of my son someplace safe.

We talk about my fears and concerns, about my time on the ward, about me and Drew, about Sammy, about my cutting back my hours at the library.

"I've applied for a new position," I say.

"Oh, that's fabulous. Tell me more about it."

"It's a paid job."

Part of my strategy. Anything to expedite our freedom.

"At the library?"

"Different one. The big library in the next town. Four days a week. Longer commute on the bus if I get it, which I probably won't, but I thought I'd give it a go."

First pay envelope. Buy two bus tickets. Go someplace far away.

We say our goodbyes and I wait for Drew to come home early from the yard.

"Well?" he says.

"What?"

"Nurse visited you. What did you say?"

"She was a social worker. We just talked about my recovery."

He nods. "You talk about me?"

"No."

"No? What did you talk about, then?"

"Me. Pills and my work."

"Happy pills?"

I nod.

He cleans his fingernails with the tip of his pocketknife.

Rain starts tip-tapping on the roof of the boat.

He lights the fire from a kindling packet he constructed last night.

"How was the yard?"

"Oh, it speaks."

"What?"

"It was the yard. Same as it ever was."

"We talked a lot about money," I say, grinding my teeth.

"Money?"

"Money, bank accounts, savings, retirement, bills."

"You talked about my money?"

"I want to be more involved, Drew. If anything ever happens to you at the yard. I don't know any of our details. I want access."

"Anything ever happens to me?"

"I wouldn't know where to start."

"You're right. You wouldn't."

"Can you write down our account numbers at least?"

I can't help speaking out. Once I start I can't quit. It's like a drug.

He clears his throat. Cracks his knuckles. "I might do that, yeah. But, Peggy..."

"Yes?"

"Don't ever talk about our private life with any mental hospital do-gooder again, right? Tell her you're doing all right and leave it at that. I'll give you account details in due time but don't ever come asking for anything else, understood?"

He seems rattled. He knows I am taking myself back from him, tiny piece by tiny piece.

"OK."

"I'm not looking after of this family, working my fingers to the bone at the scrapyard and dairy, then coming back here to focus on the book, only to have you gossiping about our private business with strangers."

"OK, Drew."

He is weakening.

"I'm always working at one or the other. Remember that. Working with my hands or with my head. No philandering, no going to a dive bar with the guys and getting hammered on payday, none of it. Your job, love, is to make sure I can get on with my book at night. No nagging, no interfering. If you can't do that anymore then what use are you?"

44

SAMSON

I buy my mother a Hershey's bar in Smith's Bookstore and Stationers.

"Is that all?"

"Yes, thanks."

I walk outside. The light is dirty and gray. Subdued. The streetlamps are on and seniors are smoking in huddles to stay warm.

We watched a video on childbirth today in biology. Gunner passed out, much to my astonishment and delight. He had to wait outside in the yard, gulping down fresh air, while the school nurse checked him. Hammer Adams almost threw up. His face lost all its color. The rest of us were fine.

I stand at my bus stop. No fear like before, but I'm still aware of those around me. I keep a lookout for groups of kids.

"Watch out," I say, turning around, after someone nudges me.

Only, it's Jennifer.

She is wearing lip gloss.

I can't help but smile.

"Oh, it's you."

"What are you doing, Samson?"

"Waiting for a bus."

She smiles.

"What's up? You all right?" I ask.

She nods.

Should I ask her?

I have to.

"What happened that day, anyway? In the park, I mean. It's no big deal. Just that—"

"My mom needed me."

"Oh, OK."

"You got gum?"

I push my hands into my pockets, which is ridiculous as I know I have no such thing.

"No."

She looks into one of my eyes, then the other. Back and forth.

"Why?" I ask. "You all right?"

She moves closer. Her breath fills the void between us. I sense people watching. She stands on her toes and her breathing slows. I get a little dizzy. Unsteady on my feet. The crowd around us goes quiet. The whole world falls silent. Blurs. It goes away. Buzzing in my ears.

"You're a fool," she whispers.

She looks down for a split second and then she pushes forward. Her lips meet mine and we stand there. She pushes into me and I put my arm around her, my schoolbag swinging awkwardly from my shoulder. The taste of her. Butterflies in my stomach. She pulls away. Looks at me. And then she kisses me again, harder, and I feel the shape of her body pressing into mine. She softens. Pulls away again.

"Well?" she says.

I smile and then she smiles.

My face is hot. Heart racing.

"Better go catch your bus, Sam Jenkins."

I turn and I can hardly walk, my knees aren't working the way they should. I look back and she purses her lips and turns away.

When my bus sets off the whole bus station is staring at me through the window. A group of girls surround Jennifer and there looks to be a carnival atmosphere out there; everyone asking questions, excited, electric.

My insides are spinning.

She *kissed* me?

Jennifer Adamu kissed me.

Not a peck on the cheek or a quick kiss on the lips. A real kiss. I think I even felt the tip of her tongue brush mine.

People on the bus must have seen what happened but nobody says a word. They are all thinking about it, though, they must be, a monumental thing like that. I can still feel her on my lips. They're tingling. She really kissed me.

Do I have a girlfriend now?

I have no idea.

One old lady with a heavy jacket stands up as we approach the waterworks and as she passes me she looks back for a split second and winks.

I smile so hard I have to look away.

Music in my ears. Symphonies. Crescendos.

When I reach the boat I have transformed into a full-grown man. I've leapt ten years ahead. Shoulders back, chest out. A girl kissed me today, on the lips.

"What are you grinning about?" asks Dad.

"Nothing."

He looks at my head.

"That mop on your head. You want to keep it?"

I run my hand through my hair. "What do you mean?"

"What I say. You want to keep all that hair or you want me to shave it off for you?"

I frown. "Mom'd kill me."

"Let me worry about that."

"She'd kill you, Dad. Both of us."

"The minute you let them boss you around is the minute your life's over, boy. They didn't build the skyscrapers of this world, did they? They didn't discover electricity or steam power. They have their place, but don't let them tell you what's what, Samson. Now, do you want your head done or not?"

She kissed me. Jennifer Adamu actually kissed me.

"What about school?"

"What about it? You get grief from a teacher tell them to come talk to me."

I can still taste her on my lips, on my tongue.

A surge of joy. Waves of it.

"All right then. Let's do it."

"Right."

She kissed me in public.

He takes me into the bathroom and opens the cabinet. His section has nail clippers, a shaving brush, shaving soap in a dish, his razors, Old Spice deodorant, and his toothbrush.

Dad cuts my hair real short with kitchen scissors first. Then he places a hot flannel on my head. He takes his shaving brush.

"Badger, this is. Genuine badger bristles."

He adds water and pushes his brush into the soap. Jennifer Adamu kissed me today, pushed her body into mine. I felt her hip bone. The soap froths. He slathers my head and then starts scraping the razor over my skin.

She kissed me in front of everyone.

"Crown to hairline first. Then against the grain. Get it down to bare skin."

He finishes with another damp flannel, this one cool.

I look at my face in the mirror and smile. "I look like you, Dad."

"Course you do. Scrubbed up like a man now."

He goes off to read *For Whom the Bell Tolls*, and, for the first time in a long time, I feel no compulsion whatsoever to dig my hands in the LEGO box. For kids, that kind of stuff. I sit and relive the kiss over and over in every tiny detail. I rub my palm over my smooth head. I want to see her. Soon. All day, every day. I want her to push herself into my chest again.

"That guy on the next boat. Jeff Turner's nephew," says Dad.

His cousin's son.

"Phoenix?"

"Jeff Turner's relation."

"What about him?"

"He's told you he's not well, has he?"

"Yes, Dad."

"He's explained it all to you?"

"Yeah."

"Well, OK then."

Mom comes home carrying two Safeway bags. She seems exhausted. When she looks up and notices my shaved head her face falls in on itself. She ages. I have never seen her look so desperately sad. She's not angry. I thought she might yell or tell Dad off. But no. She's quiet and she looks aghast. Like she's seen a ghost, or a sinister premonition.

Like her whole world just caved in.

45

PEGGY

I slept terribly.

Last night I laid out my clothes and polished my shoes. I ironed my blouse on the dinette table over a thin towel. Everything was set. Drew worked at his bureau desk with his shirt off, his back to the woodstove, and Sammy read in bed. I was drifting off when Drew came into the bedroom, and he seemed to have more energy than usual. He was agitated. He sat up on the bed and insisted on asking me dozens of mock interview questions for tomorrow, saying if I didn't train I would not be offered a position at the library in the next town. I tried to answer his questions about my experience and my favorite novels, but he found errors, superior alternatives, Pulitzer-winning writers, and then he would correct me and ask me to redo the answers over and over from the beginning. It took hours. There was so much repetition, so many minuscule changes he wanted; I began to doubt my own answers, my own history. I told him politely that I needed sleep, but he maintained I would fail if I didn't practice. Training is key, he said. When I finally stopped answering his questions and turned abruptly toward the nightstand to sleep I thought he would fall quiet. He did pause with the questions, but he tossed and turned for the remainder of the night, annoyed I would not accept more of his unsolicited help. At one point he muttered that if I did not like it on his boat I could stay in a Motel 6. Or at St. Mary's. They would have me back in a heartbeat.

I hardly slept a wink.

Drew has already left for his shift.

Sammy is sitting up in his bed rubbing his eyes.

"I'm starving. Any chance of some toast, Mom?"

I stagger past him, my eyes puffy and small. "Sure."

I open the larder and the cookies have gone. The bread is finished. Some of the cans are missing.

I rub my face. "What's gone on here?"

"What?" he says.

"Food missing. No oatmeal or bread."

"Oh, yeah," says Sammy. "Dad took some things with him earlier. Said he saw a mouse again. Said they weren't safe to eat."

I nod, my teeth biting tight together.

I walk outside to check the cold box we keep on deck. No milk. No juice. An empty box of Hamburger Helper and one can of meat paste he knows makes me queasy.

Bastard.

"Not much food, love," I say to Sammy, stoking the fire. "Your dad took most of it."

"Vermin," says Sammy. "Weil's disease."

"No vermin in the cans or the locked box outside," I say angrily. "Is there?"

"Better safe than sorry, Dad said."

I could scream. I could smash a window. But I swallow down the fury like I have done a hundred times before.

"Can I still have some toast, Mom?"

With his shaved head he looks exactly like the version of Drew I met all those years ago, and that notion almost ends me.

"No bread, Sammy. I'll get food in later after my interview. In the meantime you can have black coffee."

"Don't like coffee."

"You can have a tin of pears in syrup?"

"What?"

"You heard me."

I didn't mean that to sound so severe. I am so tired I can barely hold it together.

"Pears? I don't really care much for pears."

I take two dollars from my purse and place it on his comforter. The money I would have used in the big town today. "Get yourself something extra before school."

"Thanks, Mom."

"I still can't get over you looking this way, Sammy. You're still handsome, but . . . Don't forget your hat, will you? You'll catch your death."

"I won't."

"Bitter out there."

He smiles. "It'll grow back, Mom."

"I know it will, love. In the meantime I hope the principal doesn't send you home."

"He won't. Gunner has his back and sides shaved. Brad Sizemore has a crew cut to impress the recruiters."

"Recruiters?"

"Army guys."

"You looking up to Gunner and Sizemore now, are you?"

"No."

I rub my forehead. "Mind you don't."

I eat a tin of peaches and then Sammy changes his mind and eats his pears, sipping the sweet syrup directly from the can.

"Don't cut your lip."

"Walkman's gone."

"I know it is, love."

"No, I mean it's gone from the store window now. Somebody went in and bought it."

I touch his hand. "I'm sorry, Sam. You've got your birthday coming up in a while. I'll see what I can do."

Sam kisses me on the cheek and leaves. Then he runs back and says, "Good luck in the interview, Mom."

I smile at him.

After I clear away the empty cans I get myself ready. A little blusher to make me look alive. Some mascara, but most of it has dried into a hard paste inside the bottle. I cannot find one of my shoes. I look everywhere for it. I have to settle for my other, scruffier pair, the unpolished ones with the loose soles that flap as I walk.

Waiting for the bus my teeth start to chatter but I am hopeful. If the wind blows twice as fast and snowflakes start to fall from above I will still not give up. Because I am heading toward something new, something of promise. Instead of going north to the town I am taking the bus south. Fifty-five minutes. Going the other way to see what might happen.

The bus is empty save for a half dozen senior citizens and a young Asian couple with three toddlers. They've got their hands full all right. We drive past the chemical plant. Brick chimneys and factories: some old, some modern. A food processing plant pumping out steam into bleached skies. An old man uses an inhaler and then closes the window, but it is too late. The bus now reeks of whatever root vegetables the plant is frying.

Drew cannot handle the fact that I have an interview. That someone, or perhaps a panel of people, wishes to ask me questions and find out who I really am. He has never been good with things like that.

My stomach rumbles.

When we reach the main bus terminal I help one of my fellow passengers off and then I walk to the library. It is well signposted, unlike my old one. A solid brick building with small windows. I have a spring in my step. They want to see me, after all. They invited me.

I am early so I hang outside. Two men clean car windshields at the lights with a bucket and squeegee each, and a sign. A loose dog runs down the street and a man perches on a curb, smoking a roll-up, talking to himself, a folded newspaper down by his boots.

I will tell them about my experience in our town library. Using the computer, organizing shelves, helping readers. Mrs. Appleby will give me a reference or a letter of recommendation, I know she will. I can rely on Mrs. Appleby. She has never once let me down.

Hopefully Sammy bought himself a sandwich or a milk. He looks more vulnerable than ever without his lovely hair. Like a prisoner of war lost in a forgotten town, his oversize jacket still hanging off his shoulders, his shoes too long for him.

I open the doors of the unfamiliar library.

Three minutes early. I think that is acceptable, isn't it? I have not done this before. But I sense that even though my book contract is dead and buried, this place might still save Sammy and me in time, it just might. Such is the power of libraries.

"Good morning. Peggy Jenkins for the interview, please."

Her hair is up in a bun and she has probing gray eyes framed with large black glasses.

"Thank you. Just give me a second."

She picks up a clipboard with a list of names on it.

Her eye shadow is mauve but it is subtle.

I straighten my blouse.

She looks at the clipboard then looks up at me then checks again.

I smile my most professional smile.

"I'm sorry, Mrs. Jenkins. I don't have your name down on the list."

"Ten fifteen," I say, clearly. "Quarter past. With Mr. Karim."

"Just a moment."

I wonder if they pay weekly or monthly. That might not be relevant to most people but it is relevant to me right now.

She walks away to speak to someone else in a cubicle.

The library is cavernous. It even has a garden with tables. I can see myself working here, helping people find the books they need, monitoring the photocopying and faxing, the use of the computers. Passwords and paper jams. Lunch in the cafeteria, if there is one. I look forward to giving out library cards to kids. Watching them from afar as they grow up reading Judy Blume and Sue Townsend, Maya Angelou and Stephen King. Helping them find their favorite authors, and their own voices.

Using the wages to flee. A Greyhound ticket, a few nights in a motel, some food to keep us alive.

"Mrs. Jenkins?" She walks toward me.

"Yes."

I smile. Hold myself properly. Shoulders back.

"It's just that, I'm sorry but there's some confusion. You see, earlier this morning we received a telephone call."

"Yes?" My voice is small.

"It's just that, I think maybe there's been a misunderstanding. Your brother called, Mrs. Jenkins. Said you'd accepted another position out of town and asked for your name to be removed from consideration."

The air leaves my lungs.

"Are you OK, Mrs. Jenkins?"

He hasn't.

I can't catch my breath.

She looks at me, her eyes wide behind her glasses.

"Are you all right? You need a glass of water or something?"

She stares at a dumb fool who turned up to an interview that was never meant to be.

I know I should protest and request another slot and claim there was some kind of administrative error but instead I deflate and whisper, "I'm so sorry," and then I leave.

46

SAMSON

When I return home from school she is searching in the gas locker with a flashlight.

"You all right, Mom? What are you doing down there?"

"Have you seen my black shoe, Sammy? Have you seen my shoe?"

She shouldn't say these things. They'll take her away again and I can't have that. Never again.

"I don't think it'll be in the gas locker, Mom."

I lean down and take her by the arm.

"What are you doing?"

Her hair is falling over her face.

"Come inside for a cup of coffee, Mom. I'll make it. Talk with me. Ask me questions about class and football like you used to. About my grades."

She looks suspicious. Her eye is twitching again.

I boil water on the stove until it whistles.

She looks confused.

"Are you feeling all right, Mom? How was the interview?"

She scratches her temple. "Fine, love. It was OK, the usual questions, you know. They said they'll let me know. They have my résumé. Fingers crossed."

"You'll be awesome. I'll come visit you."

"You don't need to come all the way to the big town," she says, taking a mug of coffee from me. "It's a long way, Sammy. Almost an hour on the bus."

"When I've got money, I'll come and take you out for a pizza or ice cream. We can find you some new shoes, maybe."

"You got another paper route, Sam?"

"No. Not yet."

I can't help smiling.

"What are you smirking at?"

"Dad's taking me up to the yard tomorrow. A real job. Just Saturdays to begin with, and the foreman says I'll have to do probation, but it's decent money. Almost what Dad earns."

Mom looks unsteady. She frowns and stares at me and then she takes a sip of coffee and says, "Very good. That's what you want, is it?"

"Just Saturdays for now."

"You'll still have time for your assignments? Studying for your tests? You've got a good life ahead of you, Sammy, a real future someplace. You know that, don't you?"

"One day a week, Mom. That's all it is."

"You can go anyplace in the world if you study hard. Remember that."

"I know."

She nods and mutters something under her breath. "My baby boy."

"Don't call me that."

She sniffs. "Sammy, love?"

"Yeah?"

"How would you feel about, I don't know, maybe me and you going away for a while? Not far, just having a short break?"

"What do you mean?"

"You know, like we talked about before. Me and you going someplace different. Life's been hard on you recently with me going into St. Mary's and Mr. Turner passing."

"And Amber."

"Of course. Amber, as well. I'm sorry."

"I know you are."

"Maybe we could get away, the two of us. Bit of an adventure, nothing too exotic, but some hiking perhaps, see a different town, a national park, or look at other high schools, maybe."

"Other *high schools*?"

"Just looking. We can put our money together. Go on a trip."

What is she talking about? Has she stopped taking her medication?

"I don't know what you mean, Mom."

She takes a deep breath and another gulp of coffee. "Don't worry. Just me and you. Some special time, you know."

"I'm not moving anyplace else."

She coughs. Puts her hand flat against her chest.

"Wrong hole," she says, covering her mouth with her other hand. "Coffee went down the wrong hole."

I pat her shoulder. She's lost weight. "Are you OK, Mom?"

She nods.

"Because school's going real well for me now. You always wanted that and now it's happening. They don't screw with me. No gum in my hair or wet clothes. Nothing like before. I'm making proper friends. I fit in now. I'm getting normal."

"You've always been normal."

"You know what I mean. I'm happier. And I've got . . ."

"What?"

"Nothing."

"Come on."

"It's just . . . there's this girl."

She smiles. Her eyes twinkle. "A girl, really? Tell me more."

I smile too. Can't stop. "It's nothing."

"Does this girl have a name?"

"No, she doesn't."

"Come on."

"Please. It's no big deal."

She raises her eyebrows.

"Jennifer."

"Lovely name. Classic. Pretty."

"Mom, please. Don't."

"You're dating?"

"Please." I sense my cheeks redden. "We're just seeing each other sometimes. That's all. I like her."

"I'm happy for you. She's the lucky one if you ask me."

She places her hand down on mine.

"I know you're angry about Dad shaving my head. I should have checked with you first."

"It's not that."

"We didn't plan it out or anything. We weren't scheming behind your back."

"Sammy, love. It's just. Your father isn't always the man you think he is."

I pull back a fraction. "What do you mean?"

"Your dad is . . ." She sighs. "I know you love him. But he can be, I don't know how to say it, he's not always . . . safe, Sammy."

"He's a real man, Mom. That's all. Real men can't always be safe."

"I worry," she says, raising her eyebrows.

"You don't need to worry," I say, smiling, kissing her on the cheek.

When Dad gets home with groceries, they hardly say a word to each other the rest of the night. She looks everywhere for her missing shoe. The next day Dad hands me a brown paper bag after breakfast.

"What's inside?" I ask.

"Open it and find out."

Inside is a black T-shirt. Adidas. New.

"For me?"

"Who else?"

"Thanks, Dad."

I put it on and we walk to work together. It takes forty minutes from where we're moored up. The air is cool and the sunlight comes and goes as brilliant white clouds scroll across the sky. We don't talk much.

"Temporary job. Construction site's got problems. They're running late on plot three. Struggle to get good men in. Keep your head down, do what you're told, and don't hurt yourself, all right?"

I work eight hours. One break in the morning. The other men drink coffee and all but two smoke cigarettes. At lunch they sit in the break shack eating and reading newspapers. The air is filled with smoke and hard, wrinkled faces and laughter. Rough hands. They ask me if I've got a girlfriend and if I have naked photos of her. One electrician tries to tip me off the bench but a big scaffolder called Shaun looks at him and he stops.

Walking home, the light fading, I have never been more tired in my life. I wore gloves all day but you wouldn't know it to look at my fingers. My back aches and my legs ache. I've dug holes and moved pea gravel and sand in barrows. I helped clean out garbage from a half-built condo.

When we reach the towpath Dad stops me. He licks the tip of his finger and pulls out his leather billfold from his back pocket. He peels off four ten-dollar bills and hands them over to me.

"I'm not taking a cent of this, Samson. That's yours. Don't give it to me or your mother. Cash in hand, best way. You've worked a man's day, so you earn a man's wage."

I look at the money. The four bills.

"For real?"

He nods. "Honest money. *Real* money. How does it feel?"

"Magic."

"That's all yours. You can do with it what you want. Buy whatever you like."

We set off walking again. I can see our boat in the distance, the silhouette of Mom in the kitchen window, smoke rising vertically from the metal chimney.

Life's turning around.

It's turning sweet.

47

PEGGY

There wasn't a single moment of blinding realization. More of a building of momentum: a snowball gaining speed. Perhaps Mary-Elizabeth gave that snowball the first push. I should thank her. Then the fog from the medication lifted and I was left with brutal, unforgiving clarity.

Every time I have the boat to myself, I search. For my missing shoe, for my rings, my hair clips, my birth certificate. Documents that might trace where the money has gone over the years. I look frantically for answers, and for cash. How much of this is down to me and how much is down to him? It is partly my fault. I should have protested earlier. I am partially responsible. But he pretended to be my brother and canceled the interview. I know he did. How else could that have happened? And yet we have not spoken of it. For a decade and a half I have lived, existed, in the shadow of a vague and largely unspoken threat. A dark cloud that hangs heavy over every decision I make. And now he and Sammy are so close it breaks my heart. It is all I have ever wanted and now that it has finally happened I feel adrift, and sick with worry.

I remove the boards covering our diesel motor and probe the

darkness below. I look at the weed hatch to see if anything has been hidden close to the propeller shaft. In the bedroom I lift the mattress and check behind the hot water tank. Nothing. I take out every can and packet from the larder and all I find is fresh mice droppings. After scrubbing with Clorox I continue my search. Manically. If someone from St. Mary's saw me through the window they would drag me back. Thorough strip search to note down every single scar on my body. They would count each one. An accurate catalog to use as a yardstick for the future. They'd weigh me and then not tell me the number. I would chat with the mental health team and they would not be at all shocked at my return. That would be the most heartbreaking thing. Me arriving back would be perfectly normal. Expected, even.

There would be sadness in Fatima's eyes that I did not make it.

Instead of resting or eating or drinking, I search. What has he done to me over these years? My adult life has been shaped by his actions and needs. So many specific needs to ensure *he* can reach *his* writing potential. Detailed instructions and limits. There is nothing of mine in the gas locker or in the area where we keep the hooks and tiller. Nothing of mine in the battery housing. I open up Sammy's dinette bed and find the life preserver vests, each one scarred with mildew spots. I take them out. Musty. I shake them frantically, but nothing.

I need to adjust my plan.

I don't want to ask Mrs. Appleby for a loan but I might have no choice.

In the bathroom I search the cupboard under the sink. The usual toiletries. Cotton balls and empty Tylenol packs. Drew's nail clippers, a well-used shaving brush, shaving soap in a dish, his razors, Old Spice deodorant. Then I notice the floorboard underneath. A small circle cut out of one corner. I poke my finger through and lift the plywood. A water pump for the shower. Perfectly normal. And, underneath that, a plastic Tupperware box full of screws and bolts, and an Old Holborn tobacco tin. A crow caws outside on the canal bank. I take the small yellow-rimmed tin in both hands. It is cold to the touch. I open the metal lid and inside I find every piece of jewelry I have ever owned.

I search through the items, at once delighted and disgusted. Mom's necklace is not here. I hold a pair of earrings, also from Mom, and the silver necklace I inherited from her aunt. Seven rings, all of them sterling silver, three of them from him. Another necklace with a pendant. Why is all of this under the sink? I open the pendant. It once had a miniature photograph of Mom and a miniature photograph of her beloved aunt Dorothy. Not anymore. Both photographs are gone.

I stand but I sway, unsteady. I replace the tobacco box and place the boards back, my heart pounding. What do I do now? If I talk to the sheriff he'll send me back to St. Mary's, surely. I would sound completely insane. How do I find the exit to this maze?

Just find one and take it.

The boat sways.

Someone is here.

I close the door and dash out into the kitchen. Another boat passes us by. The man at the tiller waves and I look down.

They will be home soon.

The clock ticks on the wall and a rage builds in layers deep inside my chest. How dare he take my things. How dare he. I stamp over to his desk. Locked bureau with locked drawers. His trophy. A stack of Hemingway novels read and reread. I try each drawer in turn. All secure. There might be money in here. If I smash the bureau and destroy his locks I know it will be the end. One way or the other, there will be no going back from that action. Not with Drew's desk, his papers, his sacred work.

The clock ticks.

Raindrops against loose windowpanes.

I keep watch for them.

ADRIFT

The clock sounds louder than before, matching my own heart.

I will ask Mrs. Appleby. I'll pay her back as quickly as I can, she knows I would.

Three of the padlocks have revolving number codes and the rest use keys. I try the numbered ones. His birthday, my birthday, Sammy's. The date of our marriage. Nothing. They remain intact. Hemingway's birthday. It does not work. I reach up and take one of the Hemingway biographies, a book Drew has read at least a dozen times. I flick to the end. To the timeline. The date of Ernest Hemingway's death. Two locks fail. Then, *click*. The third lock snaps open and I smile but I am also disturbed. The day Hemingway *died*. I recall *how* he died: that image. I pull the drawer. It is tight. Wood scraping against wood. Early drafts of a novel. Paper turning yellow. Beautiful prose, as always. Achingly beautiful. Clean and direct. Taut. But this is all about him. His head. There is nothing of me in here. None of my possessions. I am violating his privacy.

I lock it up again and try the other numbered padlocks.

The clock ticks on the wall and I fail to open the locks. Does one of these drawers contain my birth certificate? My missing shoe? I sound insane even to myself. I try the date we moved into the bungalow. The date his parents died. *Click.* A lock loosens in my hand and the door creaks open. He uses death days for his locks. Notebooks and drafts of query letters submitted to literary agents, some in New York, some dating back more than a decade. A stack of rejection letters filed in date order. He's been close to signing a few times, but he complained they wanted compromises, or had editorial feedback, or wished to discuss tweaks. Each letter has the word "Incorrect" written on it over and over again in neat red ink.

Incorrect.

I try the next numbered lock. He wouldn't? I try my own mother's death date. The lock opens abruptly and I stand staring at it. How dare he use that date. The drawer is empty save for a dozen or so Staedtler pencils all sharpened down to nubs, and one Moleskine notebook. There are sketches inside. Heartbreaking poems. A sheet of paper falls out. It has a watermark, the expensive paper he uses for his finished work, to send off to esteemed publishers in Los Angeles and New York. I pick it up and immediately recognize his handwriting.

Eulogy.

I look around me, furtive, on guard.
Eulogy?

It is with an overwhelming sense of sadness that we gather together here today. But out of that sadness, there is a chance we can each find beauty and fresh light. I ask that we embrace forgiveness, understanding, and, perhaps most of all, hope.

My pulse is racing, and my chest rises and falls with each panicked breath. He wrote this for my mother's funeral? He never read out a eulogy. *I* read a eulogy. A poem written in the 1950s. A poem I found in the library.

I read on.

We may never understand all the reasons. We may never grasp her true pain. But I believe, in all honesty, she would have wanted us to celebrate her joy rather than dwell on her battles.

I freeze.

Margaret was a wonderful wife and mother.

ADRIFT

My arms turn to lead and I cannot take a breath. What is this? Why would he write such a thing?

We will never forget her humor and her kindness. Margaret, Peggy, Mom, will live on through us forevermore.

I am ice cold.

I ask that we all learn to live with the choice that she made. We will never understand it, leaving behind a child, but we must respect it as we respected her.

The choice that she made?
My mouth is wide open.
The choice?

She endured her struggles. Many of these will be familiar to you, but some she kept to herself. I can say now, from the heart, that she is released. She was a fine woman and now, at last, she suffers no pain.

48

SAMSON

I walk to the park.

    She'll show up this time.

The air feels warm against my skin. We're turning the corner into a brand-new season. There are droves of bright daffodils uplighting trees, and a wood pigeon coos peacefully in the near distance.

I'm on time.

She's not here.

There are other kids drinking from large plastic bottles. One group wrestling on the short grass, forcing one another to concede defeat.

She's not here yet.

I'm wearing Dad's beanie hat. Mom insisted.

The confidence drains from me like water through a sieve.

But, she kissed me.

A dog barks by the old bandstand.

The smell of weed in the air.

She walks toward me. I see her smile and my heart doubles in size. Triples. She glides rather than walks. Hovers, really. The way her shoulders move. Her backpack low and loose. She heads straight to me.

I try to act relaxed like it is totally normal for a girl like Jennifer Adamu to walk toward someone like me, looking at me, gazing at me, ignoring all the other boys in the park, all the commotion. Straight to me.

A cruiser drives past with its sirens blaring and she keeps walking toward me.

I'm cold and hot. Nervous and strangely calm.

"Nice hat," she says.

"It's my dad's."

"Figures."

"How was your day?"

Every time our eyes meet there is a flash of light, of heat.

"Average," she says. "Medium, I guess."

My day is far from medium. As far as it is possible to be. The polar opposite of all things medium.

"Same," I say.

She smiles.

"What?" I say.

"I missed you."

I try to act relaxed. I aim for nonchalance and experience. I fail. A partial shrug.

"Come," she says.

We close the gap between us and she cups my face with her hands. Orange nail polish flashes in my peripheral vision. Can she feel I haven't started shaving yet? She doesn't seem to notice. She moves closer and I place my hands on her hips and this moment is sublime. She lets me keep my hands there. The shape of her under her clothes. A wolf whistle in the distance. For us? My smile opens up even broader than before. She closes her eyes, gradually. Time slows. Stops. Ceases to exist at all. I move my face to hers and I cannot believe I am permitted to do this. She likes me. How did this happen? I am with her, truly with her. I push my lips close to hers, softly, gently, and there is a small electric shock as we connect.

"Feel that?" she whispers.

I kiss her properly and she wraps her arms around my neck. I hold her tight. The taste of her. Familiar yet unfamiliar. Soft. I grow into myself. Time passes in irregular waves. A minute or an hour. No consequence. People come and go around us and all of my focus, every unit of my attention, is concentrated on Jennifer. The only person in the world. She kisses my cheek. Three kisses on each and then she looks at me and tilts her head and she kisses my lips again. Her eyes are clear and her chest is pressed into mine. We're both wearing winter jackets, but I know her body now. I know it better than my own. We stay locked together for a long time.

She suggests we go sit on a bench.

"This one OK?" I ask.

She laughs and sits on my lap. It is not very comfortable, but I never want her to leave. I make every effort for her to think that girls often sit on my lap sideways like this, it's something I have grown accustomed to, I hardly even notice it.

"Does it hurt?" she asks.

"I can hardly feel you."

I can feel her. The exquisite weight of her pushing down into me. There are many others in this park and I could not be more proud to have Jennifer Adamu on my knee. The two of us, here, crushed together. Undeniable.

She tells me about how she thinks she wants to do a liberal arts prelaw major but she also likes painting and drawing. How can she know all this stuff already? She says her parents are divorced but it all happened when she was a baby and they still get on well. They even celebrate Thanksgiving together. She tells me she has a cat named Percy and he only trusts her mom.

"I want to know your thoughts," she says, rubbing my collar between her finger and thumb.

"What?"

"What you're thinking. Your dreams. You know, the things you want."

I cough. "I don't know yet, really."

"You do know."

"My thoughts?"

"Who you are on the inside."

She doesn't want to know. I cannot tell her. I can hardly tell myself.

"When I'm older I want to live someplace else," I say. "A city. Austin or Denver. London, maybe. Somewhere with nightclubs that stay open until the next morning, until breakfast. Where I can go to see a rock band one night and a ballet the next."

"Ballet?" she says. "You serious?"

"Or another rock band. Whatever. Just, you know, things happening. All sorts of people mixed together speaking different languages and stuff. Lots of people everywhere so nobody ever knows who you are, what your business is."

"What is your business, Samson?"

"Me? You're asking real scary questions, you know that?"

She smiles. "I just like you, is all. I want to know about you."

"You do know about me. You know my school, my name, my age, the fact I live on a long British boat."

"I want to know it all. See it all."

I look at her.

She kisses me and we squeeze tight together on the bench. A knot. Another glance of her tongue. I melt into her. Dizzy.

"I like you too," I say.

"I know."

"What do you mean?"

We kiss again and I run my fingertip across her upper lip. It has a shape. A perfect bow. A ridgeline.

"What happens now?"

"You walk me to the bus is what happens now. Come on."

It takes us decades to walk there. Minutes, maybe. Entire centuries. We stop in alleyways to kiss. She smells like all of the best things that might ever happen to me. All the sweetest possibilities. We talk about music and the time she went to Florida with her grandpa and mom. I pull her into a private doorway. We kiss in an instant photo booth and she pinches my butt outside Smith's. A whole lifetime of joy in one evening. She catches her bus and I watch her face through the window.

Mom's already at our bus stop when I arrive.

"Am I late?" I ask, glowing, floating just above the pavement.

"No, Sam. I just got here. You all right?"

I cannot stop my smile from breaking free.

"What's with you?"

"Nothing."

She's got a Greyhound timetable in her hands.

She puts it into her bag.

We climb aboard the bus and it is completely empty except for the driver and an old man in an Army jacket right at the front. He's chewing tobacco. We walk to the back. This is where the older kids usually hang out. Mom and I spread out like we're limousine passengers in a movie.

She starts to scratch her wrists and her forehead.

"What are you worried about, Mom?"

"What?"

"You're scratching. I know you're troubled about something. What is it?"

She holds my hand and smiles an unsteady smile.

"You know in the past we've talked about leaving one day."

This again.

"Leaving town?"

"Going away for a while. To the city or somewhere."

"So?"

"I think it might be time quite soon. You and me. Some nice mother-son time, you know?"

ADRIFT

Not yet.

Not now I have Jennifer.

"With Dad?"

"Just you and me for a time, I thought."

I remove my hand. "I think we should give Dad the option, Mom. He doesn't do well on his own, even for a weekend. I saw how he lives. He gets too obsessed with his work. Doesn't look after himself properly. He forgets to eat, even. Goes kind of feral. We could do a day trip?"

She smiles but her eyes are so impossibly sad I cannot hold her gaze.

"Yeah." Her voice is hoarse. "A day trip might work."

"When I'm older we could do it, though."

"What would you think if we found a little apartment someplace, you and me?"

"Where? I'm confused, Mom. What do you mean? You and Dad haven't had another fight, have you?"

The bell rings and the old man steps off the bus and we're left completely alone.

"It's just an idea, love."

I remove my beanie. "Thing is, I'm kind of, you know, with Jennifer now. School's better and I need to maintain my grade average. I think I can go away with you for a trip after all that's done with."

"Right."

"You look worried, Mom."

"I'm just tired. Sammy?"

"Yeah."

"When you work with your father. Train with him. Does he ever talk about what happened to his mom and dad?"

"Grandma and Grandpa?"

She nods.

"Why, what happened?"

"Nothing. I shouldn't have brought it up."

"Dad says if you start talking in riddles, saying weird things, accusing other people, bringing up things that happened years ago, saying you're in danger, we're to call the hospital right away."

She sits bolt upright. "Don't do that, Samson. All right. Listen to me, it's very important. Do not call them. Never call them."

"He told me you'd say that. Those exact words."

She holds both my hands now, holds them too tight. "You trust me, don't you?"

I nod. "Of course I do. You're hurting my hands, Mom."

She lets go.

"Forget I said anything, all right?" She's breathing fast. "I'm happy you've found a nice girl, Sammy." She smiles. "You deserve that happiness. Look after her well. Be nice to her."

I move my hand over my smooth scalp. "I will."

An acute pain, suddenly, deep inside my belly.

Maybe this is a warning, or a punishment.

For hiding her jewelry.

49

PEGGY

Snow floats gently from a featureless sky.

Flakes settle on the dinette windows, join together, obscure the empty landscape.

"You're back early, Peg," he says, stepping onto the boat. "Snowing out there. Like Alaska."

How would you know?

"I need to talk to you, Drew."

"Talk to me?"

"We need to talk, Andrew."

"Full day working out in this weather, trudging home through slush, and I come home to: *We need to talk, Andrew.* How about a coffee?"

I do not put the water on.

"Have it your way," he says, pulling off his jacket and his hat. "Have out with it, I haven't got all day."

Instead of slinking away I will confront this head-on. If I don't he'll just track us down and I can't put Sammy through that. I won't.

"Sit down, Drew. Please."

He frowns and keeps standing.

I stay seated on the dinette cushion and he moves directly in front of me, staring, his gaze boring down into me.

"All right, then," I say. "I've been thinking."

"Look out. She's been thinking."

"This is nothing spontaneous, you understand. I've been thinking on it for a while now."

He clenches his teeth.

"It would be best for us all if we go away for a while."

"Best for us all?"

"Just for a while."

He smiles. "Go away?"

"It's not working out, Drew."

"What isn't?"

I bite my lip. "I'm going to leave."

"Course you are, princess."

"I mean it."

"Oh, she means it."

"Please."

"You want me to call the hospital? I've got a doctor's direct number in my desk. I can call her up, have you looked at. You want that? Little break to get your head straight again. Might work this time. Longer stay. Might fix your hysteria, your emotions."

He says *emotions* with venom, spitting out the word.

"I need to go. Sammy and I need to go."

"Not likely."

My heart races.

"We're going to go, Drew."

"Incorrect."

"Drew."

"Not even a cup of coffee after a day like I've had. Not even a hot drink to come home to. My mother would turn in her grave."

"I don't want any shouting. Sammy'll be back from Phoenix's

boat soon. Fixing something on the roof. I don't want him to hear us argue."

"There's nothing to argue about."

"As long as you understand."

"No, as long as *you* understand."

"It hasn't been good for a long time."

"It is what it is, Peg. Fifteen years. You two aren't going anywhere, mark my words."

"He's thinking ahead to his SATs, college maybe."

"Samson? Samson Jenkins, that who you're talking about? He thinks you're deranged, Peggy. His own mother, incompetent, should be institutionalized. He thinks you're a lunatic, love. Knows it, in fact. The boy and I work well together these days. He's not going anywhere."

"I think . . ."

He raises his index finger, silencing me. "It's not about what you *think*, Peggy, love, we've been over this before. It never has been about what you think in that skull of yours. It's about what is. And what is, is the three of us getting on with it without all this nagging. All right?"

I shake my head.

He raises his finger again. Lowers his voice. "Not another word."

I pull out the eulogy from under a cushion.

He stares at it. Blinks.

"I found this."

He squints. "You found it."

"Yeah."

"You've been looking through my papers? What was going through your head, woman? Private papers, locked up. My work. What were you thinking?"

"I was thinking I might take this to the sheriff."

He looks agitated. Moving on the spot. Biting the inside of his mouth. "St. Mary's. Electric therapy, I expect. He'll put you back in

St. Mary's before he's finished reading the first paragraph. Where you belong."

I shake my head. Try to stay calm.

"What did you have planned for me? I'm curious. An accident, was it? Like Mr. Turner's tragic fall into the canal? Like Amber eating poison? How many more of these accidents before you get taken in?"

"Planned, for you? I wouldn't waste the paper, love. Not worth it."

"Samson and I are leaving tonight."

He smiles and scratches his lower eyelid. "Again, incorrect."

"I'm not arguing."

"I'm not arguing neither. Nobody's going. What's for supper?"

The snow intensifies. Pristine beauty outside these rotting walls.

"You can make your own."

He nods six or seven times and says nothing. Keeps on nodding.

"You want to finish up like your mother?" he says, finally, quietly. "Ending it alone with nobody to talk to, nobody liking you. Alone in the world. You want to end up like your mom?"

"You made her that way."

"You're delusional. Mental age of a minor."

I take a deep breath. "I don't want Sammy seeing this. I'll make us some hot food; he'll be chilled to the bone. I'll make supper and then we'll go quietly. I've done most of the packing. You can't stop us, Drew."

He snorts. "I can't?"

I close my eyes for a few seconds.

When I reopen them he seems to have grown in stature. His torso widens and his jaw swells.

I smile.

This is almost over.

"Don't you smile at me like that. Wipe that grin off your face. Wipe it off or . . ."

I stop smiling.

"We're going, Drew. I'm not frightened anymore. Just exhausted. We're leaving."

He nods to himself over and over.

"You wrote a eulogy, for God's sake."

Now he's the one who smiles.

"How could you?"

"It's an epilogue," he says, quietly. "Get it right."

"What?"

"Read it again, Peg. Take your time with it and engage your brain. It is an *epilogue*. Means the end part of a novel."

"I know what it means. But this says *eulogy*."

"Read it again, Peggy. Carefully. Take your time with it."

His handwriting is sprawling, almost illegible. I suppose it could say *Epilogue*. I don't think it does, but it could say it.

"You sure?"

"Am I sure?" he says, softening, pointing to it. "That's creative writing, that is. My own work. That's the end of a story I wrote a while back. Prose. Fiction, Peggy. Nothing to do with you. Nothing to do with any of us."

I can feel the chill from the windowpane.

"It has my name in it."

He nods. "I often use your name, or mine, or Samson's, as a placeholder. Don't read more into it. That's fiction."

"We're still leaving, Drew. Either way."

"Listen." He sits down gently on the dinette bench. His facial features loosen. "Listen, Peggy, love. You've been through a tough year, tougher than I can imagine, really. The things you've seen in that hospital. Well, it'd change a person, wouldn't it? Any person. And I know adapting to life on the canal has had its ups and downs. I understand that. Maybe I should have been more understanding. My failure, that, not yours. I should have listened to you."

I let out a breath. "You should."

"But that's not a eulogy. What a terrible thought. I don't even know what you mean by it. That's a story, the end of one, not my best work but you can read the rest if you don't believe me. I'll get around to draft two eventually. It's the end of a story."

I am exhausted.

So many blind turns.

"OK."

"You want to read the whole thing?"

"No."

He closes his eyes for a long time.

"Our boy will be home soon, Peggy. Our boy. You remember the way he'd try to push himself up as a newborn in the maternity ward, after his health cleared up, trying to do a little push-up, and again when we got home to the bungalow. Little tyke. Used to try to push himself up on his arms at a few days old. You remember, Peg?"

I don't trust him. "Yeah."

"Little guy thought he was superman. Still does some days."

"We need some time away, Drew. I'm sorry. Maybe not for long, but I need to get my head straight."

He takes a deep breath in through his nose.

"I understand."

"You do?"

"I haven't made it as easy for you as I should have."

We look at each other.

"Remember the old days, Peg?"

I dig my thumbnail into the soft flesh of my index finger. "We're leaving tomorrow, Drew. We'll write you."

"You'll write? To me?"

"We will."

"Give me another chance, Peggy."

He never talks this way.

The ground is shifting.

He rubs his hands over his smooth head.

"One last chance, then." His voice cracks, weakens. "Is that too much to ask after fifteen years of marriage? The vows, the hardship we've struggled through together, the son we made. I don't want you to throw it all away on a whim, Peggy. And I know you'll say you're thinking clear but are you still taking the tablets?"

I nod.

I'm not taking anything.

"Well, there you go then. Who knows what you'd be thinking without all the chemicals. Peggy, love, for the sake of our boy, for little Sammy's sake, give it one last chance. Don't tell him you're going yet. Don't leave tomorrow. Give me one more day. One day is all I ask for, so I can make an effort. Everyone deserves a second chance, wouldn't you say?"

"We need to go."

His eyes are shining.

He furrows his brow. "You *can* go. Look, if I haven't changed the mood, my manner, the boat, our way of life, by tomorrow night, I'll help you both pack and I won't come looking for you. Can't say fairer than that. I've been thinking about it, too, you know. How we can make home life a little more comfortable. I was the one who wanted to speak to the shrink at the health center. Remember that, Peg?" He looks so desperate. "Maybe I'll change my writing routine to weekends. So we can have more family time in the evenings. And now the boy's working we can go out for Chinese buffet every now and then at the place by the Dollar General. I'll cut back on my paper, on my stamps. Maybe take a trip once a month to the movie theater."

I rub my eyes with my fingertips and take a deep breath.

I am so tired.

Worn down.

"Sleep on it, Peg. I don't want to push you into a decision. Take your time. Sleep on it. I'll tell you what. I'll make supper for us. Spam and eggs, and you take it easy. Be a shame to mess up the boy's education when he's almost done. You can decide tomorrow after your shift at the library. Yes?"

I can see Sammy outside the boat.

He draws a smiley face in the snow on the window with his gloved fingertip. Encloses it within a triangle sign.

"Yes?" Drew asks again.

I still need to persuade Sammy and pack his belongings.

"Fine," I say, drained. "One more day."

50

SAMSON

I start work on my geography assignment and Mom takes a quick shower. I can hear the water hit the linoleum-clad wall behind my head. Less than an inch separating us.

Snow outside.

Dad stands at the gas burner frying Spam slices in the pan. The eggs are spitting.

Cloud types: stratus, cirrus, and cumulus. Half a dozen others.

Then: English lit. *Macbeth*.

Spanish. Verbs.

The boat smells safe. Toasted bread. Every time I read a word in a textbook that begins with a "J" I dream of Jennifer.

I miss her.

After I clear away my textbooks we sit down together at the dinette. Dad places our plates, the good ones, the three without chips or cracks. Three glasses of water. Steam rises from my plate, hitting the arched ceiling. Forks. He hands out knives as well. Something he never does. When he brings over a bottle of Worcestershire sauce Mom looks up at him.

"You still like it, don't you? On eggs?"

"I didn't know we had any," she says.

He places the bottle down gently next to her hand.

I wonder if Jennifer likes Worcestershire sauce.

Perfectly cooked eggs with plenty of salt and pepper. Toast with just the right amount of butter. Sweet coffee. The familiar sounds of a small family eating together.

"I saw Phoenix's caregivers when I got home earlier," she says.

"Oh, yes," says Dad. "How's he doing?"

They're talking like normal people.

I like it very much.

Mom puts down her fork. "One asked me to keep an eye on him. A close eye. Said he's stubborn."

"I keep an eye on Phoenix," I say. "I look out for him."

She takes a sip of water. Licks her lips. "I know you do, love."

The atmosphere on the boat. Like the air after a storm has moved on, after the charge has left.

Quiet solace.

"Still snowing out," says Dad.

We both look at the window and nod.

He does the dishes and I look at Mom as if to say: *What is going on*? She looks away.

Does she know I took her things?

Dad brings over apple pie. He puts Safeway's cream down on the table.

"Is it somebody's birthday?" I ask.

"Family supper," says Dad. "Family meal."

Mom eats her pie, but she looks unsettled. This is a bit weird. I don't know how to feel about how normal Dad's acting.

"What's going on, Dad?"

"What?"

"You know, all this."

"Eat your pie."

ADRIFT

Dad tells us he's not writing tonight. Says he needs a break from it to see it more clearly, gain some distance from the characters.

"There's a play on the radio starting soon," he says. "Historical. Jane Austen, I think. What do you say?"

"You like that, don't you, Mom? Dad says it's Jane Austen."

She looks tired and wary. She nods.

We sit together on the three folding camp chairs listening to the car radio the boat fitter recessed into a panel of mahogany many years ago. The snow keeps on falling.

I look at their faces. Trying to decipher what has happened, what has changed. Do they both know I moved the jewelry? Is this some charade before they confront me? Do they know I skipped class with Paul?

Mom makes cocoa for us and Dad accepts the offer for once in his life. He tells her it's better than he remembers. Not too sweet. The wind buffets the boat and the woodstove roars.

Dad doesn't shave his head tonight.

He doesn't prepare his writing desk.

We all get ready for bed quietly, uncomfortably, one after the other.

When Mom is flossing her teeth Dad whispers to me, "Tomorrow, after school, can you be home at five? Not before and not after. Can you do that for me, Samson?"

"Why?"

"I want to make things pleasant for your mother. A surprise what with everything she's been through. Our secret, though, yes? I want to make the boat comfortable. Make it easier on her."

He's buying her a fridge.

"I'll be home at five. And, Dad?"

"What?"

I look at him and he seems uncomfortable with my gaze.

"Thanks."

"Snow's still coming down," Mom says, walking out from the bathroom, her hair brushed back.

We all go to bed.

She comes through five minutes later and tucks me in like she used to. "Good night, my boy. Sleep tight."

"Mom?"

She strokes my cheek with the back of her hand.

I swallow hard. "Is everything all right?"

"It will be, love. It soon will be."

51

PEGGY

I wake up anxious.

He is not beside me. The bed is cool. I pull the drapes and the world outside is white.

It is time.

He walks through with a cup of coffee.

"Sleep well?"

"Not bad, thanks."

"Fresh batch."

He places the cup down on my nightstand and leaves.

We eat oatmeal together at the dinette. He cooked it. Sammy pours too much syrup onto his. Drew begins to scold him but then he stops himself. We do not talk much. Sammy watches us. He looks at me and then at his father and then back at me.

Samson puts on his winter jacket.

"Be careful," I say. "Icy on the towpath so keep well away from the edge, won't you?"

He kisses me on the cheek. "Don't worry so much, Mom."

"I mean it. You'd perish in the water when it's this cold. Strong swimmer or not."

"Bye."

Drew whispers something in his ear as he walks away leaving footprints in the snow.

Ten minutes later I take my purse and jacket.

"Can you be back at four?" says Drew. "If that's OK."

"Andrew. I'm not . . ."

He raises his finger in the air. "Don't say anything yet, Peggy. You agreed to give me the day. Let's talk at four like we said. We agreed, remember? I'm making a few changes and I think you'll be . . . well, just wait and see."

I smile a sad, resigned smile and walk off the boat.

The world is serene. Silver birches glistening with fresh powder. Rocks and fence posts coated with it. The sky is cerulean blue and I spot a plump robin dancing from tree to tree.

On the bus my stomach is unsettled. I am leaving. It won't be easy, but Sammy and I must forge a new life. I have pawned all the jewelry I found in the bathroom. Every single piece Drew took from me. Mom would have approved, I think. She would have told me to run away and never look back.

Just as she once did.

I will get a cleaning job. Night work, if necessary. I will get us through.

Inside the town the snow is already gray sludge. Plows are out and people walk awkwardly, cursing the weather. My right foot is wet, but I do not mind because I have a future for myself and my son.

Poor Sammy.

So many mixed messages. He sees normal domestic family life for the first time in years, maybe even the first time he can remember, and then I drag him away. It is a lot for him to deal with. It is too much.

I pass the post office. A man in a parka jump-starts a rusting Bronco from his Toyota Tacoma.

Part of me thinks I am being selfish. We have managed for fifteen years. I could wait until after Sammy has finished this grade.

No.

This is over.

* * *

At lunch Mrs. Appleby takes me to one side and sits me down. We talk for fifteen minutes. I have never chatted with her for so long. She knows. I don't know *how* she knows but she does. Not the specifics, but the general gist. Mrs. Appleby has seen some things in her life. As a nanny, as a secretary, in this library. She tells me she has been thinking long and hard and she has decided to retire.

"Oh, no," I say, taken aback. "Not yet, surely. We'd all miss you too much."

"It's time for me to move on, Peggy. Ed and I have been talking about it for years, truth be told. We might move to the coast. He's got a niece in Fort Myers."

"I can't imagine this place without you."

"Oh, I can," she says. "Exactly the same as it is now. You'll all get on just fine. You'll do a swell job."

"I don't know."

"I do. Which brings me to my question."

"Oh."

"Maybelle told me you canceled your interview with Mr. Karim. She said you canceled it."

"It's complicated."

"I'm sure, dear. None of my business, of course, but what I want to say is part of the reason for me retiring, really, is it's time to make room for you youngsters. It's only fair. Ed and I are set up just fine. We're comfortable. He's got a decent pension from the state. RV is paid off. I'd like to recommend Susan for my position."

"She'd be perfect," I say, nodding. "She'll be thrilled."

"I hope so. And that'll mean, if things fall into place, that her position will become vacant."

I look at her.

"I'd like you to consider it, Peggy, if you would, please. I'd put in a glowing recommendation for you. Decent pay, though nothing to get too excited about. Health insurance and dental. You'd be perfect for it."

I sigh.

She looks down at her hands. "I'm sorry, I thought you'd be pleased."

My dream job. I need to take my son away from this town. But I also need to be realistic about how I will support him.

"I'm delighted that you asked me, Mrs. Appleby."

"Grace."

"Grace. Thank you, really. Can I have a few days to think it through? I'm not being ungrateful, honest. It's just that life's a bit . . ."

"Complicated?"

"Yes."

Maybe I should stay until summer break after all.

I could save up for a deposit on a single-wide.

"There's no rush, dear," she says. "Take some time to mull it over. No stress."

I walk home from the bus. The snow is melting, drips falling from the trees as I slip and slide down the wooded embankment toward the canal. Two broken rye bottles and a charred JCPenney catalog. I wish I had my mother to talk this over with.

I walk past Phoenix's boat. The lights are off and the drapes are still shut.

As tempting as the job offer is, Sammy and I should make a clean break for it.

I approach our boat.

Something colorful catches my eye.

There are hyacinths in planters on the well deck. I stop in my tracks to stare at them. Intricate blue petals. Behind them is another pot full of miniature daffodils. The blue and yellow in stark contrast to the pale nature around us.

I step through the entrance cover and in through our painted steel doors.

He has lit two candles.

"Candles? Not like you, Drew."

He says something unintelligible.

"The batteries flat?"

"No, they're filled up."

I remove my jacket and boots. Pull on my slippers.

"I should have made more of an effort these past years."

He's wearing his best plaid shirt and jeans.

"I'll just change out of these clothes."

When I arrive back in the kitchen Drew is holding a bottle of wine in one hand and a corkscrew in the other.

"Like the old days," he says. "Shall I open it?"

I frown and shake my head. "Not for me. I need to pack."

He shrinks a little.

"And I've got a headache coming on."

He nods. "You want a pill for it?"

"No, it'll clear up on its own. Thanks, though. You heard from Sammy?"

"Running late," he says, blowing air through his teeth. "Forget his head if it wasn't screwed on tight. Good boy, though, isn't he?"

"Yeah."

"We're bringing up a decent young man."

I swallow.

"Got something for you, Peggy. It's not much."

"Drew, I'm sorry. It's not . . . I'm not . . ."

He raises his finger. "Let me show you first. Can I? Can I, Peg?"

I nod.

He pulls a thin plastic bag from his jeans. He removes my gold necklace from the bag.

"How?" I say, staring at it, at the faint, familiar indentations in the metal. "How did you . . . ?"

"Bought it right out of the pawnshop window display. Know it means a lot to you, Peggy. Boy's teething marks. Your mother's, originally, wasn't it?"

"Yes," I say, smiling, moving toward it. It's my last piece from her. My last remaining link. "Thank you. I mean it."

"I'll put it on you."

"No, not now, Drew."

"Come on. Turn around and I'll clip it on."

I turn my back.

His breath, warm on my neck.

Juicy Fruit.

The hairs on his forearms brushing gently against my shoulders.

He places the necklace delicately around my neck and instinctively I move my hands to it.

Only, it is not a necklace.

I start to turn.

He tightens the belt so I cannot scream.

I cannot breathe.

52

SAMSON

The bus windows are steamed up. We smell stale. The air is warm from the heater, the floor is wet.

I jump off and walk down through trees toward the water.

Most of the snow has disappeared now. A little whiteness remains in the shadows.

I stop by a gnarled oak tree for a pee.

Dad said five but I couldn't hang around the bus station for the last bus, not in this weather. I'll go visit Phoenix for a while. Maybe complete a crossword puzzle together. The care visitor said to drop in on him.

A boat makes its way slowly down the canal. It looks like it's been converted. A camper bolted onto a barge.

Our boat is farther up the towpath. No smoke from the chimney. Mom's probably cleaning with the radio on in the background. She listens to classic hits.

I was invited to Steve Chapman's birthday party today. He's having people over to his house in the suburbs past the old vacuum factory. There will be about thirty, he reckons, and the rumor is his dad's letting him have beer. One each. Light beer, nothing too strong. Steve says the only reason his dad's offering it to us is because it tastes godawful. I suspect there will be no beer. Steve told me I could bring Jennifer if I wanted. Maybe *that's* the real reason I'm invited? He says there'll be a good number of girls there. Cheerleaders, even. It's my first real birthday party invite since I was ten.

I'm not sure. Jennifer might come but she might not. You never really know with her. If Mom and Dad carry on being friendly, I might be able to bring her home for supper one night later this year. Is that normal? Mom could cook her pasta. I think Jennifer would like that.

Still no smoke from our chimney.

She must be cleaning the glass doors, emptying the ashes.

I walk toward Phoenix's boat. To think Mr. Turner bought it before I was even born. He used to travel with it on vacation. Showed me the photos one time. Rivers and canals. I think Mr. Turner and his wife had their best days on their boat. Phoenix is not home, I don't think. The drapes are still shut. I look past the boat and there are little flowers on ours. Blue and yellow ones. Mom must have picked them on her way home. I step onto Phoenix's deck.

"All right? You home, Phoenix?"

No reply.

I try the door.

Unlocked.

I walk inside. "Phoenix? Can I come in, man? You OK?"

No answer.

Inside I switch on a light.

The boat doesn't smell like it usually does. There is a tang of decay in the air. I walk through, checking the bathroom and the bedroom and the engine room. He's not here. I walk back into the living room. There are three envelopes on the sofa. One has my name on it. One has Mom's name on it. The other one is made out to someone called Mr. Soames Esq. of Harbottle and Schneider.

No idea who they are.

"Phoenix?" I shout out again.

Nothing.

The air is thick.

I do not take the envelope with my name on it because he hasn't given it to me yet. It would be stealing. I close the door behind me and step onto the towpath.

Mom will be making supper, I expect.

She might even have a brand-new fridge to fill.

53

PEGGY

I cannot breathe.

Sammy and I should have left last night.

We should have escaped when we had the chance.

I kick out with my feet, fighting with my hands, but he holds me firmly in place.

"No," I scream, but the sound is muffled.

I will not let him do this. I have Sammy to look after.

"You disgust me," he whispers, calmly, wedging the top of his belt over the steel door and squeezing it shut. "Women like you are everything wrong with this country. The harm you've done."

I kick out at him and try to pass my fingers between the leather and my neck but it is already too tight.

He holds my legs so I have no purchase.

"Look at that," he points to his bureau, to his trophy, and his voice is louder now. "I could have done it, you know. If you hadn't come along. You and your mother. Ruining my life, my career, my focus. I could have made it. You know it better than I do. You stopped me, didn't you?"

I wriggle and squirm, elevating my head, trying to take in air.

He is too strong.

"You. And your mother."

"No," I croak.

He lifts my feet higher and my vision blurs.

The pressure on my neck.

"You never looked out for me, not really. You looked out for yourself. Turned my son soft. Why did you do it? Why did you have to embarrass me?"

"No," I say, but it's just a croak. "Drew."

"Walking out? You walking out on me? Don't make me laugh. Nobody walks away from me, do you understand?" He's talking through gritted teeth. "Taking my boy away. You two, walking away from *me*."

"Help!" I try to scream. My peripheral vision is darkening and I'm hearing noises that aren't there.

"You don't tell me what's what. You want to leave. Leave me? No, princess. Won't permit it. Leave *me*? Incorrect. Leaving *me*?"

I look up at the belt. Try to move my body to the side.

"Your mother didn't do it, Peg. She should have done, would have saved us all a lot of time and a lot of hassle. She didn't have it in her. Old girl was in our way. Dear, oh dear. Writing was on the wall, wasn't it, the way she carried on. It was her or me."

What is he talking about?

It is not possible.

Out of pure fury, primitive rage, I manage to fight and dig out a finger of space between my neck and the rancid belt.

"You didn't," I croak. "No."

"Yes," he says, knocking my hand away with ease. "Yes, Margaret, sweetheart. You thought life was easy, you pair. Cozy little bungalow to grow up in. Chip on her shoulder about being a Brit. Dragged us all down, though, the pair of you. Never stopped. Heavy weight around my neck, Peggy. Us against the world, right, you never understood it, did you?"

I cannot hear his words clearly anymore. The boat is growing dark.

His lips move.

I am slipping away and all I can think of is the expression on Sammy's face when he finds me. History repeating. Drew winning once again.

"It's your fault, Peg. The boy. The books. All of it's your fault."

Blackness.

"You should have done better."

54

SAMSON

I walk over to our boat, then pause.

My coat is soaking wet from the melted snow. Mom won't like that. She's warned me not to make the rug dirty. I go to the far end, to the engine room near their bedroom. I take off my gear carefully and hang it all up one piece at a time to dry out.

The boat is quiet.

Damp socks and cold toes.

I've decided to tell Mom about her jewelry. She will be furious but she'll understand my reasons in time. I'll tell her how at first I was afraid she'd lose it. Then I was scared she might sell it all, or pawn it, and then use the cash to run away. I'll tell her the truth. That they would have put her back in the hospital but this time it would have been far worse. She might never forgive me, but I think she'll understand I was trying to take care of things for her. Buying us a little extra time.

I pad through their bedroom.

Her nightstand catches my eye. Her water glass. Her library book.

Past the bathroom.

They're over by his desk.

What is he doing?

"You ruined my life. You ruined my books. You wrecked everything I ever worked for."

Dad moves and I see that she's hanging by his old leather belt from the doorframe. I freeze up. My heart stops. The belt is draped over the top. Wedged tight. What is happening? I move forward, staggering, unable to swallow. I'm shaking.

"Useless. You and your mother. You ruined this family. Ruined my plans. I could have been . . ."

I creep forward, my heart bursting through my ribs.

He is going to kill her.

"Useless, the pair of you. Soft. You thought she killed herself? How dumb do you have to be? You and the boy have been nothing but disappointments, one after the other. Pathetic, the pair of you."

I tiptoe forward and see her face for the first time. Swollen. Eyes bulging.

Pain, deep inside my gut.

A sharp ache.

Mom.

I scream, but there is no sound. I run at him with all my might and as he turns to face me, still holding her feet, his expression isn't that of horror like I expected. He smiles. Like I am no threat to him at all. His eyes widen. I lose my footing and stumble again, reaching out in desperation, yelling for Mom. He smiles harder. So I grab the trophy. The Hugh Higgins Memorial Prize.

He stops smiling then. Pivots, bends, approaches.

I lift it.

And then I drive it into his head.

55

PEGGY

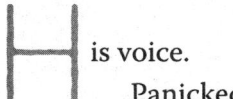is voice.
   Panicked.

Sammy's sweet face looming over mine. His eyes, wide, horrified.

I can't hear him clearly.

I try to reach for him, but I cannot move my hands.

Something is broken in my throat. I can't swallow. Shallow, painful breaths.

I gasp, suddenly recalling what he did to me.

"Sam?" I croak.

He is crying, his face over mine, his tears falling onto my skin.

"Sammy?"

"Oh, Mom."

I cough, then retch.

"Are you OK, Sammy?"

He nods, tears falling again from his eyes. Hitting my face, my cheeks, my lips.

"I'm so sorry, Mom."

I sit upright, my hands at my neck.

Drew is between us and the woodstove. The rug is turning crimson. I shift away from him. A fine splatter on the door. I can't even look at Sammy's school shirt.

I pull my boy close to me, tight to my chest, squeezing him, filling in the gaps. "You are OK, my love."

He sobs into me. Wailing. I pull him tighter still. My son has his face buried in my shirt and I sit staring at my husband. Thinking clearly, coherently, for the first time in years. Watching him on the floor while comforting my perfect child.

Sammy pulls away, tracing the ligature marks on my neck with his fingertips.

"I'm sorry."

"Nothing to be sorry for." My voice is croaky. A barely audible bark. I lift his chin so our faces are almost touching. "Look at me, Sam. You've done nothing wrong. You are not to blame for any of this, do you understand? You did what you had to."

He wipes his eyes with his palms. "I didn't think. I just . . ."

Meltwater drains from the roof.

It streams down the angled windows.

Drew moves.

"Mom. Did you see that? Mom?"

"No, love."

"He moved."

"No, he didn't. Come here."

Sammy looks at me for answers. His eyes are red and his lower lip is trembling.

"Leave your father."

The sound of our breathing. Three of us. Meltwater dripping. I touch my neck and caress the indentation burns from his belt.

"He laid his hands on you," says Sammy.

"What?"

"He said he'd never do it. Lay his hands on us. He broke his promise."

I stroke Sammy's hand, urging it to stop trembling. "This, all this, is over now. It's over. We'll be all right, you and me, I give you my word on that. Look at me. We'll be safe."

Gasping noises.

We hold on to each other.

"I'm so sorry," he says.

I squeeze him tighter.

Drew hasn't moved.

Sammy sobs and says, "I want to say goodbye to him."

"Oh, no. You don't have to do that."

"I do."

I watch as he stands up unsteadily. I see the state of his shirt properly for the first time. The stains. He steps heavily over to his father. Sobs again. Sammy kneels down close to Drew's head. Apologizes over and over. He whispers something into his dad's ear. Something about helping him at school. I start to break down and weep properly for the first time. A boy and his father. Samson rocks back and forth on his heels, shaking his head. And then he bends down carefully, his fingers shaking, and he gently kisses his dad's smooth cheek for the last time.

A bird flies up to the boat and lands on the roof. It flies on.

"What do we do now, Mom?"

I touch my neck again. "I don't know. I'll take care of you."

"But what do we do?"

The window darkens.

Wind rushes into the chimney and then there's light again from the window, illuminating Drew's body on the floor.

Footsteps outside.

"Mom."

Terror in his eyes.

I try to get to my knees.

Someone knocks on the door at my back. The door I almost hung from.

56

SAMSON

"Come back tomorrow," I shout, my voice unsteady. My heart is racing.

I look around the boat.

"It's me," says Phoenix. "Let me in, Sam."

I look at Mom. Fresh panic in her eyes.

"We have to."

She puts her head in her hands. "But . . . they'll take you away. I'll go back to . . . They won't understand."

"I'm coming in," he says. "I'm coming in now, all right."

I shout, "It's not how it looks, Phoenix," through the door. "This is not how it looks."

A long pause.

Coughing.

"I know, bud. Let me in, though, eh."

She starts crying again.

I want to hide him. Hide my shirt. Hide my own mother and the marks on her neck.

I crack the door ajar and see his gaunt, pale face staring back.

His leather jacket. His black Levi's. He is shivering out there. I open the door wider.

"Is anybody hurt?" he asks.

I squeeze my eyelids together to stop crying. Then I open the door wider still and he stands there taking it all in.

He does not step inside.

"Are you hurt, ma'am? Are you bleeding?"

"No," says Mom, struggling to stand up. "But . . . he's gone."

Phoenix comes in and closes the door softly behind him. He walks around Dad, treading carefully, moving slowly, avoiding the rug, adjusting the drapes.

"Are either of you hurt? Any injuries?"

We both shake our heads. He leans down and checks Dad's neck for a pulse.

"Did he try to hurt you? The marks on your neck. Did he have his hands around you?"

She points to the belt on the floor.

Phoenix takes a sharp breath and rubs his mouth and jaw with his hand. He's lost more weight. "The ordeal you two have been through."

He rubs his temples.

She says, "We need to call someone. I don't know who."

Phoenix says, "I'll help with all of that. Don't you worry. I won't leave you alone."

I gesture toward Dad's trophy. "I had to do it. I had no choice, Phoenix, honest. Her eyes were rolled back. I'm telling the truth. He was yelling at her, holding her feet up. Her eyes were white." My voice cracks. "She was nearly gone."

"Listen to me, both of you." He smiles a pitiful, hollow smile. Checks with his eyes to make sure we are following. "Look right at me. I'm going to take this over from here, yeah? Deal with the authorities for you. It'll be a lot of questions, a lot of time. I'm gonna take the strain off you both, all right?"

"You can't do that," she says. "This is my problem. You're not up to it."

"Listen to me, Peggy, can I call you that? You've both been through a trauma. Not just today, I don't mean that. For years. I don't pretend to know much about what you've lived through, but I do understand some of it. And I want you both to know that this, all this, isn't yours to pay for. Neither of you. It just plain isn't. You mustn't pay for any of it."

"I didn't have a choice," I say, choking on the words.

"He's gone, Samson, buddy. It's over now. He's bullied you both for years, hasn't he? Isn't that right?"

Mom squeezes her eyelids together and nods.

Phoenix has tears in his eyes. In a gentle whisper he says again, "He's done it for years, hasn't he?"

I nod.

"He won't do it anymore."

She looks at him. "How did you . . . know?"

"Can you both do me a favor, please? I want to shoulder this. Grant me that wish. I don't want you pair splitting up, accused of things you don't deserve, agencies involved, months of inquiries and questions. I couldn't bear to know that's what's happened to you two. Do you understand what I'm trying to say?"

Mom nods. Tears in her eyes.

"I don't understand anything," I say.

"Look back to the bedroom door," he says. "Both of you, for me, look the other way at that door."

I turn to the bedroom door then glance back.

"Keep looking at it, Samson. Over there. Focus on it. Trust me."

Mom holds me tight and we stare at the distant door.

I squeeze her.

An audible *thump* behind us. I start to turn but she holds me firmly in place. I struggle harder and Phoenix is spitting on his hands and rubbing his fingers all over the Hugh Higgins Memorial Prize. More dull thumping noises.

"Don't," I cry out.

Mom squeezes me tighter still. Holds on, her arms digging into my chest.

"What are you doing, Phoenix?"

She pulls me back toward the kitchen, smothers me with her arm. It goes quiet.

He walks over to join us. Kneels down on the floor right next to us. Puts one hand on each of our shoulders. He's out of breath, can hardly talk. Droplets of blood on his jacket.

"I came in and saw your mom hanging from the door." He pauses to catch his breath. "She was on the door, yes?"

I nod, a tear rolling down my cheek.

"Right then."

"He was killing her," I say.

Phoenix sighs. "I came in and saw that, and then I hit him with the trophy." He winces in pain and tries to catch his breath. "Then you came home, Samson. Have you got that? Is it clear? Who came to the boat last?"

I squeeze my eyes shut. "I did."

"Good man. That's it, buddy. Who hit your father?"

My lip trembles. I bite on it. Tears erupt from my clamped-shut eyelids. "You did, Phoenix."

"I did, didn't I? I had to. Peggy. I had to do it. For both of you." He's more agitated now. Panting. "He made your lives hell, didn't he? Yeah? Messing with you. Just like he made my life hell for years back at junior high."

Mom frowns at him.

"I had to move away in the end. It was the only way."

"At school?" I say, opening my eyes, wiping them.

Phoenix takes a deep, labored breath and wipes his own eyes with the sleeve of his leather jacket. "Two years. Every single school day. Haunted me on weekends and holidays. Back then I had blond hair. I was a big kid, emotional eater. Andrew was bullied by an older guy for a bit, I remember it, whole school saw it, and then he turned into one himself. You go one of two ways, I guess. I was in the firing line, that's all. Two years that felt like twenty. Never got over it, really. But you've both had it so much worse."

"Did he know?" I say, frowning, gesturing to Dad at the far end by the woodstove.

"Him?" Phoenix frowns. "I was nothing to him. He probably never even remembered it. I've had work done since, changed my looks over the years, trips to Mexico, changed my hair. And then sickness changed me even more. Anyway, it's over now. For all of us. You two deserve to live, I mean it. You've been looking out for each other all these years, living defensive. I know how exhausting that is. Now it's time to really live. Live your lives."

"And you, Phoenix," I say.

Mom pinches the bridge of her nose to stop herself crying.

"I don't have long left." He smiles at me. "A month, maybe. Taking this burden is no hardship for me. If anything, I'm grateful to you both."

"What?" I ask, reaching out and touching his shoulder.

"Taking all this from you. I know I'm doing a good thing. There's not many moments in a man's life when you know that for sure. You looked out for me, and Jeff, both of you. And now I'm going to look out for you and make it all worth something."

"No, Phoenix."

His lips are blue. Gaunt cheeks. He's struggling to catch his breath again.

"We'll get the sheriff out here soon, Samson. I'm leaving all this anyway, remember that. I've made my peace with it all, honest. I'm going. It's all right. I'm off and you two are sticking around. He can't get at you anymore, that's the crucial thing. This isn't yours to pay for, remember that. This isn't yours to pay for."

EPILOGUE

The air is warm and the leaves are beginning to turn.

An ice-cream truck passes by.

Dennis Davenport is waiting for me outside the library. He waits because he wants to see me and he wants to walk with me, not because he is checking. It took me many months to trust him, to hear him. When he asked me out for a coffee, the year after, I said no. Then I changed my mind and suggested we go out for lunch. I have grown very fond of him. Dennis does not ask me who I have been speaking with or what I have been wearing.

We have lived in town these past years, close to the high school. Eventually we moved in with Dennis, to his bungalow opposite Jeff Turner's old place. Sammy enjoyed being back on Bakersfield Avenue, visiting the corner grocery, cutting through the park with the public pool they empty every fall. He and Dennis liked to gaze at nebulae and shooting stars together on clear nights.

I can sense the weight of the bracelet on my wrist. It is made from Mom's gold necklace. I am still not comfortable wearing anything around my neck, even after all this time, but the jewelry store at the mall did an excellent job adapting it.

We walk hand in hand past the pawnshop, the post office, the hair salon.

My heart: full of sadness.

Aching.

I fought hard to give Sammy a new life, with stability and reassurance. For years I've worked two jobs. He has always been my priority.

I am far more confident now, and I finally believe I deserve the library job Mrs. Appleby helped me to get. I have reorganized some of the admin and the place is looking better than ever. I am in charge of inviting local, and even not-so-local, authors to come and give talks. It is the children's authors I focus on. The kids around here need their stories. It is important for local children to see that things might be possible and exciting, even for them. It is vital they feel seen.

It took a long time for Sammy to work through what happened that night. Talking to a professional with me there. Talking to her on his own. His grades recovered when he finally felt comfortable in Dennis's bungalow, although that was not a smooth process, especially in the early days. It wasn't only that Dennis was head of Lower School. I think it would have been challenging with any new man in the home. But then Sammy fell in with the wrong crowd. Dennis called them troublemakers. Tensions grew. I don't know why Sammy hung around with them, but he would not leave them alone. They accepted him, I suppose. Smoking weed and shoplifting. Probably worse I don't know of. He believed he was strong in their presence.

A bus passes. The bus I used to ride each day out to the canal.

I have had two novels published by a small press. They have been well received. I am working on my third. Writing helps me process what has happened.

The ache in my chest intensifies.

He was doing ever so well. Grew tall and began to impress his teachers. But people started saying he was crazy like his mother. He would defend me, bless his heart, say there was nothing wrong with his mother's mind.

Thin, wispy clouds high in the sky.

I was more concerned that he might have inherited his father's mind. When he confessed how he had hidden my jewelry I felt like the whole cursed cycle might continue through him and beyond. I was bereft. But then he explained to me, eloquently, calmly, how he worried I might flee if I had the means to do so. He knew I would be committed again, and he was scared of losing me forever. It took me months to unpack and come to terms with his reasoning. I told him I thought what he did was wrong. I explained how he did not have the right to make that decision on my behalf. And then, thank God, I forgave him.

I walk past Jeff Turner's bungalow most days. A young family live there now and they have a terrier that looks a little like Amber.

It is terrifying to imagine how many crimes go unsolved or mislabeled in this world. How many perpetrators take their dark secrets to their graves.

A pigeon picking at the crust of a discarded slice outside the pizza place.

If I see someone scared or lost in the library I try to offer them some comfort, some support. I have placed helpline leaflets by the entrance. I do what I can.

Two dogs barking at each other.

Dennis does not hold my hand because he wants to own me or control me. He holds my hand because he wants to hold it. And I want to hold his. The difference is nothing from an outside perspective, but here, on the inside, it is everything.

If I didn't have Dennis I don't know if I would manage the long years ahead.

We walk on past the discount furniture warehouse and the pet food store.

Clear skies.

The churchyard is up ahead, a narrow steeple basking in the last warmth of summer.

"All right?" asks Dennis, squeezing my hand.

I squeeze his hand back.

"You sure?" he says.

I squeeze his hand again but I cannot answer him.

Drew took me away from Sammy for weeks. A black hole missing in my life: that hospital, that Christmas. He separated us and I will struggle to ever forgive him for that.

Sirens in the distance.

Fatima helps me work through it all. To process what has happened since. We meet for coffee each week at the bakery. I can talk to her about things nobody else understands.

An empty Dr Pepper rolls down the road, spinning and rattling in the drainage gully.

Drew did not try to kill me that time in the bath. He tried to soften me, to quiet me, to deplete me. He wanted me subdued but alive: medicated, shamed, and living with reduced credibility and self-belief. Alive, yet contained. Hospitalized and shrunken. I fear a similar thing happens in one of a thousand ways to women all across the globe every day of every year.

My dear boy wore Phoenix's jacket for years after he passed on. He wore it with such pride. Sammy only knew Phoenix for a few months but, in a way, for that brief time, he was the paternal figure he needed and deserved. I saw a photo of Phoenix as a schoolboy at the memorial service. Big kid with thick blond hair and a bent nose back then. Dreadful what Drew and the others put him through. Horrific bullying. Maybe that is why he and Samson formed such a quick bond. After the service, Sam wouldn't wear a raincoat, not even in a November downpour. It was Phoenix's black leather jacket or nothing. He told me once it smelled safe.

We walk to the graveyard railings.

My boy never deserved what happened to him.

Fresh flowers on some of the graves. A squirrel dashing up the trunk of a twisted ash tree.

ADRIFT

Sammy deserved so much better.

So much more.

I look over at the far corner of the cemetery and squeeze the LEGO brick I keep in my coat pocket.

I squeeze it so tight it hurts.

EPILOGUE II

I can see seven concrete streetlights from the entrance to the train station.

Seven.

A bus hisses and moves away and in its place are Mom and Mr. Davenport, hand in hand, walking toward me past the churchyard railings. Three years ago I would have been furious to see them like this. Two years ago I would have been irritated. Even though I knew by then that Mr. Davenport was a decent man. I've probably always known it. But it took me years to trust him with her.

I call him Dennis now.

My heart sits high in my chest. Full. Swollen to the point where it beats like an orchestral bass drum. When I bought the ticket yesterday the man in the booth passed it through to me. An orange cardboard rectangle. A standard single from this place to someplace else entirely. A new world. When I left I passed Gunner working in the coffee kiosk. We had a long chat. I asked him about his daughter and he asked me about the Bears game last weekend even though I don't watch football. We've both grown up a lot since the old days.

Mom's smiling as she approaches but her eyes are wet. She's making strange faces to stop herself from crying, to avoid ruining her makeup. An invisible hero. The strongest person I will ever know but nobody else can see it. There are many like her. Holding on, keeping it together, looking for a way out, feeding those in their care, protecting and loving.

So many invisible heroes.

I said goodbye to Jennifer earlier today. She calls herself Jen now and she's started her own import-export company, choosing to postpone college for a year or two. It's tough, she says, but I know she'll make a success of it. We haven't been together for a long time, but she'll always be my first love. She took a chance on me when I had no confidence and she had plenty. I was an untouchable, a social pariah, and she kissed me in front of everyone at the bus station and she completely transformed my life.

Smoke rises from the factory and passes the hills in the distance and moves up into a mottled sky.

Phoenix left envelopes. Mine talked about living for myself and moving on from whatever went on before. He said I'd need to find a way, in time, to find peace inside. He said I should learn to love who I am, and how that isn't easy and sometimes, too often, it takes the best part of a lifetime to figure it out. But he said if I learn to be at peace then I can help others. He said he knows that because it's eventually what happened to him.

Mom picks up her pace and Dennis accelerates to keep up. She looks at him then at me.

They're coming closer.

I'm wearing his leather jacket, of course. That's probably why she's so upset. She knows exactly what Phoenix gave up for us both. It has a special power, this old leather. Sounds ridiculous, but it's true. When I'm untethered and afraid, like when I accepted the college offer, applied for the scholarship, I wear the jacket. It's thick leather. Phoenix used to say it could stop a bullet.

Paul Pricklett did better in his SATs than anyone expected, him included. He's going to UMass to study English. First in his family. His mother's driving him there with a station wagon packed full of ramen noodles and frozen homemade lasagnas. He's going to come down and visit me when he's settled. I owe him more than I can put into words.

Mr. Turner, Phoenix, Dennis. Mom, of course. Paul. I owe all of them. Small things and enormous things. Keeping me going. I'll never forget what they did for me. And in a way I still can't fully comprehend, Dad helped me as well. The good part of him helped me turn my life around.

"Hello, love. You ready?"

I nod. "We'd better get to the platform."

She squeezes my shoulder.

"You packed your paperwork?" says Dennis. "Your forms? Certificates? ID?"

I smile at him and nod.

"Ticket? Cash?" he says.

"Yes, Dennis."

It still feels a little awkward to call him that.

A little girl passes by on her bright turquoise scooter. Her mom follows, carrying three Safeway bags.

I understand my mother better now than I did even a year ago. She is impressive; she's just very quiet about it. It's as if she treads lightly on this world. Acts without ceremony or expectation of reward.

It's good that she has Dennis. If she was alone I probably wouldn't be doing this today. I wouldn't be able to leave her. But he's releasing me from this town and some of the complex memories it holds. Dennis is the one setting me free.

We've talked about visiting England after I graduate. After I've worked a few years. I want to save up, if I can, and take the three of us on a trip to see Mom's relations.

She never told me what Phoenix wrote her in that letter. And because of the way she looked when she read it I have never once asked her.

I step up onto the train and place my bag on a seat. It's the same bag that was moved, stolen, placed in wet planters. The bag is coming with me.

I think she knows now that I'm not like Dad. She worried about it for years, as I was growing taller and stronger, after I started shaving. She looked at me and sometimes she saw him, I know she did. But I think she has put the matter to rest. I am made up of both of them, but also of myself. I still don't know who I am, exactly, but I think I know who I am not.

The sheriff was gentle and considerate after Dad died. We gave our statements and they listened to Phoenix. I'll never forget what he did for us.

I check my seat number and stow my bag.

They're down on the platform. I step off and hug them both. Mom squeezes me so tight she hurts my back.

"I'm always here for you, Sammy."

"I know, Mom."

"Whatever you need. Night or day. I'm always here for you."

"We both are," says Dennis, not looking me in the eye.

I step back up onto the train. Mom holds out a Milky Way wrapped up in a fifty-dollar bill. I reach out for it and my gold bracelet, made from Nanna Ruth's necklace, catches the light. She wears an identical one.

"Look after yourself, love."

I smile. "You too, Mom."

Jen will be waiting on the footbridge where we first met. She said she'd be there watching the train leave the station. She said if I wasn't on the train she'd track me down and damn well put me on the next one.

I can sense the hardness of Dad's pocketknife in my pocket. I keep it clean and sharp these days. Maintain it like he showed me.

A train guard blows a whistle and the doors beep and close.

She smiles through her tears.

I miss Dad. Never saw that coming. Right now I miss him very much. The good parts. His training, his reading, his face. Despite everything, I miss him.

She places her hand on the glass window of the train door.

This town will always be my home, but it never will again.

I love you, Mom.

She smiles and mouths, *I love you, Sammy Jenkins.*

They won't know me in New York. They won't know about her hospital stay and what Dad did. They won't know the names kids used to call me and how we lived on a boat with no working fridge. I'll be away from this place.

I always dreamed of sitting in a train car like this.

Mom smiles from the platform, wipes her eyes.

Then she winks.

The train pulls away slowly from the station.

I am gone.

ACKNOWLEDGMENTS

I would like to thank my wife. We met on the steps of the London School of Economics back when I was eighteen and she was twenty. I was a rough, untraveled country boy from the Midlands and she seemed like a movie star or a heroine from a novel. Much to our son's (constant) embarrassment, we are still very much in love over a quarter of a century later.

Any author needs luck, and I am fortunate to work with the best agents and publishers in the business. Thanks to my US editor, Emily Bestler, and the team at Atria, Simon & Schuster (Lara, Megan, Hydia, Maudee, Morgan, Jolena, David, and colleagues). Thanks to my UK editor, Jo Dickinson, and the team at Hodder & Stoughton (Alice, Alainna, Sorcha, Kate, Sarah, Catherine, Richard, Sinead, Dominic, and colleagues). Thanks to my literary agent, Kate Burke, and the team at Blake Friedmann (Conrad, Isobel, Julian, Juliet, Sian, Lizzy, Nicole, Daisy, and colleagues).

Heartfelt thanks to all my international publishers and translators.

Thanks to the cover designers, printers, delivery drivers, audiobook narrators. You bring the books to life.

To everyone who shares a review (whether you're a journalist, a blogger, an online reviewer, a book club member, librarian, or bookseller): thank you from the bottom of my heart.

ACKNOWLEDGMENTS

This particular story was difficult to write. That's partly why it took me five years from idea to publication. I felt like I was right there on that claustrophobic boat, and from the very beginning I was fearful for Peggy and Samson. They are incredibly real to me and I hope I have done them both justice.

Most of the time I live an extremely quiet and offline life here in the forest. I'm happy to go for weeks or even months without leaving these silent woods. That is because I have a wonderful family (Bernie and Monty included) but it is also because I am surrounded by books written by other authors. I am happy to say many of them are now my friends and I am thankful for their skill and effort and comradery. Their books help me understand the world.

Without storytelling I would have struggled as a child, and I would probably still be struggling to this day. I am so grateful to all the writers out there who help us make sense of change. We need that sensation of stepping inside a book, walking in someone else's shoes for a while, empathizing with their life situation. Reading helps us all to exercise our compassion and empathy muscles.

Now, more than ever before, we need stories.